W9-BUV-578

PRAISE FOR THE NATIONAL BESTSELLING CATS IN TROUBLE MYSTERY SERIES

The Cat, the Mill and the Murder

"A charming novel that highlights the love of felines with a mystery that tugs at the heartstrings. For a mystery that features a custom cat quilter as the heroine, the novel nevertheless tackles very serious themes and contains a strong plot that engages the reader until its very satisfying conclusion."   —Kings River Life Magazine

"Ms. Sweeney is a talented writer who has peopled this series with some extremely likable characters. . . . She is adept at weaving the history of the textile industry into *The Cat, the Mill and the Murder*, giving the reader just enough to keep their interest without boring them. This series just gets better and better."   —Fresh Fiction

"Leann Sweeney has written another well-plotted page-turner. I loved this book. I enjoy a good mystery that features my furry favorites as well as quirky characters. Jillian is such a loving character that you can't help getting drawn into her life and wish that you could help her solve the problems she encounters. So if you enjoy mysteries that feature adorable cats, then *The Cat, the Mill and the Murder* is a book you should read."

—MyShelf.com

"I cannot recommend this series enough to animal lovers and fans of a darn good mystery. The mystery was multilayered and kept me guessing right to the end, and, as always, I'm anxious for the next Cats in Trouble book!"
—Cozy Mystery Book Review

continued . . .

The Cat, the Wife and the Weapon

"A light and easy cozy mystery that strikes a nice balance between the murder mystery and the intricacy of human relationships. . . . I give this book four paws up!"
—MyShelf.com

"[An] amusing and enthralling regional amateur sleuth tale starring an eccentric cast led by a likable, peacemaking heroine." —Genre Go Round Reviews

The Cat, the Lady and the Liar

"A lighthearted, fun cozy starring an engaging cast of characters. . . . Feline frolic fans will enjoy."
—The Best Reviews

"Tightly plotted, with likable characters, and filled with cat trivia, this entertaining mystery will become a favorite for cozy and cat lovers alike." —The Conscious Cat

The Cat, the Professor and the Poison

"A fun, entertaining story. . . . The mystery will keep the reader guessing." —Fresh Fiction

"The characters and friends Jillian makes along the way, and the care she gives to the cats she encounters, will make her a fast favorite." —The Mystery Reader

The Cat, the Quilt and the Corpse

"The cats are entertaining four-legged assistants . . . [and] kitty lovers will enjoy the feline trivia."
—Publishers Weekly

"[Leann Sweeney's] brand-new series about adorable cats that just can't stay out of trouble is bound to be a hit!" —Fantastic Fiction

Other Novels by Leann Sweeney

The Cats in Trouble Mysteries

The Cat, the Mill and the Murder
The Cat, the Wife and the Weapon
The Cat, the Lady and the Liar
The Cat, the Professor and the Poison
The Cat, the Quilt and the Corpse

The Yellow Rose Mysteries

Pushing Up Bluebonnets
Shoot from the Lip
Dead Giveaway
A Wedding to Die For
Pick Your Poison

THE CAT, THE VAGABOND AND THE VICTIM

A CATS IN TROUBLE MYSTERY

LEANN SWEENEY

AN OBSIDIAN MYSTERY

OBSIDIAN
Published by the Penguin Group
Penguin Group (USA) LLC, 375 Hudson Street,
New York, New York 10014

USA | Canada | UK | Ireland | Australia | New Zealand | India | South Africa | China
penguin.com
A Penguin Random House Company

First published by Obsidian, an imprint of New American Library,
a division of Penguin Group (USA) LLC

First Printing, August 2014

ISBN 978-0-451-41542-4

Printed in the United States of America
10 9 8 7 6 5 4 3 2 1

This book is for Meika. I love you.

Acknowledgments

Every book is special; every book I write teaches me something new about myself; every book is a challenge. No book is written alone. Without my husband's support, I would be lost. I must thank my former writer's group — Charlie, Susie, Kay, Dean, Laura, Amy, Bob and Millie. It was your voices I heard as I wrote, guiding me along, even though we no longer meet face-to-face. I miss you! Dear cozy readers and those who encourage me to keep writing, I thank you. This book couldn't have been created without you. Jenn and Lorraine, I love you both. Cozy Chicks, you are always there to encourage and help. Carol Mann and your assistants — thanks for working so hard for me this year. Claire, you are my hero. Thank you.

It is in the nature of cats to do a certain amount of unescorted roaming.

— ADLAI STEVENSON

One

Visitors don't often knock on my front door at eleven o'clock at night. But my friend Allison Cuddahee from the local no-kill shelter had called me in a panic to ask a favor. She arrived thirty minutes later bearing a gift.

The opportunity to foster a cat is always a gift as far as I'm concerned. This particular feline's name was Clyde, and I already knew he was a celebrity. The press was onto him and his amazing story. See, various out-of-town reporters had been hanging around the Mercy Animal Sanctuary, hoping for photo opportunities. That was why Allison resorted to this late-night, stealthy delivery. I guess you could now call my home his "undisclosed location."

I'm Jillian Hart, I live in Mercy, South Carolina, and I have a history of helping cats. After all, my three beauties—Syrah, Merlot and Chablis—are all Hurricane Katrina rescues. I found each of them in different shelters in the Houston area where I once lived. They'd been removed from flood-ravaged New Orleans and remained unclaimed months after the storm. But my now-late husband, John, and I gladly gave them a new forever home. I wondered how they'd get along with Clyde, who was being surprisingly quiet in the crate Allison set at her feet in my foyer.

"Thanks for stepping up again, Jillian," Allison said. "We sneaked Clyde out the back door of the shelter and into my car because two particularly pesky reporters have been following Shawn around ever since this big boy was transported to our place. We were afraid they'd follow Shawn's truck if he drove Clyde over here. Now let's hope they weren't paying attention to *me*."

Shawn was Allison's husband, and together they ran the local pet rescue shelter.

I glanced down at the crate. "I caught Mercy Animal Sanctuary in the background when the *Today Show* aired Clyde's story. I suppose they found out about him because of the piece that ran in our town paper?"

"Who knows? It seems to me anytime a cat travels more than fifty miles, he or she makes the national news."

"You two come on into the living room," I said. "Can I get you some sweet tea? Water? A soda?" I took the bag of food and treats she'd placed on top of the crate and led the way through the foyer.

The sweet perfume of early summer's pine and Carolina jasmine wafted through the air as Allison carried Clyde in his crate with some effort. Although of a slight build—three inches shorter than my five foot four— Allison had well-toned biceps and strong legs from her work at the sanctuary. If she was struggling with that crate, my guess was that I was about to meet a big boy—maybe bigger than my nearly twenty-pound Maine coon, Merlot.

"Nothing to drink," she said. "I am exhausted and want to sneak back home before one of those weird reporters accosts me with questions. And I'm not talking about your Kara. She's been nothing but wonderful."

Kara was my stepdaughter, my late husband's daughter, and the editor and owner of the local newspaper, the *Mercy Messenger*.

Allison set the carrier down near my chenille sofa, and my three kitties immediately surrounded Clyde. Syrah is a sorrel Abyssinian, Merlot a red tabby Maine coon, and Chablis a seal point Himalayan. I heard no growling coming from inside the crate—unusual, but a relief. Maybe Clyde would fit in here quickly.

. I turned to Allison. "So you're not upset that Kara broke the story about Mr. Jeffrey and Clyde in the *Messenger*?"

"Of course not. It's these out-of-towners who bother me. It all started as a simple human interest piece as far as Kara was concerned." Allison knelt by the carrier. "Shawn was happy to talk to her about Clyde—even though he'd rather be speaking with dogs, cats or birds. Who knew the major networks would run with this? Maybe that's because it doesn't quite have a happy ending yet."

"It is sad about Mr. Jeffrey's death and how poor Clyde never made it home in time to be with his friend," I said. "But Candace won't tell me much about what they found at the man's house except to say that if not for Clyde, his body would still be lying there undiscovered."

Deputy Candace Carson, a local police officer and my best friend, was investigating the man's passing. Kara reported that his death was assumed to be from natural causes, but the coroner had not released an official report. Only three days had passed, though. Maybe tomorrow we'd know more.

Allison rested a loving hand on top of the crate. "Norm, poor Clyde's best buddy, is gone, and I know this guy feels the loss."

"I'm not sure I understand why Mr. Jeffrey—Norm— placed Clyde away from his home," I said. "He sent him to stay with his sister or his nephew, right? At least, those are the two people on the news I saw giving interviews."

She nodded. "Clyde was supposedly with the sister, a woman named Millicent Boatman. That other person on

TV was her son, Dirk. Anyway, Mr. Jeffrey took the cat down to Hilton Head where the Boatman woman lived two months ago, but Clyde ran off. Then he showed up on Norm's doorstep several days ago and raised a ruckus. Woke the neighbors, who wondered why in the heck Norm didn't hear his old friend meowing at the door."

I peered into the crate and said, "But there was no waking your friend, huh, buddy?"

Clyde, a gigantic orange tabby with the kind of up-turned mouth that looks like a perpetual smile, blinked at me. This boy had traveled more than two hundred miles to get home. A combination of sorrow and admiration created a lump in my throat.

Allison said, "Shawn is not inclined to hand this cat back over to the sister without first talking to her away from the cameras. He wants to know how Clyde escaped from her house. And would you believe she hasn't even shown up in Mercy yet? Too busy giving interviews to CNN, I guess."

"And I gather they're still thinking Mr. Jeffrey died of natural causes?" I said.

"Far as I know. The man did have cancer." She whispered the last word. "Don't know what kind—not sure I want to know." Allison's eyes filled as she fixed a short, burnished wave of hair behind her ear.

I said, "I guess Mr. Jeffrey must have been too frail to care for this big fella. Anyway, I promise to heap tons of love on him if he'll let me." I was feeling the need to comfort both Allison and Clyde now. "This guy knew his owner was ill and he needed to get home." I watched Syrah, my bravest kitty, nose in close to the carrier door.

"Kara kept anything she knew about Mr. Jeffrey's private medical issues out of the paper," Allison said. "But those reporters must have got someone to talk. Like this Millicent person, maybe?"

Chablis rubbed against Allison's knee, her curiosity

about Clyde satisfied for now. Besides, she knew Allison needed a little comfort.

Allison sat cross-legged on the floor so Chablis could climb into her lap.

"Did you know that Norm adopted Clyde from us?" She stroked Chablis, who closed her eyes and raised her chin to offer her throat. Allison complied and stroked it.

"I had no idea." I pushed two fingers through the carrier grate to let Clyde sniff my fingers. "When was that?"

"Clyde walked right up to our sanctuary door a couple years ago," she said. "'Course he was a kitten and a third the size he is now. You can imagine our surprise when Candace brought him back to us the other day. We recognized him right away by his smile."

I shook my head, troubled. "All they want to talk about on the news is Clyde's voyage home. I heard next to nothing about poor Mr. Jeffrey and how much he probably missed his cat during his illness."

Allison said, "Thing is, it's not all that amazing for a cat to travel long distances to return home. Those TV folks don't understand the true feline nature if they think it's odd." The passion for animals that both Allison and Shawn felt came through in her voice. "Animals love with all their hearts. There're a few humans I know who could take a lesson from them."

"That's for sure. But I don't understand why these reporters are still hanging around. I mean, the story's over, right?"

"Oh no. Not over yet. One of those reporters was shouting at my husband this morning, yelling that he knew Shawn wasn't in any hurry to turn over the cat to Millicent Boatman." She shook her head in annoyance.

"How could they possibly know?" I said. "No. That was a silly question. The folks in Mercy do love to talk."

"True," she replied. "As far as Shawn is concerned, this cat will not be turned over to a woman who couldn't hang on to him, so I am sure there will be a bit of a *disagreement* over who gets possession of Clyde. Like anyone can really possess a cat." She grinned, and it warmed my heart to see her lovely smile.

"You got that right," I said.

"Anyway, the story continues. Candace says—and you know how thorough Candace is when it comes to an investigation—anyways, she agrees that until she knows for sure who Clyde should go home with, he stays with us. Well, now with you."

"Still, Mr. Jeffrey did give Clyde to his sister, so if she persists about wanting him back, then—"

"Nope. Not yet, anyway. Shawn worries that Clyde will leave Hilton Head again and might not make it back to Mercy the next time." Allison continued to pet Chablis, who purred loud enough to wake the birds sleeping outside.

Clyde finally broke into the conversation, and the sound made me start. His meow was louder than a small dog's bark. No wonder Mr. Jeffrey's neighbors had heard him.

Merlot backed off a couple feet from the crate, and this time, his tail puffed and he growled. Syrah's coat stood on end, too. But Chablis? She was content in Allison's lap, completely unaffected by Clyde.

"Wow. That's quite a voice he's got," I said.

"He can be very vocal. He had to be to get the neighbor's attention. Hope he doesn't keep you awake tonight." Allison gently moved Chablis off her lap and stood. "And now, I need to go home."

I rose, too. "Is Clyde on scheduled meals? I mean, he seems awfully big and—"

"Big, yes. Overweight, no—probably because of the long trip he just made. We've been filling his bowl as soon as it's empty because he's hungry all the time," she said.

"What about his feet after his trek? Are they okay?" I asked.

Syrah had jumped on the sofa behind me so he could look down at the crate—and be higher than our new friend, Clyde.

"His feet are fine," she said. "All he suffered was a little dehydration. He didn't even need worming. My guess is this guy made friends along the way—and he made good time, too. Took him a couple months. Probably walked five to ten miles a day."

"Wow. I'd be exhausted—and probably lost—if I were him. But since cats have their own little GPS in their brains, they aren't quite as directionally challenged as someone like me." I picked up the bag of kibble. "I'll be starting Clyde out in the basement guest bedroom. As soon as you called, I ran down there and put out a clean cat quilt, a litter box and fresh water."

Allison smiled. "You'll spoil him rotten. And he deserves to be spoiled. I'll carry him down for you. This boy is heavy."

"I believe I'll let you do that. I don't want to drop him."

Fifteen minutes later, a tired Allison was on her way home and Clyde was already digging into his food while I sat by and watched.

I knew my three cats would not be joining me in bed tonight. They'd be parked outside the guest room door until dawn. Cats do not like a closed door, especially when a visitor is on the other side.

I'd miss them, but cats have to do what cats have to do.

Two

At first, the loud and insistent knocking on my front door seemed to be part of a dream. Was I experiencing Allison's late-night visit all over again? But the noise persisted and grew even louder. I sat up and squinted at the nightstand clock. Seven a.m.

Seven a.m? What the heck?

I grumbled as I got out of bed and found the jeans I'd left on the floor last night. My friends do *not* knock on my front door; they come to the back of the house. And they call first—at least most of the time. So, though I wanted to cover my head with my pillow and grab another hour of sleep, I had to find out who was being so demanding. Maybe a neighbor had lost a pet . . . or maybe Allison needed me to do something else for her. But she could have phoned. No, this was something else, and I had a bad feeling about it.

Groggy from staying up too late playing with my new friend, Clyde, I felt almost hungover as I rummaged in my dresser for a T-shirt. What a fun cat that big boy was, and once he started playing the "paws under the door" game with my crew without any hissing or growling involved, I decided it was okay to let my three curious felines into the room to meet him right away. It helped that mine were used to an occasional feline guest, but I still thought it best that after I supervised their getting to know one another, I'd shut them out for the night.

Now, when I could have used another hour of sleep, I'd been awoken by some person pounding—yes, now they were *pounding*—on my front door.

I grabbed my cell phone as I hurried to see just what was so urgent. When I peered through the peephole, I saw something I certainly didn't expect: a man who I could have sworn was wearing makeup—and maybe even hair spray.

Huh? Since I couldn't see beyond the distortion of his large sandy-haired head through the peephole, I hurried back to my living room, grabbed the remote and turned on my television. It was a new smart TV, and my security expert and boyfriend, Tom Stewart, had set it up so I could access a screen that showed the view from every security camera installed outside my home.

Sure enough, I could see the entire picture of what was transpiring out there.

"Darn it all," I muttered. But I was glad for all my cameras. Tom installed them after Syrah had been catnapped a few years ago, and I could have never anticipated how much I appreciated being able to see most of my property, both inside and out. Plus all the feeds were connected to my smartphone. Even if I was away from home, I knew what was happening here. I'd told Tom he could probably make a fortune selling his techniques for this sort of thing, but he said other companies already did similar work and that he didn't really care to get involved in business that might involve travel or take up more time than his PI and security business already did.

Various other people besides this man loitered on my lawn, drinking coffee or staring vacantly at the front of my house. The man at the door had on a suit and there was a woman with swept-back blond hair who wore an expensive-looking print dress and high heels, but others wore shorts, T-shirts and headphones. And not small ear-bud headphones, either. Big headphones. Cables snaked along my driveway to a van with a satellite dish on top. Yes, the TV folks had found Clyde. And, of course, they'd found me, too. I was again reminded there are no secrets in the small town of Mercy. Not for long.

I found Candace's number in my speed dial. Though worried I might wake her, I had no idea what to do about this situation. I might need her police presence here.

Fortunately, she seemed quite alert when she said, "Hey there. What's up, Jillian?"

"What's up?" I eased onto the sofa, still staring at the media tableau before me. Chablis joined me, promptly sprawling across my lap and blinking up at me. "Here's what's up. My front yard is cluttered with people holding cameras, and one of their vans is blocking my driveway."

She sighed heavily. "Great. They know you've got the cat. I promise I didn't tell them a thing."

"Of course you didn't. But what should I do?" I ran my hand over Chablis's silky champagne-colored coat and felt calmer almost instantly.

More sighing came through the phone. "I'm waiting for a fax from Mr. Jeffrey's pathologist. His autopsy report should come in today. Can I send Morris to get those press-types to back off? They do have a right to be on the street, but we can get them away from your front door."

Morris Ebeling, Candace's partner, seemed the perfect choice for the job. A grouch in uniform was just what I needed. "Thank you," I said. "I only want them to stop pounding on my door and not block my driveway."

"Will do. Just don't talk to them," Candace warned. "They're sorta like kids and candy. You give them a taste of sugar and they'll keep begging for more."

"I have no intention of giving them the time of day—which is seven o'clock in the morning, last I checked. Should I call Kara to come over and intervene? She's their colleague, so to speak."

"No. Don't do that. If they figure out you two are related, they won't leave *either* of you alone."

"Okay. Morris it is, then. Talk to you later." Ready for much-needed coffee, I disconnected and picked up Chablis. "Keep me company in the kitchen, baby, and we'll pretend there's no one out there trying to get our attention." I was certain Syrah and Merlot were waiting downstairs. A closed door and a strange new friend named Clyde could not be ignored.

By the time the coffee was brewed, Morris had come to my rescue. I heard his familiar gruff voice shouting at the folks assembled on the front lawn. In case they decided to invade the back of my property as well, I'd closed every blind in the house so no one could sneak a peek into one of the many windows overlooking Mercy Lake. It bothered me to be denied the view of the salmon-colored sunrise spreading its glow across the water. I'd only had a glimpse this morning.

A good five minutes later, Morris knocked on my back door, shouting, "It's me, Jillian."

I let him in and gave him a grateful hug, which seemed to catch him by surprise. He blushed bright red, a Christmas-like contrast to his forest green uniform.

"Just doin' my job," he said after I thanked him. "They got no right steppin' all over your flowers and rattling your door like you've got Elvis Presley's ghost floating around in here."

"My pansies? Darn it all. They were doing so well." I walked over to the coffeepot and held it up, eyebrows raised.

He nodded at the carafe. He might even have been drooling. "Your flowers are flat as the earth used to be. I can make them pay you for those. I got all them TV idiots rounded up in the road and I'm bettin' not one of them is leavin', neither. How much those flowers set you back?" He took a mug off the little stand by the coffeepot and handed it to me.

"Not much. I'll let it go. I don't want to talk to any of those people, not even about crushed pansies." I filled his mug and pushed a spoon and the sugar bowl toward him.

Just then, Syrah, Merlot and Clyde appeared through the door leading to the basement. That darn Syrah had probably been working all night to get the guest room door open. Latches to him were merely a puzzle to be solved—and he always succeeded.

Morris glanced down at the cats as he doctored his coffee. "This big one's the guy causin' all this ruckus? He's just a dern cat. What's the big deal?" Realizing his mistake at once, he offered a rare, conciliatory smile. "Sorry. That's the wrong thing to say to you."

"True, Morris. No such thing as *just a cat* to me." I knelt and greeted all the felines. "I suppose this is a human interest story and these press people have nothing better to do right now. I called Kara last night after Allison brought the cat over here. She says a slow news cycle will make reporters go after a tale like this—pun intended. Plus they got a photo of Clyde—from where, I don't know. She told me since he's got this lovable face and he's so big and pretty, the story of his travels has gone viral."

"Yeah, like a *disease*. Reporters are prone to those types of illnesses." Morris held up his mug. "Best coffee I've had since . . . about an hour ago."

I laughed. "You do love the stuff. You hungry? I was just about to toast a bagel."

"Nope. I gotta get back. With Candace all tied up making sure Norm Jeffrey died a natural death and wasn't a victim of foul play . . ." He paused to roll his eyes. "Anyways, she's busy, and I got to pick up the slack. Who knows? Some kid mighta spray-painted the high school bricks with his girlfriend's name now that school's near out."

Vandalism and public intoxication were the most common crimes in Mercy. But if Candace was still investigating a death three days after a man's body was discovered, I was certain she had a good reason. "Candace has a concern about how Mr. Jeffrey died, right?" I stood and all four cats began weaving around my legs. They were hungry.

"What do you think? 'Course she has a concern." But then Morris's annoyed expression disappeared. "Sorry. I know she's your best buddy and I shouldn't be actin' like she don't know what she's doin'. She's good at her job and a lot less lazy than this old SOB." His cheeks fired up again. "Pardon my language, Jillian. It's early and I need at least six more cups of joe before my mouth cleans up proper." He glanced down at the cat crew. "Bet these four don't care, though." He smiled.

"All they care about right now is their next meal. Anyway, if Candace has a concern . . . well, we both know it's not without cause." I leaned a hip against the kitchen counter as the cats stared up at me in patient anticipation. "Tell me what the heck is going on."

"Okay, there is something—but don't you go repeating it."

"Of course not," I replied. I *knew* there had to be more to this story.

"The number of pills in Mr. Jeffrey's heart medicine bottle wasn't right. Not enough there for when the prescription was last filled. She thinks that could mean something. Me? I wouldn't have been even lookin' in that bottle to begin with, much less countin' the pills. Anyways, she pestered the coroner to have the man autopsied—something that wouldn't normally have happened seein' as how he was old and sick. But you know Candace. Never leaves a stone unturned."

I smiled. "That's my girl. If there's foul play involved, you know she'll find out."

"Got that right." Morris drained his mug and set it in the sink. "You have any more trouble with those folks out yonder, you call me and I'll arrest their sorry butts for trespassin'. They've been warned."

"Thanks for coming over, Morris."

Grumpy as the old guy was, he was still huggable, but he left before I could hug him again.

After Morris had gone, I dealt with the most pressing issue—hungry cats. Then I rechecked my security feeds to make sure the newspeople were complying with Morris's warning to stay away from my house. They were. For now. So after I gobbled down my bagel, I showered. While toweling my hair, I heard knocking again—but fortunately at the back door.

By the time I reached the kitchen, Tom had already come inside and was crouched down, his hand extended to a sitting Clyde. My three cats were rubbing against Tom's knees and thighs, begging for his attention.

"Hey there." I raked my hands through my still-damp hair. "You're here early."

Tom looked up at me, his amazing blue eyes gentle as a whisper. "I was worried after I checked your surveillance feeds this morning. But now I understand." He glanced knowingly at Clyde.

"Yes, the celebrity cat has a new temporary home. He was staying in the guest room, but Syrah decided he needed to be released from captivity." I eyed Syrah. "You love a challenge, don't you?"

Tom patted each cat's head and stood. "You need knobs rather than latches if you want to keep Syrah from opening any door he pleases. He's got it down to a science."

I laughed. "But what fun would it be then?"

Tom walked over and took me in his arms. We shared a fresh-from-toothpaste, minty kiss. "When do I get to join the fun here full-time? Because I've been patient and—"

I touched a finger to his lips. "First we have to tell the folks in our lives that we're getting married. I think I'd like to invite everyone for a barbecue. How's that sound?"

He smiled down at me. "You're ready to let the secret out that we're engaged?"

I nodded. "Time to let the cat out of the bag." He'd asked me to marry him several months ago—and I'd said yes. But I told him I needed time to let the idea sink in, learn to live with my decision to move on after losing my husband to a heart attack more than five years ago. But I felt ready now.

Tom smiled, tilted his head to the ceiling and let out a whoop that sent all my cats scurrying to far corners—all except Clyde, who stayed put and seemed to study us both as if we were statues at a museum. Then Tom hugged me close. "My mom thought after my first marriage, I'd never get married again. She'll be pleased, even if we middle-aged folks won't be giving her the grandkids she always wanted."

I lifted my face to his and we shared another kiss.

Five minutes later we sipped coffee at the small mosaic-tiled table in the kitchen nook that overlooked Mercy Lake. I opened the blinds enough so we could enjoy the water lapping the bank under the morning sun.

Tom said, "Should I set up a few more cameras so we can tell if those TV people get closer to the house? They do have to respect private property, after all."

I laughed. "More cameras? Have you bought new techie toys you want to try out on me? Because the White House might be envious if they saw how well-protected my house is."

"I do have upgrades that I planned to put in anyway. You liked how I did the four-screen feed on your smartphone, right?"

"Yes, but I can wait on that. The reporters' interest will surely wane in a day or two. Another story will catch their fancy and they'll be gone as quick as they arrived."

"Having once been a cop, and even now in my PI work, I've tangled with reporters a lot. I can tell you that newspeople from big-time TV are aggressive and manipulative. I don't like them hanging around here—especially when I have a security installation to do fifty miles away today."

I leaned toward him, forearms on the table, brows knitted. "You don't think I can handle them?"

"Guess that sounded too old-school, huh? I know you can take care of yourself."

I reached over and grabbed his wrist. "Glad you get that, so hush. I'll be fine."

For an instant his eyes seemed to glisten, but the tender moment was interrupted by Candace's unique knock on the back door. She let herself in before Tom or I even had a chance to stand.

"Hey there, y'all. I see the show goes on right in front of your house." She made a beeline for the fridge, took out the pitcher of sweet tea and set it on the counter. She opened a cabinet and removed a glass. "It's a nice kitty story, but isn't there a war somewhere that deserves their attention more than one vagabond cat?"

Candace's voice brought my three friends meandering in from the living area. They gathered around her legs and promptly deposited cat hair on her uniform trousers. They loved Candace. She knelt to greet them. Clyde sat just outside the kitchen, observing. He was such a calm and handsome boy—a patient watcher.

Tom went over to Clyde. "This celebrity is one cool customer, huh, Candace?"

Candace smiled at Clyde. "Loved that guy from the minute I laid eyes on him outside Mr. Jeffrey's house." She poured her tea and put the pitcher back in the fridge. "If I weren't so busy all the time, I would have taken him in myself. Clyde must have known something was wrong here in Mercy to travel all that distance. And he was right-on. Which is why I'm here. I fear those reporters will be around a tad longer once the autopsy report goes public."

"Uh-oh." I glanced at Tom and saw concern furrow his brow.

"What's the problem?" Tom said.

"Overdose of digitalis, his heart medication." Candace took a long drink of tea.

"Did he take his own life?" I was thinking about what I'd learned concerning Mr. Jeffrey's terminal cancer. Some folks would rather control the end of their life than have a disease make the decision about when they would go.

Candace's eyes narrowed and she cocked her head. "Suicide would be the logical conclusion. But if you're gonna go do something like that, why not take the entire bottle of pills? Why leave *any* behind?"

Tom folded his arms and nodded in appreciation at Candace. "You're right. Why *not* take the whole bottle?"

"I didn't think about that," I said. "But please tell me the killer didn't leave behind an unsigned, computer-generated suicide note."

Candace allowed a small smile. "Don't you hate it when you see that on TV?"

I knelt and extended a hand to Clyde, who was looking at me now. "Obviously the killer had access to Mr. Jeffrey's medication. That should narrow the field." The cat trotted to me and rubbed his head against the back of my hand.

Lips tight, she nodded. "Narrows it to about one or

two people here in town. Enough said about *that* piece of information for now. Anyways, before I pay a visit to one of them, I need to know exactly what happened in that house and why the poor man had to die right now. Because, see, he was dying anyway."

"Really?" I tried to sound surprised, not wanting her to know I'd already been given this information. But then I saw a look on Candace's face I'd become quite familiar with—her "I need you to do something for me" expression.

"Yup. The man had the big *C*. And right now, I need time and space to investigate this case. Learn everything I can about Norm Jeffrey. And that's where you come in. Jillian, I need a favor."

Three

I hefted Clyde up into my arms—gosh, he had to weigh twenty-five pounds—and carried him into the living room. "I'll help any way I can."

Tom and Candace followed me—and so did my three cats, no doubt unhappy I wasn't carrying a cat named Syrah, Chablis or Merlot.

Clyde purred like an idling motor as I sat on the couch. He was so big, he could rest his head on my chest while the rest of him stretched out all the way to my knees. Syrah jumped up on the back of the couch and stared down at Clyde, his sleepy glare not concealing his jealousy. Meanwhile, Merlot and Chablis sat at my feet and looked up with undisguised indignation. But Clyde had traveled so far for loving comfort, I felt the need to offer him what I could.

Tom came to the rescue. He picked up Chablis and sat with her on his lap at the opposite end of the couch. She would be the one most offended by my cuddling another cat. Merlot turned and decided Candace was the best option for his share of affection.

Merlot was content to rest against Candace's legs when she sat opposite me on the overstuffed chair, her glass of tea held with two hands. Syrah, meanwhile, sat in his favorite spot, a place where he could keep a close eye on Clyde.

Candace leaned toward me. "You and Clyde present the perfect picture. This is what the newspeople want to see."

"But I thought you weren't happy with the press presence here," I said.

"I'm not pleased, but I want you to invite a couple of them in for an interview. Let them see Clyde like Tom and I are seeing him right now. You can answer questions about him and about cats in general—because you know more about cats than any person I know."

"But—"

Tom interrupted, saying, "You *want* her to invite those people into her house? What's the plan, Candace?"

But I understood. "Distraction, right?" I stroked Clyde, whose face now rested in the crook of my neck.

She lifted her glass in my direction. "You got it. If we give them what they came for, I'm hoping they won't notice I'm investigating a suspicious death. They'll continue to focus on the journey of one determined cat."

I shifted, rubbed a thumb against Clyde's cheek. His already loud purring amped up another notch. "I don't know. Can't Tom sit with Clyde and talk to them? If you haven't noticed, I'm not exactly a Kardashian."

"You're better than any reality TV princess," Tom said. "Better looking, more genuine. I'd be glad to help, but I have to work. I've put off this client once already—last week when it rained like God opened a spigot. But in my book, you are *so* made for a TV appearance like this, Jilly."

"I agree." Candace drained her glass and stood. "It's settled. I'll talk to them, give them a time—I'm thinking this afternoon right about when the autopsy goes public. They'll be here interviewing you, get their story and then hopefully leave town. And meanwhile I can pick up my search warrant, sneak back to the Jeffrey house and look for anything we might have missed in light of these autopsy findings."

Tom released Chablis. I could tell she was becoming a tad pissed off that I was holding Clyde. She made her way over to me and sniffed at him. He was so content, he didn't even open his eyes. I stroked Chablis with my free hand and this seemed to mollify her—for the moment.

Tom bent and kissed my forehead. "I have to get going. You'll do great. And maybe you can sneak in a mention of your cat quilt business. Nothing like free advertising."

"Bye, babe. Drive carefully." Clyde wiggled free, apparently feeling the need to accompany Tom to the back door.

"Be careful when you open the door, Tom," I called. "Clyde's following you."

After we heard the back door close, Clyde soon ambled back to join us, that darling smile on his impish face.

Before leaving, Candace said she would talk to the reporters and call me with the time they'd be arriving with their cameras and lights.

"You owe me, Candace Carson," I called as she left through the back door. I tried to sound like I was joking, but a gnawing had begun in the pit of my stomach. I'm no fan of the spotlight and I am not one for inviting strange humans into my home. Fur babies are quite another story. But then, animals that you love and care for rarely turn on you. I had the sense this upcoming encounter might not be as simple a solution as Candace believed it would be. Not by a long shot.

The two reporters and their crew of four who knocked on my door at two o'clock had less equipment than I'd imagined. As they noisily invaded my living room, the reporters immediately informed me Deputy Carson had assured them they could each have a separate interview. So this would be doubly difficult. One of them was the man in the bow tie who'd knocked on my front door so early this morning. His name was Gerard Holcomb and my first impression was that of an abrupt and distracted man. I wasn't getting a good vibe off him, especially when he pretty much ignored me after introductions, peppering the cameraman with orders instead.

The other "correspondent," as she called herself, was Tess Reynolds, the blonde I'd seen first thing this morning. She now wore a cream silk blouse and pencil skirt. She shook my hand, made eye contact and seemed interested in talking to me. I had seen her on a morning show she once hosted years ago. When I mentioned this, she quickly explained that she was a "special assignment" correspondent now.

Up close, Tess looked every bit her age—which had to be early sixties. On television, she had never seemed to grow old and it struck me that I preferred seeing her in person. She seemed softer, more human. In contrast to Gerard Holcomb, she even acted interested in Clyde. But when I offered to pick him up and bring him to her so she could pet him, she held up her hands and stepped back. "No, no, no. Can't have any cat hair on me. But he is sweet looking."

Mr. Bow Tie then insisted that I remove my "other animals" from his "set." Yup. He called my house his *set*. I refused, but it didn't matter. Merlot and Chablis scurried down the hallway to my bedroom once they felt they could safely get past the cameras and extension cords. Syrah, however, wasn't about to relinquish his territory. He perched on the picture windowsill and stared at the man with impervious disdain.

A young woman, maybe midtwenties, approached me with authority once Tess and Gerard began busying themselves deciding where to best "place the woman and the cat." I was simply *the woman*. Clyde was just *the cat*. Regret and anxiety began warring for priority inside my head.

"I'm Cindy and I'll be doing your hair and makeup," the young woman said. "You're very fair, and with those red highlights in your hair, we'll go with lighter rose shades." She smiled and asked if she could set her makeup case on the dining room table. But she didn't even wait for a response. She just walked to the table, set the case down and opened it.

Hair and makeup? Why had I ever agreed to this? I thought someone would simply shove a microphone in my face, ask me a few questions and then these folks would leave. But they'd gone all Barbara Walters on me and I felt as if my life belonged to them now. Meanwhile, Clyde sat calmly at the junction of the kitchen and living room, unperturbed by this mayhem. I needed to take a lesson from him, get through this and hope they all left town as soon as they walked out my door.

A good thirty minutes later, I was seated in my over-stuffed chair. It had been moved so the view of the lake out my picture window was prominent in the background. This forced them to push aside the leather re-cliner that my late husband once sat in every night before bed for as long as we'd been together. I swallowed down the lump in my throat as I watched them move it, eager to shout, *Be careful with that,* but not wanting to sound rude.

The cameraman was the only person who seemed in-terested in the scenery. After the sound man clipped a small microphone onto my shirt—a pink blouse the makeup lady "suggested" I wear after a thorough exam-ination of my closet—he smiled as he looked out on the shimmering water. "What a view, Mrs. Hart."

I nodded appreciatively, grateful for the presence of someone who didn't seem completely self-involved. As

Tess began her interview, I found myself drawn to his encouraging smile rather than to her. At least he sensed my discomfort.

"We're here in the living room of Jillian Hart in Mercy, South Carolina. She's graciously invited us inside so we can visit with a now-famous orange tabby named Clyde. Clyde is a wanderer, we have learned. He traveled more than two hundred miles to find his original owner." She stared fondly at him sitting in my lap. "Such a bittersweet tale. Can you tell us how he came to be living here with you today?"

I told her about his needing a foster home after his owner's untimely death and how I had fostered cats in the past.

Without a mention of poor Mr. Jeffrey, she went on. "The world is amazed at Clyde's stamina. Did he have any health issues after such a long journey?"

"No, ma'am. He has a great appetite and his paws are in perfect shape. Our local vet found absolutely nothing wrong with him." I forced a smile and stroked the cooperative Clyde. He lay on one of my kitty quilts that I'd draped over my lap. Tess thought it would be a nice touch to have him sitting on a quilt.

Meanwhile, Syrah had taken his favorite spot on the sofa back and his expression seemed to mock us both. It was as if he were saying, *Why are you doing this? You sound ridiculous—and Mr. Big Cat? What's with you? Have you no pride?*

I fought a sheepish grin, knowing this would be a perfect assessment had Syrah been able to talk.

"We understand you helped out another famous cat—one belonging to local socialite and philanthropist Ritaestelle Longworth. How do these two cats compare?"

I was momentarily stunned by her question. How did she know about Ritaestelle and her cat, Isis? And what else did these people know about my life? I took a deep breath before I answered. "Isis and Clyde are very different, but both special. Just like each person is unique. I haven't known Clyde that long, but he is a calm and loving boy. And I can tell he is missing Mr. Jeffrey. I could never be a substitute for the man who originally rescued Clyde."

"Yes, he *was* a rescue cat, wasn't he?" She tilted her head and again smiled at Clyde. "I understand rescues are often very bright. And this one must have his own GPS to have come so far."

"Actually, scientists believe cats do have a kind of GPS in their brains and—"

"So interesting, indeed," she interrupted. "What's in Clyde's future? Will he live with you or go to one of the former owner's relatives? Or perhaps one of our viewers will have the opportunity to adopt him. I know the e-mails and tweets are already flooding into the network."

Her suggestion struck a nerve. This wasn't a game show with Clyde as the prize to be offered up to their viewers.

"That's not up to me," I answered, trying to keep my tone Southern sweet. "Please remember, Mr. Jeffrey will always be Clyde's owner in his heart. Right now, this boy needs love and attention. That's my only focus."

Her interview ended with a question about my kitty quilt business and whether Clyde had decided the one he sat on belonged to him. I wasn't sure what I answered as I was still stunned by her lack of empathy for a dead man.

Gerard Holcomb was up next and his questions were similar. But though Tess seemed pretty much the same on camera and off, Gerard turned on the charm. He became a totally different person than the man who had pounded on my door and marched into my house.

I even found myself smiling broadly when he said, "You and this cat have already formed a bond. When you watch this interview once it airs, you'll see what the world is seeing. I understand you have cats of your own."

I told him about my three Katrina rescues and beyond the cameraman, I saw Tess's face fall. She hadn't thought to ask about my other cats and knew she'd missed an opportunity to add even more emotion to the interview. Her research hadn't revealed *all* the details of my small-town life. But somehow Gerard knew, probably by instinct, that my own cats might have an interesting backstory similar to Clyde's.

He finished the interview by asking the cameraman to get a close-up on Clyde's wonderful, gentle expression and I felt more relaxed than I had all day.

But the minute the red light on the camera went off, he reverted to being a jerk. People, unlike cats, have the ability to often disappoint.

Four

Once the television people went out the front door, I was thankful to see them pack up all their equipment and drive away. If Candace and I had our wish, they were off to the airport. I felt as if a weight had been lifted— until Clyde began pacing around the house and meowing mournfully. This was not his home, no matter how easily he had embraced me and my cat family.

In my opinion, cats grieve. After all, the part of the cat's brain where emotion is centered is almost identical to a human's. Clyde had worked so hard to get home to Mr. Jeffrey and instead he found himself in a strange house. I tried to comfort the big boy, but Clyde didn't want treats, or tuna cat food or even real tuna water, and believe me, that was something cats rarely turned down. He simply needed time and petting and, most of all, acceptance.

My kitties seemed to sense his suffering as well and they let him be. I decided to follow suit and get on with a day mostly lost to watching or worrying about the media people. I'd wanted a chance to make the interview more about Mr. Jeffrey, and about how a cat traveled all those miles out of need to be with his friend. But little of that would air on television tomorrow because they hadn't asked me those sorts of questions. Now, I felt like a trial witness who had a complete story, one that would shed light on a crime, but I hadn't been able to tell it because I could answer merely what was asked. So Clyde's story would only be half told.

I busied myself with Internet orders for my kitty quilts the rest of the day. The time flew by, and before I knew it, Tom texted that he would bring over dinner.

Thirty minutes later, Tom arrived. What he hadn't told me was he was also bringing a big box of fresh peaches. He kicked open the back door, his arms loaded with peaches and pizza. When I came to help him, that was when it happened.

Clyde slipped out and ran toward the lake.

"No," I cried. I was barefoot but had a pair of flip-flops near the door. I grabbed them.

Tom juggled the box as I pushed past him to chase after Clyde. At the top of the back stairs, I put on the almost-shoes and ran down in the direction Clyde had gone. But I couldn't see him anywhere.

Tom was right behind me.

"I'm so sorry," he called as I hurried along the shore, looking ahead and then up the slope toward the empty wooded lot next to my house. Tom caught up to me and I stopped, hands on hips.

"He'll be hard to find between all those trees." I glanced at Tom's stricken face. "Don't blame yourself. It's my fault. Clyde was . . . *distraught* after being put on display. I should have figured he was planning an escape. That is his MO, after all."

"I don't see him anywhere." Tom looked left and right, then up the hill until his gaze stopped at the tall pines and black walnut trees at the top. "Is he a climber, you think? We could get Billy Cranor out here with the fire ladder if we need to."

Billy was a local volunteer fireman and a good friend.

"That's a big if—and it's getting dark." I shook my head, feeling guilty and helpless. "My cats know the word *treat* and would come to me in a heartbeat, but this guy couldn't care less about food—at least today. All those cameras and strangers in my house probably unnerved him. He didn't like it any more than I did." I stared at the grass, shoulders slumped. "I should have known better, should have anticipated this."

Tom rested a hand on the back of my neck and gently squeezed. "My turn to say it's not your fault. This is what cats do—especially Clyde. We'll find him, but it might take time."

I leaned into him. "I know exactly where he's going— it's just a matter of what route he'll take and how long until he gets there."

"Are you thinking he'll head back to the Jeffrey place?"

"That's right." I scanned the trees again. "But I can't give up until we at least look for Clyde in that miniforest. I won't be able to sleep if I don't hunt for him."

After I traded the flip-flops for tennis shoes, we found a couple of flashlights and spent an hour calling for Clyde in the empty lot. Then we trekked up and down the road in front of my house, the heat of the day dissipating into the darkness. Nothing but squirrels and birds to be seen. So we got in Tom's Prius and drove down the road leading out of my neighborhood in the hope of catching sight of him. Still nothing. The entire time, I worried for Clyde's safety as he roamed the rural landscape of Mercy all by himself.

Finally, pitch darkness forced us to give up and return home. Syrah, Merlot and Chablis sat by the back door and stared up at us when we came in. Merlot craned his neck as if looking behind me for Clyde to appear.

"We lost him, friends," I said to my three.

Tom took my hand and pulled me into the kitchen. "I know you feel awful, and I do, too, but we'll get him back."

The pizza Tom had brought with him, cold by now, sat on top of the box of peaches he'd set on the counter. But I'd lost my appetite.

Tom was hungry, though, and while he heated up a few slices, I made the phone calls I didn't want to make — to Candace and to Shawn.

Candace, like Tom, figured the cat would be fine and would show up on his own either at my house or at Mr. Jeffrey's place. Shawn was another story. He was always emotional, and now he was angry.

"How could you let this happen, Jillian?"

"I'm so, *so* sorry. But we'll find him."

"If he doesn't get hit by a car or chased down and torn apart by a stray dog." I heard him take a deep breath and let it out slowly. "Sorry. Me and my big mouth. I don't mean to make you feel bad. I've lost cats myself. He'll find Mr. Jeffrey's house again — maybe as soon as tomorrow. We'll get him back. Meanwhile, I'll make up some Lost Cat flyers to post in a few businesses like Belle's Beans. Can't risk those city folks coming here with their cameras and trucks. They're pests and they spook my shelter animals."

Usually Shawn would tweet about Clyde's escape or put his information up on a missing pet Web site and Facebook, but neither of us wanted those reporters to come back — and they do watch the Internet like hawks. Word of mouth in Mercy is almost as good anyway.

I offered to phone Doc Jensen and have him inform his vet staff about Clyde so they'd know if anyone called in to report having found him. Shawn said he'd take care of it, and after we said our good-byes, I hung up with tears stinging my eyes. The weather was perfect, with no rain in the forecast for tonight, and it wasn't as if Clyde didn't know what he was doing. But I still felt terrible and was sick with worry.

I hung my head and soon felt myself enveloped in Tom's loving arms. I allowed the tears to fall, remembering the panic I'd felt when Syrah had been snatched a few years ago. Miserable thoughts love the company of unhappy memories.

But I would find that cat—if it was the last thing I did.

I spent a restless night worrying about Clyde, fearing the worst—that he'd been hit by a car or maybe attacked by a raccoon. I finally gave in to the insomnia and got out of bed around five a.m. Fortified with strong coffee, I walked out on the deck and called Clyde's name. I leaned on the railing and scanned the landscape, the rising sun illuminating my wooded backyard. I saw no cat, and only the mockingbirds answered. I thought that was sadly ironic.

I went to my craft room with Syrah, Merlot and Chablis leading the way inside. Syrah immediately found an empty wooden spool—one of his favorite toys—and Merlot sat and watched him bat it around, waiting for a chance to take over if Syrah lost control of it. Meanwhile, Chablis joined me in my comfy chair where I did most of my handwork and settled on the padded right arm next to me.

I attempted to distract myself by finishing off the hand-quilting on an order for a woman in Minnesota with five cats. Though I usually machine quilt my kitty quilts since they require laundering pretty often, she'd asked her order of five quilts be hand-quilted. *Nothing but the best for my babies,* she wrote in her e-mail.

I was creating a pattern on the fifth and final quilt— an outline of a seated cat inside each block. But after stitching for more than an hour and having to take out almost every thread and redo my work, I gave up. I couldn't concentrate. I kept wondering if Clyde might be hanging around my house even though I hadn't seen him. It was worth another look.

Though it was still too early to alert the neighbors about a missing cat, I could walk up and down the street and check the wooded areas again. I tied my tennis shoes and opened a fresh can of salmon cat food for my three buddies. They had already informed me that it was their breakfast time.

They were chowing down when I left through the back door to search the yard and look under the deck one more time. Having no luck, I walked around to the front of the house. As I went along, I called "Here, kitty," or "Here, Clyde," even though I knew exactly where we'd find that cat later today or tomorrow—at the Jeffrey home.

But it wasn't Clyde who came in answer to my voice this warm morning, but rather a stranger. I looked up to see her at the end of my driveway, right near the mailbox. The young woman had Asian features, shiny black hair cut in a pixie style and a bright smile. She looked vaguely familiar, but I couldn't quite place her. She didn't walk up my drive to meet me, and then it dawned on me why.

Morris had warned the media to stay off my property and she was being careful to remain on the street. This person was with the press.

I groaned inwardly. She probably heard me calling for Clyde and no doubt guessed he was missing. I was willing to bet her big smile was because she was about to get a major scoop—something that might read OUR WANDERING FELINE IS OFF ON ANOTHER JOURNEY.

I pasted on a smile of my own and strode toward her, trying to convey via my body language that all was right with the world—when it was anything but.

"Hi. Can I help you?" I asked on reaching her.

She extended her hand. "Emily Nguyen, Channel Five, Asheville. Are you Jillian Hart?"

I took her tiny hand—she seemed no bigger than a twelve-year-old—and we greeted each other with nods and smiles.

Then I blinked as I took in her face. "You're the weather girl, right?"

Her dark eyes stared into mine. "I do other things. Special features on the weekend."

I'd upset her and I wondered what the politically correct term was. *Weather presenter?* "Sorry. You're a reporter, too, then. I guess I've only seen you do the early morning weather and traffic reports."

Her face relaxed and she offered that winning smile again. "That's okay. Not many people understand you have to start out somewhere. For a year, all I did was bring people coffee while I was studying to become a meteorologist."

"Wow. You're a meteorologist?" I didn't recall her doing the weather during the main newscasts.

She couldn't keep the frost out of her voice. "Once I got a full-time job on air with the station, I saw no need to continue in meteorology. It isn't my calling. I'm just doing fill-in weather reports and the morning commuter info to start. I have to say, the meteorologists have been so helpful. But my dream is to become a newscaster. And I will make it happen."

"I understand. Well, how can I help you, Miss Nguyen?" I knew I was in for a grilling.

"Did I hear you calling Clyde's name—Clyde, the wonderful cat our country has embraced?"

I had no idea what to say. She'd given me an opening to put her off with a lie, but lying didn't come easily for me. Thank goodness, out of the corner of my eye, I saw Candace's RAV4 speeding toward us down my street.

"You might want to step onto the lawn or you'll risk

life and limb." I tugged the sleeve of her short denim jacket and nodded in the direction of the oncoming vehicle.

Emily Nguyen moaned her displeasure. "Not *her*."

I smiled inwardly. "Ah. You know Deputy Carson?"

"Let's just say we're not best friends," Emily said.

Candace pulled into my driveway and joined us by the mailbox. Since she'd arrived in her own car and wore boyfriend jeans and a T-shirt, I assumed she wasn't on duty yet.

"What are *you* doing here?" she said to Emily.

"Following up on the story, Deputy. The interviews were given to the major outlets. We little people have to keep a finger in the pie *somehow*."

"How long have you been hanging around Mrs. Hart's house?"

"Why is that important?" Emily tried to appear clueless, but I decided she might need acting lessons. Then a little shiver climbed my arms. Had she been here last night when we'd been hunting for Clyde as well?

"Have you been here since the crack of dawn? Earlier than that?" Candace demanded.

Emily stood taller and raised her chin. "The sun has clearly been up for an hour. Besides, if you eat kale on a regular basis like I do, you can wake up with enough energy—"

"*Emily*. Wannabe Reporter Girl?" Candace moved within a foot of the woman-child and looked down on her. "Let me rephrase the question. How *long* have you been outside Jillian's house?"

"It's not a crime to be an early riser, you know. Maybe since about four a.m?"

"Next question," Candace said. "Don't need an essay in response, either. *Why?*"

"Because it's important to tell the whole story. Follow-up is crucial." Emily sounded almost sincere. Almost.

Candace tried to hide a smile. "We're talking about a cat here, not civil unrest in a foreign country."

"But from what I've seen and heard this morning, it sounds like he's missing again. And the world needs to know." This time her smile was triumphant. "And guess who'll be the first journalist to report on this? I'm thinking you should give me the story. I'm here and I can report this piece the way it ought to be told. Poor Clyde the Cat, after months on the road, once again—"

"Stop." Candace held up a hand in exasperation. "Here's what we're gonna do—and if you want the scoop on this, you'll go along. Yes, the cat is missing. But if you report it, all those big-time news folks will come rushing back to town. So, you're gonna keep quiet for now. When we find Clyde—and we will." Candace glanced my way. "We *will*. Anyway, I promise you'll be the first to tell the story of his latest escape from beginning to end."

Emily's eyes narrowed. "You promise?"

"I keep my word," Candace replied. "You leave us alone for now. But tell me where you're staying so I can get back to you when we find him."

After giving Candace her information—a cell number and the chain motel she was staying at up by the interstate miles away—Emily Nguyen tottered away on too-high summer wedges and left in a beat-up Altima parked down the road.

Candace shook her head slowly in disgust. "Just what we don't need. Someone ambitious like her. She hung around the station for hours yesterday, so she may know something is hinky with Mr. Jeffrey's death. How, I don't know." She turned to me. "And now, I can't function one more second without sweet tea."

Five

I usually have sweet tea ready and I'd made a new batch last night before bed with plenty of cane sugar syrup. Candace poured us each a tall glass while I popped a few frozen buttermilk biscuits into the oven. Since Tom had brought over plenty of peaches, I sliced some of those up, too. Biscuits and a bowl of sliced fruit sounded good to both of us.

We soon sat in the breakfast nook and Candace mumbled her delight after her first bite of the succulent peaches.

"I forgot to eat breakfast, and this is way better than the Pop-Tart I left sitting on the counter," she said.

"Hits the spot," I said. "Why are you here so early? I mean, I'm so glad you came when you did—you saved me from that reporter by showing up at exactly the right time. But is everything okay?"

She took a long drink of tea before answering. "I was worried how you're holding up after what happened. I figured you'd be beside yourself and need a friend. But a cat like Clyde? One who's traveled a couple hundred miles already? He was bound and determined to get on the road again, Jillian. Don't go blaming yourself."

"I should have been more vigilant. I feel terrible about letting him escape—and he was gone in a flash."

"But just like you told me last night, he'll show up at the Jeffrey house and you'll get him back."

"Another thing has been bothering me," I said. "I've been condemning the media in my mind for paying more attention to Clyde than to poor Mr. Jeffrey and his tragic death. But I've been guilty of the same thing myself. I want to know more about the man. Can you share what you know?"

"Not much to share yet. I intend to learn about him myself. For now, I believe he was murdered. And I always ask myself what made him a candidate to be a victim? Who might have wanted him out of the way sooner rather than later? See, that's what's important in this case. He was gonna die, but apparently not soon enough, according to someone out there."

I shook my head, feeling sad. From all accounts, the man died alone. "So you're certain it's murder and you're on the case. I can't think of a better person to be on Mr. Jeffrey's side."

"Until the complete toxicology report comes back, it's not officially a murder. The missing digitalis is the only reason they agreed to an autopsy, so the pathologist drew blood and looked specifically for the drug. He found levels that were far too high, but there could be other findings in the tox report. All I can do for now is to investigate his death as suspicious—and even Chief Baca believes I'm stretching it on that one. He's thinking suicide. But whatever he believes, it won't stop me."

I licked remnants of honey from my biscuit off my fingers. "I'm sure of that. How exactly will you investigate?"

"First I'll be interviewing Buford Miller. He's the home health aide who cared for Mr. Jeffrey. If anyone knows about that digitalis, it'd be him."

I perked up. "Could I go with you? Do one of those ride-along things?"

"Why, Jillian?"

"Like you said, this man knew Mr. Jeffrey. Probably knew him better than anyone while the old guy was so ill. I'd like to hear what he has to say. It would ease my mind if I knew as much about him as I do about Clyde."

"Can't see any harm in it—but Buford would have to agree. If he doesn't, you'll have to sit in my car and wait, okay?" She glanced down at her shirt and jeans. "I have to change into my uniform."

"So we have to go back to the station? Or to your apartment?"

"I planned on heading to work after coming here. Got my uniform in the RAV. We can swing over to the courthouse after I change, get my squad car and be on our way."

"But what about Morris? Will he want to go, too?"

Candace laughed. "Are you kidding me? Maybe when I have solid evidence he'll be on board with the investigation. Besides, the chief was adamant this case was *my thing*. He didn't want two officers tied up on a hunch. Since we have a paperwork backlog, Morris said he'd handle it while I interviewed Buford."

"Doesn't sound like *just* a hunch," I said. "The medication count is wrong."

"It is. That's why I need to speak with Buford. Perhaps either he or Mr. Jeffrey kept some of the medicine in a different container—like one of those pill organizers—though I never saw one of those. I specifically looked when I was at the Jeffrey house yesterday afternoon, thinking maybe I overlooked it. Came up with nothing. But I bagged every medicine bottle as evidence. Maybe Mr. Jeffrey mixed up his pills—had them in the wrong bottles. Who knows what the complete tox screen will show."

"You mean there could be other drugs that caused his death, ones he took by accident?" I said.

"Maybe. Or he took too much because someone switched things up on him. I simply don't know. I would think Buford should have answers."

I nodded, understanding that Candace always looked at a case from every angle. "Guess you're right to explore the possibilities. Could Mr. Jeffrey's family have come to town? Moved things or put his pill organizer in a different place?"

"I don't know that, either. They'll be in Mercy tomorrow to make funeral arrangements and I can ask them. But I learned last night that Mr. Jeffrey has several cousins, many of whom live close by. A widowed childless cousin, LouAnn Rafferty, resides right here in Mercy. The other families live in Woodcrest. Not far away at all. Learned all this from the pathologist, who in turn had been informed of this by Lydia Monk. Apparently she tracked them down and made the death notification. Of course, she never told any of us at Mercy PD."

Lydia Monk was the coroner's investigator, a peculiar woman who happened to have an obsession with my Tom. She had the deluded belief that deep down he loved her and that one day they would be together. Needless to say, she disliked me with a passion.

No surprise Lydia hadn't spoken to Candace, but what about these relatives? I said, "None of the family even made a phone call to Mercy PD about Mr. Jeffrey's death? And why didn't the neighbors who informed you about Clyde's loud arrival home tell you about these relatives?"

"You're assuming the neighbors knew about them. Who knows what the family situation is? Could be the sister has spoken with the cousins. Or maybe there're bad feelings in the family. Old grudges. Or could be they're all on vacation."

"Maybe," I said, "but it's been days since he died. Something doesn't feel right about this."

Candace pointed at me. "Exactly."

"From all you've told me, sounds as if Mr. Jeffrey was pretty much alone dealing with a terminal illness. How awful."

She nodded. "I agree. But it could be that's the way he wanted it. He wouldn't be the first person facing his Maker who pushed family and friends away. Anyway, it's time to visit with Buford. Be warned, he and I went to high school together and he's . . . *different*. Always was a troublemaker—pranks mostly. I was surprised to see he ended up in a job caring for others, but I guess he finally decided to care about someone besides himself."

Candace called the home health care agency that employed Buford Miller and learned he wouldn't start his shift until the afternoon. She phoned him after jotting down a number the agency gave her and told him to expect her soon at his residence and not to go anywhere.

Candace stood and smiled. "I know this address, know exactly where he lives. And I sure don't want to give him too much time to think. Let's go."

Buford Miller rented a room in the top floor of an old house off Main Street in downtown Mercy. His landlady, a large black woman named Birdie Roberts, greeted us with narrow-eyed interest after she answered the front door.

"Good morning, Mrs. Roberts. We came to see Buford." Candace smiled.

The woman gestured us into a foyer. The smell of bacon hit me immediately, but the air carried the scent of laundry detergent and lemon oil as well. Mrs. Roberts had already been busy today.

After she shut the lace-shaded front door, she opened her arms. "Why, it's you, Candace. That sun had me

squintin' and I couldn't see nothin' but your uniform.
Come here, girl." Candace was soon gathered in the
woman's warm embrace. Birdie then held her at arm's
length and said, "What's Buford done—'cause if that
boy's arrested, he can pack his belongings and find a new
place to live. I don't tolerate fools or criminals in my
house."

Candace smiled reassuringly. "Nothing criminal. We
just have a few questions about Mr. Jeffrey."

Her eyes shifted and I was almost certain she was
blinking back tears. "Ah, this is about poor Norman,
then. Such a good man."

"You knew Mr. Jeffrey?" I said.

Birdie cocked her head, the inquiring squint returning. "You're that cat lady, right? The one's always running 'round with Miss Candace here?"

I smiled. "That would be me. Jillian Hart."

"Seen your picture in the *Mercy Messenger* once or
twice. I been knowing Miss Candace all her life—her
grandma, rest her soul, was a dear friend from church. If
you're with her, then you're fine by me. Let me get Buford
before I forget why you came callin' in the first place."

She lumbered to the old staircase and didn't bother
with an intercom or a phone, probably because she didn't
require anything more than her voice. "Buford, get your
butt down here. Miss Candace is here for you." Birdie
offered me a quiet aside. "I know the boy wasn't awake
until I heard his phone ringin'. If ringin's what you call a
blast of music only Satan could endure. What's wrong
with phones ringin' like they's 'sposed to?"

"I agree," I said with a laugh. My thoughts drifted to
Finn, Tom's nineteen-year-old stepson. "But there's a
teenage boy I know well and his phone plays a loud
song, too—something about a pay phone. A ringtone
about something as obsolete as a pay phone just shows
his sense of humor."

"You talkin' about Finn, Mr. Tom's boy? I'm thinkin' y'all are practically family, right?"

I nodded and smiled. Birdie certainly knew everything about everyone, but she did live in Mercy, after all, gossip capital of the South. She was so up front with her knowledge and such a warm person, it didn't bother me in the least. Finn was a young man I held very dear to my heart.

The pounding on the steps foreshadowed the appearance of Buford, a pudgy, flushed young man with thinning blond hair. He wore khaki shorts, a camo T-shirt and a pair of Crocs.

"Your breakfast is sittin' on the table and cold by now," Birdie said. "Gonna get colder, too, lest you want to talk to Miss Candace in my kitchen."

Buford nodded, but he was staring at me. "Who's this?"

"Mrs. Hart. She's doing a ride along. You don't mind talking to me with her present?" Candace said.

His small eyes shifted between us. "I don't know. Seems weird. And if this is about Mr. Jeffrey's medical stuff, that's private."

"He's dead, Buford. There's nothing much private when you're dead."

Birdie grabbed Buford's shoulder, turning him in the direction of a long hallway. "Quit arguing with the police and get yourself in that kitchen. Those eggs is stone cold, but you'll eat every bite or there won't be another breakfast made by my hand for the likes of you."

Apparently that was a threat Buford took seriously. We soon found ourselves sitting at a Formica-covered kitchen table in the country-style room. Birdie placed a pot of coffee, slices of homemade bread and a pot of jam in the center.

"I got cleanin' left to do, so if you need anything, you just holler." With that, Birdie left the kitchen.

I poured cream into my coffee and watched the rich colors swirl together. It smelled heavenly.

Meanwhile, Buford shoveled congealing scrambled eggs into his mouth and alternated those bites with crispy-looking bacon. He listened to Candace as she asked questions about how long Buford had been caring for Mr. Jeffrey and what his duties were.

I sipped the smoky coffee, wondering immediately what kind of beans Birdie used. I *had* to get some. I then began to pay attention to Candace's interview. Despite the distraction of delicious homemade bread and amazing coffee, I heard he'd worked for Mr. Jeffrey for about a year and came in the afternoons three days a week to prepare protein shakes, help the man bathe, shave and take short walks with assistance.

"What kind of medical procedures did you do?" Candace asked.

Buford pushed his clean plate away and leaned back in a chair so creaky I feared it might break under his weight. "Took his blood pressure and pulse. Checked his eyes for jaundice. That's where the eyes get all—"

"I know what jaundice is," Candace said. "I did see him after he died and his skin was pretty yellow. Was that from the cancer?"

"Yup." Buford intertwined his thick fingers and rested them on his belly.

"He was dead for probably three days before he was found. If you checked on him every few days, how'd you miss him lying in that chair in the front room?"

Buford sat up straighter and the first sign of discomfort shadowed his features. "I took two days off to have a long weekend. Feel bad about that, but Mr. Jeffrey was fine with it. Sorry I wasn't there when he passed."

Candace rested her forearms on the table and stared into Buford's eyes. "When did you last see the man?"

"Last Wednesday. I took off Thursday and Friday.

Needed a little vacation. I do get vacation days. You found him on Monday, right?"

"Right. Three days ago." Candace sipped her coffee, her eyes still trained on Buford. "How was Mr. Jeffrey's mental state?"

Buford appeared confused by the question—and perhaps wary as well.

Finally he said, "W-what do you mean?"

"Was he sad . . . happy? You tell me, seeing as how not many people saw or talked to him but you."

"He was dyin', Candy. How do you think he felt?" There was an unpleasantness in his tone for the first time.

The muscles in Candace's jaw tightened. He'd called her Candy and that was a big no-no. "Let me break it down if these questions are making you have to think too hard. Was he sad?"

"No more than usual. He was a quiet old man for the most part. Only time I saw him happy was when he had that cat in his lap. He did miss Clyde." Buford laughed. "And now Clyde's come back as a celebrity."

"Back to Mr. Jeffrey. He wasn't despondent, then?" Candace pressed.

"Despondent? You pullin' out your hundred-dollar words on me, Candy?"

"Despondent as in so miserable he might want to take his own life?" she said slowly.

Buford considered this so long, I wanted to clear my throat to get him to focus and answer the question.

Finally he said, "I suppose he coulda been feelin' that low."

"You never wrote that down anywhere or told a supervisor he might be suicidal, though, did you?" Candace's tone told me she already knew the answer, had probably talked to someone at the agency about this.

"I *said* I *suppose* he coulda felt like that. I know I would if I was about to meet my Maker."

"Let's move along. Did his illness make him confused or forgetful?" she asked.

"Nope. Not in the least. He had a routine and that's good. I always tell the folks I care for that routine will keep their minds sharp. I deal with the elderly for the most part and—"

"That's nice, Buford," she cut in. "Back to Mr. Jeffrey. You give him his medicine? 'Cause we noticed he had quite a few pill bottles."

"Nope. He had that all under control." Wariness had returned to Buford's eyes, but added to that, his intertwined fingers drew up and tightened into a white-knuckled knot.

"Did he have one of those pill organizer things—you know, to keep his medicines straight?" she asked.

"Why are you asking these questions, Candy? You think somethin' fishy happened?"

"It's my job to ask questions when someone dies, so just answer me."

Candace can be abrupt, but her attitude toward Buford bordered on rude. I got the feeling something in their past relationship had more to do with this than with Mr. Jeffrey's death.

Meanwhile, Buford licked his lips before continuing. "No pill organizer. Man had a lot of health problems, so he was taking stuff for his heart, stuff for pain, stuff for his stomach. But he knew what to take and when. Like I said, he didn't have any trouble with his mind. It was liver cancer, not brain cancer, that was killin' him."

For the first time, Candace took her small notebook from her shirt pocket and jotted down a few notes, then said, "I see. Helping him with the medicine wasn't part of your job description, then?"

He shook his head vigorously. "No way. I ain't finished my schoolin' yet to become a medication aide. But I'm getting there." He smiled proudly. "Might be done by next month. For now, if you want to know about the medicine, talk to his doctor or the home health care nurse who visited once a month. She's my supervisor— but then I get the feelin' you already know as much."

She ignored his remark and went on. "You never touched those pill bottles, then?"

Buford's hands slackened and he began moving them as if lathering up. His forehead wrinkled as he considered the question and I noted that his earlobes were reddening, too. Then his hands stopped moving. "Wait a minute. Are you sayin' I took his pain pills or something? Because I mighta' pushed those bottles aside on the kitchen counter once or twice to make room for groceries I'd picked up, but I never took no drugs. *Not never.*"

"Did I say that?" Candace rested against the chair and since I knew her well, I saw a familiar look of satisfaction in her eyes. "I'm thinking I'm making you nervous, Buford. Why's that?"

Buford glanced at his hands and, as if realizing they told more of the truth than the words he'd spoken, he dropped them to his sides. "I never had a patient turn up dead before, is all. I've taken a few to hospice or called an ambulance, but then my job is done."

"Did you pick up Mr. Jeffrey's medicines from the pharmacy for him?" Candace asked.

Beads of sweat had popped out along Buford's receding hairline. "I did."

"Take them out of the paper bag?" Candace asked.

"No way. Never touched his pills."

"But I'm guessing you knew exactly what he was taking—because it would be on his medical history notes. So, why don't you write down the names of the medications for me—so we can make sure nothing is missing." Candace tore a page from her notebook and pushed the paper and pen across the table to Buford.

You'd have thought she put a rattlesnake on his empty

plate. After Buford wet his lips with his tongue, his attitude clearly shifted. "What's goin' on here, Candy? I swear you're accusing me of something."

"Not at all," she replied sweetly. "This is a suspicious death and—"

"The man had cancer," he practically shouted. "How's that suspicious?"

Candace leaned in again. "We found a dead man. That's all you need to know. Write down the drugs, Buford."

He snatched up the pen and scribbled for what seemed like forever. Maybe it seemed so long because the tension in the room was as thick as morning fog.

When he'd finished and shoved the paper back at Candace, she folded it and put it in her pocket. "Thank you. Anything else you can tell us about Mr. Jeffrey? Like why his family isn't around?"

Buford let out a breath and seemed relieved to be moving on from the medication topic. "His cousin Lou-Ann came 'round to visit maybe a week ago. You talk to her?"

"Not yet. What about his sister?" she asked.

"Miss Millicent and her son are on their way, or so I've heard."

Candace's eyebrows arched in surprise. "Oh. You know them?"

"'Course I do. Talked to Miss Millicent on the phone lots of times when she was checking on him. Dirk is the one who hired me. He comes into town every so often. I know them cousins of Mr. Jeffrey in Woodcrest, too. You sayin' you came to me first, rather than talking to the family? What's with that?"

"Are you telling me how to do my job, Buford?" This was stated with enough frost to coat a lawn in winter.

"Far as I recall, wasn't no one could tell you nothin', Candy Carson. 'Cause you already knew it all."

The chair legs scraped against the wood floor as Candace stood abruptly, sounding as angry as she looked. "We aren't done, Buford. I'll be back." She glanced my way for the first time since we'd sat down. "Come on, Jillian. We're out of here."

Six

Candace stormed out of the house while I paused in the front living area. Birdie stood on a step stool cleaning a ceiling fan.

"We're leaving, Mrs. Roberts. Thanks so much. And by the way, your coffee was so delicious, I have to ask, what kind is it?"

With a pleased smile, she told me her son sent the coffee beans from a small place in Brooklyn called Roasted. "He's a professor, you know. Loves the big city."

"You must be so proud. I used to live in Houston, another big city, but I prefer rural America. Thanks for the information about the coffee. Maybe Roasted has a Web site and I can buy the beans online." I said good-bye and started for the front door, but she called after me.

"He's made our Candace angry, huh? Boy's gotta habit of doin' stuff like that."

I turned back. "I have the feeling he might make you a little angry, too."

Birdie resumed her dusting. "I regret the day I rented that room to him. He's noisy, messy, and his friends are as loud as he is. I believed he helped folks by doing his job and I figured God wanted me to give him a chance. I do believe I was wrong. You tell my Candace I apologize for him."

When I climbed in the car, Candace immediately said, "I messed that interview up. One of the unfortunate things about being a small-town cop is *this is a small town*. You know everyone and sometimes you know them too well."

"I could tell Buford was getting under your skin—and by the way, Birdie apologized for his behavior."

She pulled out of the driveway. "She is such a sweetheart. I should keep in touch with her more than I have in recent years."

We drove in silence for several minutes and finally I said, "Do you plan to tell me why Buford bothers you so much?"

"Sorry. I was turning over in my mind how I could have handled the interview better." She glanced out the window for a second. "Guess I owe you an explanation."

"I am interested—mostly because I worry about you trying to be too perfect. In my opinion, you handled yourself just fine. He seems like kind of a jerk—even though he was probably on his best behavior."

Candace laughed. "*Kind of a jerk?* That's about the meanest thing I've ever heard you say about anyone. But you're right. That *was* his best behavior. I thought he'd changed, considering his line of employment. Never assume."

"There's old business between you two, I take it?"

"There's old business between Buford and half of Mercy High School class of 2006. The guy was a bully. And yes, I know that says more about him than the people he picked on, but sometimes you find yourself transported back to an unpleasant time in your life and react as if you were sixteen years old."

"What did he do to you?" I asked.

"Silly stuff, really. He made fun of me, used to call me out in the hall when everyone was between classes, ask me why I spent all my time in the chemistry lab. Asked if I was hooking up with Mr. Elway in there." She glanced my way again. "Mr. Elway was the chem teacher."

"Got it. I can tell the guy's definitely never grown up. But you understand that every high school has people like that."

"I do." She gripped the steering wheel tighter, seemingly not comforted by what I said. She tapped near her temple. "The problem is all between my ears, I know. Today I got the same feeling as if I were back in that crowded high school hallway. I wanted to slap Buford, even though today he was being less of a smart-ass than I recall. Guess I haven't gotten over my issues about being labeled a nerd."

"Okay," I said. "Maybe you can get a do-over. Write down anything you didn't ask him that you believe you should have and meet with him again."

Candace nodded. "Good idea. I did plan to talk to him once I had all my old high school crap tucked away in the back of my mind where it belongs. First, though, I hope to track down this cousin who lives in town. I believe Lydia called her to the county morgue for a formal ID and to sign off on the autopsy after I insisted they do one. But of course Lydia never feels obligated to inform me about much of anything."

"I feel like some of the problems you have with her being uncooperative are my fault—because she dislikes me so much."

Candace eased to a stop at the red light close to Belle's Beans, our favorite coffee shop. "That is ridiculous. Lydia is nuts, always has been. But she does get her job done. I am sometimes amazed at how normal she can act when she's dealing with grieving relatives—which is her responsibility, for the most part."

"You're right," I said. "I only wish I could understand where her obsession with Tom began."

The light turned green and she drove on past the Main Street Diner toward the highway that leads to my house. "Why even try to understand? It won't make sense."

I sighed. "You're probably right." For the last hour I hadn't worried about Clyde, but a sick feeling came back like a fist in my gut as we made the turn toward home. I rested a palm against my stomach. "I hope we see that big boy sitting in my driveway when we get to my place."

"Jillian, we'll find him. If he's not there, I can pick you up at dusk tonight and we'll go over to the Jeffrey house. According to my calculations using the time it took Clyde to trek across South Carolina, I would expect him to show up about that time."

I slumped a little in the less than comfortable squad car seat. "If something horrible happens to him along the way, I'll never forgive myself."

"Stop worrying and get out your phone," Candace said. "Look at your cat cam and chill while I drive you home."

"Good idea." I pulled my phone from my pocket and tapped on the app that allowed me to see what was going on in several rooms of my house. As I swiped the screen and checked every room that had a camera, I found all three of my fur kids sound asleep in different places. They looked peaceful and content. If Clyde was hanging around my house, Syrah and Merlot would have been on watch at a window. I knew I wouldn't find the big cat I'd let escape, at least not now.

As I expected, Clyde was nowhere to be seen or heard when I arrived home. I spent an anxious afternoon waiting for Candace to pick me up so we could head out to the Jeffrey house to search for him there. I occupied my time surrounded by purring and playful cats as I finished several quilt orders. Thank goodness for my fur friends. Both Shawn and Tom called me to ask whether Clyde had shown up. Shawn apologized again for sounding angry last night and told me about a solution for the roaming problem when Clyde finally did show up again—a GPS collar. He rambled on about how to set it up, but it sounded like I'd need pretty thorough instructions—if Clyde did return to my care. And that was a big if.

Tom was sweet during our talk, saying he knew how anxious I was about the cat. Though he wanted to help look for him, he was stuck longer than anticipated installing a security system across the lake. He told me he'd drop by my house later tonight.

Seven p.m. finally rolled around and Candace picked me up in the RAV, her uniform abandoned for street clothes and her blond hair loose on her shoulders. The early-evening air was thick with humidity and I feared impending rain might send Clyde seeking shelter under shrubbery or some crawl space. This would make it extra difficult to find him—if he was even at his old house.

"I have a good feeling about this." Candace sounded a lot more optimistic than I was as we pulled out of my driveway. "But what can we do about Clyde's penchant for wandering if we do round him up?"

"I talked to Shawn and he has a GPS collar we can use. If Clyde gets out again, we can track him. He told me he should have put the thing on Clyde before he even had Allison bring him to my house." I smiled over at her. "He and I are both on a guilt trip."

"I don't see why," she replied, sounding a little exasperated. "Animals do what they do. This particular cat has an agenda that will not be interfered with."

"That's for sure. But this GPS collar sounds like a solution—*if* we find him, that is."

"He'll be there. I know he will."

"I sure hope you're right," I said.

We arrived in Norm Jeffrey's neighborhood after a few minutes' drive. The houses were a lot like Tom's home—small and either red or brown brick. The tall trees and mature landscaping told me this was one of the older subdivisions in town. Not that there was a whole lot of new construction in Mercy aside from apartment complexes like the one Candace lived in.

We pulled into the driveway of Mr. Jeffrey's house, which stood on a winding, hilly street. The grass was in serious need of cutting. Who would do that now? I wondered. The city? The family? And what about the empty lot next to his, which was even more overgrown? The house on the opposite side of the Jeffrey place had been updated with a garage rather than a carport, and lovely baskets of ivy and flowering plants hung from hooks on the porch. It was a cute, inviting home in contrast to Mr. Jeffrey's shabby, sad house.

But my thoughts were interrupted.

I saw Clyde.

Concern and worry melted away immediately because Clyde was sitting close to the garage—as if he'd been waiting for us to arrive.

"Oh my gosh. There he is." I was out of the car before Candace could even kill the engine.

But if I thought he'd sit and wait for me to scoop him into my arms, I was wrong.

He bounded away toward the back of the house with me stifling the *No!* I wanted to scream. I would scare him even more by yelling.

I walked toward him and he looked back as if this were a game. I sure hoped that game wasn't hide-and-seek. Clearly this was a cat as independent as they came. As I approached, hoping not to lose sight of him, heavy raindrops began to splat on the driveway, on my head, my shoulders and probably on Clyde. Then he disappeared behind the house.

"Don't hide," I muttered as I followed. "Please don't hide."

Candace caught up with me and as we turned around the corner of the house, we saw Clyde's striped tail disappear through the slightly ajar back door.

Candace stopped in her tracks. "What the hey? We didn't leave that open. I hope the place hasn't been vandalized."

I said, "Mr. Jeffrey's death has been all over the news. Doesn't that sometimes draw thieves or vandals to a home they know could be abandoned?"

"That's true. Let me get my gun. You stay here."

My heart thumped harder against my chest as soon as she said the word *gun*.

She returned within seconds, her weapon in one hand, her cell phone pressed against her ear as she spoke to the Mercy PD dispatcher. "B.J., I need backup at the Jeffrey place. Could be an intruder." She disconnected, slipped the phone into her pocket and handed me the umbrella she'd tucked under her arm.

"We have to wait?" I opened the umbrella and tilted it to give her shelter from the rain.

But she stepped away. "*You* have to wait. I'm going in." She went to the door and carefully widened it with her sandaled toe so she could enter.

But I was right behind her and whispered, "I'm coming with you. For Clyde."

Then neither of us spoke. I was stunned by what the fully opened door revealed. I know Candace was, too. Clyde or a possible intruder wasn't the only problem in this house.

Peering over her shoulder, I saw Buford sprawled on the kitchen floor, his wide, sightless eyes staring up at nothing.

Seven

Candace squeezed beside me under the umbrella while she made a few more calls—to the police chief, to paramedics and to the coroner's investigator, Lydia Monk. When she finished, she pulled me by the elbow to her car and opened the passenger side door despite my pleas that I should be allowed to find the cat first.

"Stay here," she said. "If I find Clyde, I will bring him to you. This is the scene of a suspicious death—two now. Though I called the paramedics, I assure you, that man is dead."

"But the cat will contaminate the crime scene, if this *is* a crime scene, and you wouldn't want that, right?"

Candace saw right through me. "Nice try, Jillian. Wait here."

I closed the umbrella, and as soon as I slid into the passenger seat, a Mercy PD squad car came screeching to a halt behind Candace's RAV, its lights turning like gaudy lit-up pinwheels in the lightning-streaked sky.

The newest member of Mercy PD, rookie Lois Jewel, exited her vehicle. Short, compact and African American, she may have appeared to be Candace's opposite, but the two women had the same no-nonsense attitude. She walked up to the RAV and said, "What you got, Candace?"

"DB. Don't know much more than that. I need to clear the house. You can help, but remember your training. Do *not* contaminate this scene. You got any booties handy?"

Lois, who had the sense to be wearing the forest green rain slicker provided by the department, went back to the squad car.

Candace turned back to me. "I've got a flashlight rolling around on the back floor. Can you reach it?"

I found it and handed it to her. Her hair was stringy wet by now, but I knew Candace couldn't care less. She was focused on the terrible find in that house.

Lois returned and handed a pair of shoe protectors to Candace, who shoved them in her pocket. They walked side by side toward the house, with Candace's flashlight beam trained on the ground. Her head moved with the light as she swept it back and forth. She was looking for clues, footprints, anything that might be quickly washed away by the rain. Soon the two disappeared around the side of the house.

I heard sirens in the distance, and not long after, the circus was in full swing. Paramedics, the fire department, Chief Mike Baca, and my least favorite person on the planet, Lydia, filled the tiny street with their lit-up vehicles and their faces marred by urgency. The next-door neighbors stood on the adjacent lawn and watched in horrified silence under a giant golf umbrella, its yellow, green and red stripes suitable for the big top.

When I saw Lydia in the side mirror walking up the driveway, I slunk down in the seat and lowered my head, hoping she wouldn't see me. Thank goodness for umbrellas. With hers being a giant black one, it was nearly impossible for her to see anywhere but straight ahead.

I sat in the car for what seemed like hours, though the

time that passed was probably more like forty-five minutes. I kept asking myself the same questions over and over. How had Buford died? What had happened inside that house? Why had he come here? And where was Clyde? Had he sneaked out the back door undetected and slipped off into the night? Finally I opened my phone and checked on my cat crew at home. Chablis was giving Merlot a bath and Syrah was playing with his catnip banana. I felt the tight muscles in my neck and shoulders relax as I watched them.

But all at once the Clyde question was answered. Lois came walking toward Candace's car, holding him tightly in her arms.

I opened the door and she handed him to me, saying, "He's a cute guy, but he doesn't belong in that house."

"Thanks so much, Lois. What happened in there?" I took Clyde, who had the courtesy to purr the minute I wrapped my arms around his damp body.

"Can't talk about it. Procedure. But this big fella kept wailing and wandering around. Couldn't catch the son of a gun. He knew every hiding place. It was kinda like he was looking for something he couldn't find. Anyway, he finally gave in and let me pick him up."

"He was probably searching for Mr. Jeffrey." I scratched Clyde's head between his ears and he settled on my lap to begin the process of grooming his wet body.

"Ah. You're probably right." She abruptly turned and hurried back toward the house as the rain began to fall harder.

Clyde had never gotten the chance last week to complete his mission to reunite with his best friend. Perhaps his hunt around his former home told him what he needed to know—that the man was gone for good. Clyde's wandering and cries might have actually been his way of expressing grief.

The stress of seeing poor Buford lying on that floor and then hearing about Clyde's behavior finally got to me. Tears welled and I was grateful for a cat in my lap. Nothing could be more soothing to me.

But a rap on the car window startled me. I wiped my eyes and found a face staring at me through the rivulets of rain streaming like a glistening curtain between me and the woman outside. It was Emily Nguyen.

No, I nearly cried out loud. Not *her.*

"Can I get in the backseat?" she yelled far louder than necessary. "It's raining really hard."

I sure wouldn't have put it past her to march up to the house and stick her nose into police business if I didn't do what she wanted. I nodded in affirmation, making sure the door was unlocked.

She removed her industrial-weight yellow raincoat and shook the excess water out the open door after she sat down, then laid it at her feet.

Placing her hands on the front headrest so she could get closer to me, she said, "What's happening? Did someone break into the Jeffrey house or—" She stared at my lap. "Oh my gosh. Is that Clyde? *The Clyde?* Oh my gosh. Oh my gosh."

Not only was she tiny enough to be twelve years old; she was acting prepubescent.

"Does he bite? Or can I touch him?" she said.

I quickly decided that if keeping her occupied with Clyde would stop her from asking questions about the police presence here, I was willing to do that. "He won't bite. He's quite friendly."

She wiped her wet hand on the front of her blouse before reaching over and awkwardly patting his head. "He's so soft."

"He likes it if you scratch between his ears—in fact most cats like that. I'm guessing you've never had one?"

"I haven't. We weren't allowed. My mother said they were messy, left hair everywhere and then there's that whole litter-box thing to deal with."

"Not everyone is a cat lover," I said. "But this guy might grow on you. He's so sweet."

As I'd suggested, she'd begun to lightly scratch Clyde's head. He closed his eyes and began to purr again.

She grinned. "Oh my gosh, that means he likes me, right?"

I nodded and had to smile. I was always surprised when people who had preconceived notions about cats were introduced to one. Usually, their fear or distaste or whatever they had been harboring in their minds fell away like leaves off a tree in autumn.

Hoping to keep her focus off the house, I said, "How did you find me? You weren't following me, were you?"

She tapped her temple. "Have to think logically when you're a journalist. See, I wasn't interested in you—okay that sounded bad. You're a nice lady. But I'm in town because of Clyde. I thought about where he would go and this seemed like the common-sense answer." I caught her satisfied smile out of the corner of my eye. "And I was right—wasn't I?"

"You are a smart one." We fell silent and I scrambled to make small talk before she decided that the activity outside the car was more important than petting a cat. "You don't have a southern accent, Emily. Where's your original home?"

"California. Oh my gosh. Just *try* to get a TV job there. I couldn't get past security in the studios to apply for so much as an internship in any part of the state. But I persisted, expanded my horizons. And look where I am now. Finding Clyde is a *major* deal, Jillian. I might get a weekend anchor spot when I bring this story home. You will give me the story, right?"

"Why wouldn't I?" I said immediately. Heck, if I had

my own car, I'd take her and Clyde straight back to my house and let her interview me until dawn. But we were stuck, and if I thought I would keep her occupied any longer, I was wrong.

She said, "Why are the police and the fire trucks still here? Obviously they've already found the cat."

"Um, I'm not sure." Hoping to distract her, I held up my phone. "If you like this cat, I can show you the ones who own me." I laughed nervously. "You can never truly own a cat. They own you."

She did seem interested, but not in the cats. She took the phone from me and brought it closer to her face. "What *is* this app? It's so cool with the split-screen video and all. Does it drain your battery fast?"

"Not really." I leaned toward her and started to point out each of my cats by name, but she wasn't interested.

Her gaze had switched to the back of the house. Lights had been turned on, shedding a golden haze that highlighted the driving rain. "Whatever is happening here isn't about the cat, is it?"

"I—I couldn't tell you," I stammered unconvincingly.

"Then I guess I have to find out on my own." Her stiff, rubbery raincoat squeaked as she picked it up.

I touched her shoulder. "Wait. Those people have a job to do and you can't interfere."

"But I'm a journalist and this is probably breaking news. Is it about Mr. Jeffrey? Was it a break-in after all?"

"You could say that. At this point I'm not sure of the facts and you wouldn't want to report on a piece before you have everything straight. Right now, I'm not sure who would have the time to stop and answer your questions. This is a small town with limited police resources."

"But he was an old man, right? Natural death is what we all assumed. Does this break-in mean there's more to this story than a wandering cat?"

Oh boy. She was about to latch onto this like a tick on

a dog. Here I was, a virtual prisoner with her in this car and without a clue as to how to handle a girl who considered herself a reporter, but whose behavior was nothing like the professionalism my Kara exhibited at crime scenes. "Emily, can you just—"

"If you can't answer my questions, then I'm sure someone in that house can." She handed me my phone, struggled into the raincoat and opened the car door.

But before she could get completely out of the car, Lois came striding toward us.

"Your name, ma'am?" Lois held up a hand to stop Emily's progress. She bent and glanced at me, looking confused, before her gaze settled on Emily again.

Emily stood. "Emily Nguyen, Channel Five News, Asheville. Can I have your name, Officer?"

"You don't need my name," she said. "You need to stay in this car and not contaminate our crime scene."

I wanted to groan an *Oh no* when Lois said the words *crime scene*.

But Emily did sit down.

Lois spoke to me through the open back door. "Deputy Carson suggested you call someone to pick you up, Mrs. Hart. Perhaps Mr. Stewart? Or you can get a ride home in the fire truck. They're about to leave." She turned back to Emily. "As for you, I can escort you back to your vehicle—you did come here in a vehicle, I assume?"

"Yes I did, but—"

"Because I am about to run crime scene tape across the driveway and you don't belong inside that tape. We clear?"

Emily said, "Why don't I wait here while you do that and then I'll—"

"I'm taking you to your vehicle, ma'am." Her head cocked, eyebrows raised, Lois stared at Emily.

"But if Jillian can wait here, then—"

"You're *not* Jillian. Come on now. Get out of this car right quick before you get yourself in trouble." Lois stepped back so Emily could get up. "I'll just shine my flashlight for you down the driveway."

Emily mumbled unintelligible words under her breath, but she complied. As Lois led her away, Emily called back over her shoulder to me. "I could drive you to your house and get that interview about Clyde. How about it, Jillian?"

"You can talk to her later," I heard Lois say. "Right now you need to get off this property."

Thank goodness they were now too far away for Emily to hear me if I were to respond about her driving me home. Sure, I'd talk to Emily at some point, but right now I was too rattled to deal with someone who seemed to have a few puzzle pieces missing.

Once they were gone, I called Kara for a ride. I may have told Emily I'd give her a sit-down about Clyde's most recent escape, but this situation was not about him. This was police business and Emily would have to deal with Mercy PD. Besides, if anyone was getting the scoop about what Lois had just confirmed as a crime, it would be my stepdaughter and not a young woman I found almost as annoying as Lydia. *Almost.*

Eight

I didn't have to wait long for Kara to pick me up. She was already on her way to the Jeffrey house when I called. Her police scanner had informed her about a crime at this address. I left the RAV4 escorted by Lois and protected Clyde with Candace's umbrella as I walked down the driveway. Once I got in Kara's SUV, I handed the sopping umbrella back to Lois. She turned and hurried back to Candace's RAV as we drove off.

I waved to Emily, who was sitting in her car, cell phone pressed to her ear. She didn't return the courtesy, but I gave her the benefit of the doubt. She probably was too caught up in how she could get an interview with anyone who knew anything about the goings-on inside the house.

Kara's long dark hair was pulled back, her ponytail sticking through the back of her Carolina Panthers cap. "I've got a towel in the backseat. I wasn't sure if you'd be prepared for this monsoon. Looks like both Clyde and you could use it."

After I wrapped Clyde up and cuddled him close—something he seemed to enjoy quite a bit by the sound of his loud purrs—I said, "We found a body in that house. But I don't know what happened to him. It's—"

"Buford Miller," she said. "Murdered."

"Oh my. I knew he was dead, but I wasn't sure he'd been murdered. How did you find out?"

"I am the editor of the newspaper, Jillian. I have my sources in the police department . . . not to mention the county sheriff's office, and then there's my boyfriend Liam, an assistant county district attorney, and—"

"Okay. Dumb question. What happened to Buford?"

"My sources say blunt force trauma to the back of the head."

I shuddered at the thought as I rubbed my knuckles along Clyde's cheek. He pushed against my hand lovingly. "That's terrible. I assume since we didn't see a car in the driveway, Buford went to the house with whoever killed him."

"No vehicle? Ah." Kara turned onto Main Street. "See? Now you're telling me stuff I don't know. But what about our darling friend Clyde here? You said when you called that you went there to find him. I didn't even know he was missing."

"He escaped last night and we guessed he'd show up exactly where he wanted to be." I looked down at the cat. He was so big that his legs stuck out of the towel and hung off my lap. "We went to the house to see if he'd arrived yet, and we found him right away—but we also discovered the back door open. That was when we saw . . . Buford."

"How did you know Buford? Because it sounds like you do."

"I can't get anything past you, can I?"

"Just doing my job." She turned down the road that led to the lake. "I want to know everything you do, including the cat's story. The major news outlets left town after you gave your interview, so I am assuming no one else knows about this crime. I want to tell this story in the *Messenger*. Mercy is our town, after all."

"Um, there's a slight problem."

Kara turned to me abruptly before refocusing on the puddle-filled road ahead. "What kind of problem?"

"Her name is Emily Nguyen. Channel Five News, Asheville."

"I've seen her on TV. But she's a morning-traffic girl. Does a little weather at six a.m. What does she have to do with this?"

I sighed heavily. "Candace promised her an exclusive on the cat."

"What? She's *here*?"

"That person I waved to as we were leaving the Jeffrey house? That was her."

"Great. And Candace promised her an exclusive on the cat?"

I nodded. "Yup. To get her to stop hanging around my house and pestering me."

"Why was she hanging around . . . Oh, I get it. She wanted more on Clyde."

"She was lurking around my house this morning and learned Clyde went missing again. Since the newspeople who interviewed me have left and know nothing about his latest great escape, this could be her story."

"So," Kara said, "this exclusive had nothing to do with murder?"

I smiled slowly, figuring I knew where her thoughts were headed. "No, it did not."

By the time Kara dropped me off, she had all the facts I'd gleaned about Buford Miller from Candace's interview. She then left quickly to get back to the Jeffrey house to see what else she could obtain from the officers and other professionals at the scene for her front-page story tomorrow. She had the advantage because, unlike

Emily, she was friends with those folks. They trusted her to report the facts accurately and would be willing to tell her what they could—just like her unnamed police source had. The Mercy police, like other small-town cops, relied heavily on the community to help solve crimes.

Once inside my home, I reintroduced Clyde to my cat crew. Since Clyde was still a little damp, he needed a thorough sniffing, it would seem. While my three followed him around, I took a much-needed hot shower.

As I scrubbed myself, wishing soap and water could wash away the image of Buford lying on that kitchen floor, I wondered what had brought him to Mr. Jeffrey's house. Or perhaps a better question was *who*. Was it safe to assume that he'd called someone right after he'd spoken with Candace and me? That Candace's interest in Buford raised red flags for someone? Was it the same someone who killed Mr. Jeffrey? There *had* to be a connection.

I pulled on pajama bottoms and a T-shirt, dried my hair and joined my cat family in the living room. Amazingly enough, Chablis and Clyde lay stretched out on the floor in front of the entertainment center. Chablis was giving him a thorough bath while Syrah and Merlot crouched a few feet away, observing them. It was one of those "aw" moments I desperately needed right now. I grabbed my phone and snapped a picture. Chablis was sweet to feline strangers and the scene lifted my spirits.

I'd just set my phone down when I heard a rap on my back door and then the sound of Tom's voice calling my name. He was my security guy in more ways than one and knew the entry code.

We met in the kitchen and he wrapped me in his arms, saying, "I heard what happened. How awful for you."

After a kiss and another tight hug, I asked if he'd eaten. He said no, he'd been too busy. I warmed up leftover Chinese takeout and we ate fried rice off paper plates in the living room.

I must have been hungry because I was half done with my rice before I said anything. With a few calories in me, my gray cells had started to fire again. "How did you hear about Buford?"

"Mike Baca called me," he answered.

"The police chief? He called during the middle of a murder investigation? I know you guys are friends, but—"

"He needs my help. He's leaving town for a police convention. Two murders in a week require plenty of leg-work and brainwork, so I'll be doing contract PI work for the police again."

I nodded. "That's good. You've sure helped them in the past and with your police background, it makes sense." I went on to tell him about Emily Nguyen nosing around, her presence at the Jeffrey house and how he had better watch out for her.

"Thanks for the heads-up. We don't need a zealous reporter who wants to make a name for herself messing around where she doesn't belong. She could cause all sorts of problems. In fact, it sounds like she already has."

"She's annoying, but you know, there *is* something about her . . ."

"Uh-oh. Here goes Jillian discovering the best in everyone again." He grinned. "But don't ever stop, because it's one of the many reasons I love you."

I set my empty paper plate on the coffee table and snuggled close to him. "She's pushy, but she's chasing her dream. I admire that."

"Of course you do." He put an arm around me and pulled me closer. His gaze fixed on Clyde stretched out on the living room floor. Chablis had curled up next to him. "Chablis has a boyfriend, I see."

"Just a guess, but I believe she's comforting him. He got inside the Jeffrey house and couldn't find his owner.

He knows things are different now and he might be a little sad."

"Maybe you're right. If anyone knows the mind of a cat, it's Jillian Hart." He leaned his head against mine. "Jillian Hart Stewart."

"Or Tom Stewart Hart," I replied.

"Doesn't matter to me. Changing a name doesn't mean a thing. Your changing my life is what counts. And you have."

"What you just said needs to be sealed with a kiss."

And it was.

Nine

The next morning, Tom called and invited me to meet him at Belle's Beans for coffee. We often met there before he headed out for a job that might take all day. But I had a feeling the work he'd been handed by Mercy PD might take longer than all day.

After making sure Clyde didn't sneak out the door with me, I headed to town. I'd forgotten to tell Shawn last night that I'd found Clyde, so I called him while on my way to the coffee shop. He said he'd meet me at Belle's with the GPS collar for our vagabond friend.

Tom was waiting at a table and motioned me over to the back of the busy café. As I passed the counter, the Belle of the Day—also known as the barista—told me that Tom's order that included my vanilla latte would be up now that I'd arrived. I asked her to add a raspberry Danish and she nodded.

After kissing Tom hello, I took the chair at our lacquered table facing the door. Seated here, I could see Shawn when he arrived. Soft guitar music played from speakers on the ceiling in accompaniment to the hum of conversations going on all around us. This was Mercy's favorite spot for people to meet and was run by the amazing Belle Lowry, who, though well into her sixties, had the energy of a teenager.

The real name of the Belle of the Day was Nancy—Mrs. Lowry long ago decided all her baristas would have "Belle" name tags—and she called to Tom when our order was ready. Soon the aroma of my latte sent me straight to coffee heaven.

"Thanks for phoning me," I said after my first sip. "This is just what I needed to start out the day—sitting with you in my favorite spot in town."

"Didn't want to miss seeing you today." He wore a dark blue-and-white-striped shirt that made his blue eyes seem more vibrant. "Tracking down those cousins in Woodcrest could be more of a problem than I thought. Not even one of Mr. Jeffrey's relatives has returned my calls. I have addresses, but I don't know if they're any good."

"What about Birdie? Has anyone talked to her?" I asked.

"Birdie?"

"Buford Miller's landlady." I tore off a piece of the sticky, decadent Danish and started eating.

"What's her last name? No one told me about her." He pulled a notebook from his jeans pocket.

I gave him her address. "She probably knows about Buford's death, but she might have more information about Mr. Jeffrey, too. She said she knew him, so she might be able to help you find his relatives."

"Maybe Candace plans to talk to her, but it can't hurt to call on Birdie and report back what I learn to Candace. I need the whole picture, everything about both victims."

I nodded. "Like Candace always says, 'Why did this person have to die now?' From what I've learned from her, the answer usually lies within a small circle of relatives and acquaintances."

"I love when you go all cop on me." He grinned and stood. "Hate to leave so soon, but now that you've given me another person I should interview, I'd better get moving." He leaned over and kissed me before he left.

I was wiping my sticky fingers on a napkin when I saw a very unhappy Emily Nguyen marching toward me. She slapped this morning's copy of the *Mercy Messenger* on the table in front of me so hard, my coffee cup rattled.

"You told me I had an exclusive." The chair scraped the floor as she pulled it out to sit across from me.

"Think back, Emily," I said quietly. People around us were staring. "Your exclusive was centered on Clyde's recent escape. Isn't that what Candace said?"

Her dark eyes narrowed. "You're splitting hairs. This is *my* story and now it's all over the front page of your little bitty town newspaper. That is *not* fair."

Okay. She seemed to also have the maturity level of a twelve-year-old. I took a deep, calming breath before I spoke. "Actually, this story belongs to Mr. Jeffrey, Buford Miller and Clyde. It belongs to their families. It's not yours to own."

She opened her mouth to speak, but no words came out. She tilted her head and stared at me for a second. "Maybe you're right. I guess there are dead people."

"Indeed there are. And that's a tragedy. Maybe if you took a little different angle on *your* story, you might find people who will cooperate with you."

She sat back and I could tell she was giving this real thought. I wanted to smile because I'd sensed deep down she was a decent person who thought she'd found a path to her dream job—and hopefully just realized that road was at times paved with the pain of others.

"I've always been pushy," she finally said. "It doesn't sit well with others, but in this business—"

"It works *sometimes*," I cut in. "But here? In small-town America? It doesn't, Emily. It simply doesn't."

Her face dropped. "You're saying I lost my story because I was obnoxious?"

"You didn't lose your story, but I'm guessing if word gets out about Clyde's return home in the rain last night, the other newspeople will come back in droves." Pulling the newspaper so it lay between us on the table, I tapped the headline. "See, this says 'Local Man Found Dead.' It doesn't say anything about Clyde, so you can still focus on him. That wasn't my stepdaughter's emphasis when she wrote this piece. To the media people who have already left town, they may see this story and sure, they might notice it's the same town where Clyde lived, but to them this is just another murder. To you, it could be a ticket to your dream job—if you get what's important about this event in Mercy, that is."

She twisted her lips, considering this. "Maybe you're right. Maybe—but wait a minute. You said your *stepdaughter*?" Emily sat back, dumbfounded. "No wonder this is all over the front page."

I nodded. "She owns the newspaper. She's the editor, the writer, and sometimes even the photographer. But she was already on her way to the scene before I even spoke to her. She has her finger on the pulse of this town. Maybe you could learn something from her and write a great story about Clyde's connection to murder."

Emily's chair again grated on the floor as she stood abruptly. "Are you saying I don't know anything? That I'm incompetent? Well, I'm *not*. I lost this exclusive because of . . . *nepotism*." She pointed at me, her display of temper drawing everyone's attention now. "You go all sweet on me, act like you're so nice. But you are such a *fake*."

She stormed out of Belle's Beans and every person in the place watched. Then their stares turned on me and I felt my face heat up. Had I sounded insincere? Because I'd meant every word, and I actually was almost getting to like Emily's youthful exuberance.

To avoid making eye contact with anyone still staring at me, I lifted my coffee cup and drained what little was left. I gathered my used napkins, empty Danish plate and cup and set them to my left. But I still felt as if I'd disrupted people's mornings, not to mention given them plenty to gossip about.

I kept my focus on the shiny tabletop, hoping Shawn would arrive soon with the collar and I could go home. But then I realized a man, maybe in his early forties, had approached my table and now stood looking down at me.

He said, "I couldn't help but overhear. I mean, well, no one could help but overhear." The jeans he wore, distressed and torn in places, didn't fool me. They were designer. Expensive. So were his ecru shirt and the gleaming veneers on his teeth. My heart sank. Another reporter or producer, no doubt.

"I apologize about the loud . . . *conversation*. I'll be slinking out of here soon." I offered a nervous laugh.

"Please don't leave. I appreciated what you said to that girl," he said quietly. "She's some kind of journalist, I take it?"

I nodded. "From a TV station in Asheville." Hmm. Maybe this guy wasn't with the media after all. "I'm Jillian Hart, by the way."

"Dirk Boatman." He held out his hand.

What? I stared at his hand briefly before shaking it. I felt the remnants of hand lotion and smelled a hint of cologne. "Aren't you—"

"Norm Jeffrey was my uncle. My mother and I just arrived in town." He gestured at my chair. "May I join you?"

"Um, sure."

"How about another coffee?" he asked.

"No, thanks. The brew here is pretty high-octane. One latte is enough . . ." I trailed off. "I am so sorry for your loss, Mr. Boatman."

"Please call me Dirk and I appreciate your condolences. I loved Uncle Norm." He'd moved into the chair Emily had vacated, but he hadn't dragged it, thus avoiding the noise she seemed to have enjoyed creating. "My mother and I went to his house this morning and found crime scene tape everywhere. She was pretty freaked out, so we drove away and—"

"Y-you haven't spoken with the police?" I didn't mean to sound so flabbergasted—but I was.

"They *have* called us. I believe my mother made an appointment to talk with an officer today."

An appointment? Is that what they were calling it? But then, perhaps they hadn't picked up the newspaper and had no idea a man's body had been found inside that house. "I'm sure they're anxious to speak with your mother." I rested my arm over the newspaper Emily had left behind so he couldn't see the glaring headline.

"My mother's been upset, as you can imagine. Uncle Norm was her closest relative besides me. It's taken her a few days to wrap her head around his being gone."

More like a week, I thought. "Let's rewind. You saw the crime scene tape and left. Where did you go?"

He seemed surprised by my question. "We went back to the bed-and-breakfast where we're staying—the Pink House. Quaint, nice accommodations. But about this reporter. Can you tell me—"

I held up a hand. "Sorry. Hang on." I'd just seen Tom return and he headed straight for the counter. Had he come back for a take-out coffee? Forgotten to tell me something? When he glanced my way, I smiled big and gestured for him to join us. He was about to get one of the witnesses on his wish list handed to him and he'd be a happy camper.

I saw the Belle of the Day give him his forgotten credit card before he came toward us. So *that* was why he returned. Nancy-slash-Belle had probably called him.

"Who's that?" Dirk asked.

But Tom reached us before I could answer.

He offered his hand. "Tom Stewart. Don't believe I've had the pleasure."

"This is Dirk Boatman," I said. "Mr. Jeffrey's nephew."

A slow smile brightened Tom's expression. "Really? Mind if I visit with you for a second?"

Dirk stood. "I believe I need to get back to the Pink House. We only rented one car and my mother—"

Tom pressed a hand on Dirk's shoulder. "You can spare a minute or two. See, I need to talk to you."

Dirk eased back into his chair, looking guarded and a little stunned. "Why would you need to talk to me?"

Tom sat opposite me and adjacent to Dirk. "I'm a PI contracted to work with the police on this case. Are you aware there was a homicide in your uncle's house last night?"

The man paled. "Is that what all the crime scene tape was about? A murder?"

Tom nodded. "Did you know a person named Buford Miller?"

Dirk's eyes widened in surprise. "Yes. I hired him to take care of my uncle. He's a home health aide."

"So you understand Buford Miller made regular visits to your uncle's house. Your *dying* uncle's house." Tom had rested his arms on the table and was focused in on Dirk Boatman. "And now he's been found dead there."

Dirk sat back. "Buford's the victim? You're kidding. What the heck happened? Was there a break-in?" He shook his head, seemingly confused. "But no, that doesn't make sense. What was he doing at my uncle's house? I mean, my uncle passed days ago."

"Good question. I assume he had keys?" Tom asked.

"Of course. I hadn't even given a thought to getting the keys back. They were the last thing on my mind, as you can imagine."

"I need to talk to both you and your mother, Dirk. Can you make that happen today—in private?" Tom probably sounded polite to this man who didn't know him as well as I did. But I heard the edge in his voice.

"My mother will be at the police station later today, but she's understandably distraught. This new information sure won't help. Can you meet up with her there at three this afternoon?"

Tom checked the wall clock. "That'll work. What about you?"

"I'm here," he replied. "Ask me anything."

"This isn't exactly a private place and I'm headed out, but I do have a few pressing questions," Tom said. "Tell me again what you thought when you saw the crime scene tape."

"We thought there'd simply been a break-in and since as far as we knew, Uncle Norm didn't have much of anything of value in the house, I figured thieves wouldn't have gotten much."

Nothing of value in the house? I thought. How connected was he to his uncle that he knew this?

Tom continued. "That's why you haven't returned my calls? Because you assumed nothing more serious was going on than a dead senior's house being broken into?" His tone was more stern than I'd heard in a long time.

Dirk, looking flustered, reached in his jeans pocket and pulled out his cell phone. He tapped and a screen appeared. "Oh, you're *Tom Stewart*, the one who's been calling?"

"Yes. Three times today. Didn't you think, with a death in the family and this area code showing up on your phone, that someone in Mercy might need to talk to you?"

Tom sounded so intense. I decided I would never have wanted to be interviewed by him when he'd been a cop.

Dirk must have felt it, too, because his face reddened. "Here's what I thought—and I'm embarrassed to admit it now. Your name didn't register when you introduced yourself a minute ago. Earlier, I'd decided you were a casket salesman, or a funeral home director looking for our business. I mean, all you left me on my voice mail was your name and number. We came here to arrange Uncle Norm's funeral, put his affairs in order, and since we've already contacted a local mortician—"

"You just decided to ignore me," Tom finished.

I cleared my throat. Tom's sarcasm was making me uncomfortable. "Dirk, I can understand your concern about any unwanted intrusions at a time like this." I glanced at Tom while I spoke, hoping he'd take the hint and cut this guy a little slack. He *had* just lost his uncle, after all. "But this terrible event on the heels of your uncle's passing makes it important to communicate with Tom and the police."

Dirk's features relaxed. "You're absolutely right. What else can I do to help you, Tom?"

"I'm running late because there are other relatives I have to find. I believe there's a cousin here in town? A few more in Woodcrest? Seems to be a shared family trait not to return phone calls. LouAnn Rafferty is the one who lives in Mercy, correct?"

"Yes. She's kind of a recluse since her husband died. I've reached out to her, visited when I was in town, but she doesn't seem to trust anyone. Your local coroner—Miss Monk, I believe? Anyway, she told us she'd made the death notification to LouAnn and to our family in Woodcrest."

"Miss Monk's not the coroner, Dirk," I said. "But she does help grieving relatives with the paperwork after a death. If you need death certificates for the mortician and any documents sent to insurance companies, she'll help you."

"Thanks for clarifying. I was pretty upset when she called and was just grateful she'd notified the rest of the family."

Tom's eyebrows rose. "Are you saying you haven't spoken with any of your local relatives since your uncle died?"

Dirk shifted uncomfortably. "We're not exactly a close family." He checked his watch. "I should be getting back to the B and B where we're staying. My mother wanted to check with the funeral director before she went to the police station. And I guess now we'll have to get these death certificate copies from Miss Monk. I never knew there were so many details to attend to when there's a death in the family."

"What time did you say your mother will be talking to Deputy Carson?" Tom asked.

"Three this afternoon." Dirk stood.

Tom did the same. "Thanks. And I have more questions for you and I'm sure Deputy Carson has plenty of her own. Can you verify the addresses I have for your relatives before you go?" Tom pulled out his pocket notebook, flipped a few pages and showed it to Dirk.

After glancing at what was written, Dirk confirmed the addresses were correct. The two men exchanged a brief handshake. Dirk nodded at me with a smile and left.

"Thanks for reining me in," Tom said once the man was gone. "I pressed too hard, but something about that guy feels . . . wrong."

"He's different, but I wouldn't use *wrong* to describe him. A little distrustful, perhaps? From what little he told me, I believe you'll soon find out the entire family is *different*." I quickly summarized what Dirk had said before Tom left to hunt down anyone who could help him understand the family dynamics better.

Shawn came rushing in five minutes after Tom's departure, full of apologies for making me wait so long. He placed the locator collar for Clyde on the table between us. It was a thick fabric collar with a techie-looking oval contraption attached. My own cats would throw a fit if they had to wear something like this.

As it turned out, I needed another cup of coffee to understand how to set up this GPS system for Clyde. Thank goodness Shawn brought the directions and had added notes to make them easier for me to understand. I'm the kind of person who has trouble with written directions. This might not be difficult at all—once I convinced Clyde he had to wear this collar.

Indeed, putting this thing on a cat? That would be the real challenge.

Ten

I'm not sure what it is about felines, but they know when their world is about to change. Clyde, sitting at the back door waiting with my three amigos, took off the minute he saw my face. For a big cat, he sure could move. No wonder he'd made good time returning to Mr. Jeffrey's house.

With help from Syrah, I found him hiding under the computer desk in my office. I thanked my lucky stars he was too big to squeeze behind the bookcase, because I would have had a major problem extricating him from there.

I carried Clyde into the living room—thank goodness he didn't resist—and we sat on the floor. I spent time stroking and talking to him while Chablis, Merlot and Syrah watched with great interest. They all knew something was about to go down. Maybe they even thought they'd be next. After Clyde had calmed enough to purr and nestle into my crossed legs, I put the collar on. Although he let me fasten it on without a fight, he got up immediately once I'd finished and shook his head, hoping to rid himself of the contraption.

But the head shaking and pacing stopped once I rattled the treat container. Since his visit to his old home, his interest in food had returned and especially his fondness for kitty junk food. He liked treats almost as much as my Chablis. While all four enjoyed my offering of tuna-flavored crunchies, I synced the GPS monitoring system with my computer network and with my phone, amazed that I got it right without a glitch. *Tom, you'll be so proud of me,* I thought as I smiled at the TV display showing Clyde's exact location—my house.

But my good mood didn't last because a knock on the door and the people I saw through the peephole standing outside changed everything in an instant. Not only Emily Nguyen, but Lydia Monk had come calling. I stepped back and closed my eyes as the doorbell rang this time. Syrah sat at the edge of the foyer, waiting patiently for me to answer, as he always did when someone came to the front door. Lydia had to be his least favorite human ever and I wondered what damage he'd do to her shoes or whatever she might be wearing that would be close enough to the floor for him to attach onto with his claws.

I sighed heavily and let them in, trying my best to sound polite when I greeted them. "Hello, ladies. What can I do for you?"

Lydia, wearing a subdued outfit for her—a zebra print wraparound dress and shiny black sandals—marched right past me into my living room, her bleached hair held back with a large rhinestone-studded clip. On her way, she said, "I heard something I didn't like from my friend Emily. We need to talk, Jillian."

Syrah skulked behind her, his eyes on the charm dangling from Lydia's toe ring.

Uh-oh. That could be a problem.

Emily followed all of us into the room and sat next to Lydia on the couch. She looked childlike as always in a short red skirt and lacy white tank top. But at least she appeared professional. Lydia, on the other hand, never seemed to manage any semblance of professional style. A toe ring? Really?

I sat on the edge of the overstuffed chair across from them, knowing I should offer them iced tea or a soft drink, but I couldn't bring myself to do it. I didn't want them here. I'd rather be hiding under the bed like Merlot and Chablis liked to do when Lydia showed up—as she often did when I was connected to one of Candace's cases. Clyde, on the other hand, sat out of their view at the kitchen entry, his gaze trained more on Syrah than on the women who'd come calling. I guessed he wanted to take a cue from Syrah on how he should respond to these folks before he joined us. If he was smart, he'd head for cover.

My hands clasped in my lap, I said, "What do we need to talk *about*, Lydia?"

"Emily tells me you were at that crime scene last night. Is that true?" Lydia smiled, maybe trying to show she could be nice. But her latest round of Botox wouldn't quite allow her lips to move that much.

"I was there. We were searching for a cat," I replied.

"*We* meaning you and Candace Carson?"

"That's right." I looked at Emily. "Um, how did you two meet, by the way?"

"Since you decided to renege on the exclusive I was promised, I decided the county coroner might be a more . . . *reliable* source of information. The coroner, in turn, referred me to Miss Monk since she is the investigator."

I plastered on my best polite smile. "Yes. That is her title. Lydia, perhaps you should explain to Emily who does most of the investigating when there's a suspicious death in Mercy?"

Lydia crossed her leg and bobbed her foot. I caught Syrah out of the corner of my eye. He was homed in on that dancing toe-ring charm. "We always defer to the locals, but I am in charge of death certificates, talking with families, being at crime scenes to—"

"Ah," I interrupted. "You gather information from the pathologist's reports and the coroner himself and disseminate it to the police and to the families. Maybe take a few pictures at the scene to show to your boss—but you don't actually determine cause of death or regularly interrogate suspects, right?"

Emily turned to Lydia and from her confused expression, I got the sense she'd been given an inflated description of Lydia's job, just as Dirk Boatman had.

"You *know* I interview suspects, Jillian," Lydia said through clenched teeth.

"After the police have done so first—and I do know they appreciate your presence at the scene representing the coroner." I tried to sound pleasant. The last thing I wanted was for her to go all, well, *Lydia* on me.

Emily said, "I have to say Miss Monk's been more forthcoming with the press than that policewoman has. Deputy Carson won't even return my calls. No one in that police station aside from the sweet dispatcher—B.J., I think—would give me the time of day. But he told me how to find the coroner, thank goodness."

I nodded, still wearing a forced smile. "B.J. is a kind young man. But I'm still not sure why either of you are here." Meanwhile, I noted Syrah was getting ever closer to Lydia's foot. He wanted to play with that charm in the worst way—and she was tempting him by continually moving her foot.

Lydia cleared her throat. "Then let me be clear. I'm here because Emily tells me you promised her information about this cat that was found wandering around the crime scene. You understand cats leave hair all over the place and that this animal might have seriously compromised—"

Syrah pounced on that foot and it was all I could do to

keep from laughing out loud when Lydia jumped straight up off the sofa and nearly tripped over Emily's legs as she backed away from Syrah. I didn't see any blood, so he hadn't scratched her. He just wanted that shiny object.

Lydia pointed a magenta-painted nail at me. "How many times have I told you to keep that cat away from me?"

Emily reached around and offered the back of her hand so Syrah could sniff her. "But he's so gorgeous, Lydia. I mean, look at those ears. He's almost regal looking."

"He's an Abyssinian," I said. "An ancient breed and from the name, you can surmise he's an ancestor to the Egyptian cats worshipped in ancient times."

Emily left her seat and knelt down so Syrah could approach her. One dose of Clyde last night and she'd become a cat lover, it would seem.

But Syrah still eyed Lydia's foot jewelry.

"Can't you put him up in a bedroom for now?" Lydia asked, bending over to examine her toes for any injury.

"This is *his* house, Lydia. As I've told you before, if you want to talk to me, you have to talk to my cats, too."

"Talk to your cats? *Really?*"

She glared at me, something I was used to from her. Did she believe angry looks would ever make me change my mind about where my cats belonged? I nodded at her feet. "I suggest you remove your toe ring. He might leave you alone, then."

But Syrah, I knew, took great delight in annoying Lydia. He might find another dangling object to attack— like her long beaded earrings.

"If that's the only thing that will move this discussion along," she replied impatiently.

While she struggled to get the toe ring off, Emily and Syrah greeted each other, and soon he was rubbing up against her. As she petted him, she said, "What's his name?" I told her and then she asked, "Boy? Girl?"

"Neutered male."

"How do he and Clyde get along? Because I would love to get a shot of them together for my piece."

Lydia held out her foot to get our attention. "There. Happy?" She pulled out her dress at the top and dropped the ring into her bra.

I smiled. "Thank you, Lydia."

Emily reclaimed her spot on the sofa and pulled a camera out of her oversize tote. "I've never photographed any animals before but—"

"Hang on," Lydia said. "First, we deal with *my* questions. Do you honestly expect me to believe the only reason you went to Mr. Norman Jeffrey's home last evening was because you guessed a cat that didn't even belong to him anymore ended up there?"

"First of all, Clyde will never forget the man who rescued him. Cats and dogs have memories, just like people. Second, you understand I was with a police officer?" I kept my tone even. Would Lydia ever tire of questioning my relationship with Morris and Candace and my other friends at Mercy PD?

"You mean your BFF, Deputy Carson? How *did* you talk her into snooping around over there? Did you know what you'd find?"

"Are you kidding me?" I couldn't hide my irritation this time. "How could I know we'd find a dead man?"

She raised her eyebrows inquiringly. "Because you visited that victim earlier in the day? Or at least that's what Buford Miller's landlady told me when I called her."

"Please make your point, Lydia." I noticed Clyde had moved into the room now. Maybe he wanted a little of the attention Syrah was getting from Emily.

"My point? You need to keep your nose out of official business—and I don't care if your friend wants to bring you along for Buford's autopsy, you will not step through that door. You stay out of this."

I took a deep breath, determined to remain calm. "I don't even want to think about an autopsy, much less go to one." I was certain Lydia knew as much. So why was she *really* here? "Any other warnings you want to offer before you leave?"

"I believe you should keep your word and give this girl what you promised—an interview about this cat, an animal that for some strange reason seems *so* important."

It was Emily's turn to pipe in. "Because you promised, Jillian, and the police aren't giving me the time of day."

I was puzzled. This didn't jibe with Lydia's usual practice. She never made friends or allowed anyone near anything even remotely connected to what she considered *her* investigation. "O-kay," I said slowly. "Let me get this straight, Lydia. You want me to talk to this out-of-towner about Mercy's unpleasant business? Don't you think that might draw all those media people back here?"

Lydia let out an exasperated sigh. "Their interest has probably disappeared since you gave your little interviews. Yeah, I saw you on TV. You had nothing important to say and these murders aren't something they'd care about. My friend Emily, who is such a sweet thing and understands the importance of my role for the county, is only interested in the cat. And *you* have the cat. Do what you promised and answer her questions."

Emily stared at Lydia. "*Murders?* As in more than one person was found dead in that house?"

Lydia blinked hard and I could see her wheels turning. She'd just revealed a piece of information she knew she shouldn't have—and probably because Emily had flattered her. And flattery often resembles friendship about as much as a shark resembles a dolphin.

"*Murder*. Buford Miller was murdered." Flustered, Lydia turned to me. "Tell her about the cat. Me? I have work to do."

Syrah ran behind Lydia as she scurried out of my living room and through the foyer. Once the door closed behind her, Syrah turned around and sat, staring at me as if to say, *Thank goodness* she's *gone*.

"Okay, then." I smiled politely. "What did I promise to tell you about Clyde?" I pointed behind her. "He's right there, by the way."

Clyde was definitely an interested observer, sitting there with his precious cat smile.

But Emily wasn't about to be distracted now that Lydia had let an important tidbit slip. "She was lying, wasn't she? So, tell me. Who else besides Buford Miller was murdered?"

Eleven

As I racked my brain for a way to divert Emily's attention from questions about murder, my phone rang. Tom's name and picture appeared on the display and just seeing his face settled me.

"Excuse me, Emily, but I need to take this call." I turned away to talk and saw Clyde approaching Emily. *Good. Maybe he can work some magic.* I answered my cell with a cheerful "Hey there."

"You busy?" Tom said.

I glanced back at Emily where she sat with Clyde. My two cats who hide every time Lydia comes around had decided it was safe to return. Happy for attention from our visitor, they butted against Emily's legs as she scratched their ears.

"Um, you might say that. But aren't you . . . *working*?" No way did I want Emily to overhear anything about the murders. I knew she paid close attention to what was said in her presence.

"Yes, and that's the problem. I'm at the cousin's house here in Mercy and the woman will only talk to me through the door. That's not the best way to do an interview."

"Okay. I understand you're frustrated, but I have this . . . guest. Remember Emily? She's here for the interview about Clyde's second journey." I turned to smile at Emily, but she was responding to the demands of all four cats now. And engrossed. *Yes. Go Team Kitty.*

Tom said, "Sounds like you need an excuse to escape and I could sure use your help."

"I'm listening."

"I get that you don't want to talk in front of her. Here's the deal. This Rafferty woman has at least three cats. Could be more, but I've seen three for sure in the windows. I may be reaching, but she might let us in if you can convince her how much you love cats. It's worth a shot. I even called Candace and put her on speakerphone while Mrs. Rafferty listened through the cracked door. She still wouldn't budge and open up."

"I'll be there as soon as I can." I spoke loud enough that Emily couldn't help but overhear. After Tom gave me the address and I disconnected, I turned to Emily. "I have a small family emergency. Can we do this another time?"

"Something wrong with your stepdaughter . . . Kara, right? Because my research says she's your only family."

The thought that she had *researched* me didn't sit well. But I had to get away. "I consider a few people in town my family, so Kara isn't my only relative. I promise I'll talk to you again and by then we'll both know more about the . . . *problem* at the Jeffrey house."

Emily patted each cat on the head and stood. "You keep putting me off, yet you're so darn likable, I can't get angry with you. Okay. You're off the hook for now." She placed her camera back in her bag and left without another word.

I sighed with relief when the door closed behind her. I turned on the television and watched her on the security screen as she slid behind the wheel of her car and drove off. But one thing was certain. I'd be watching in my rear-view mirror on the way to LouAnn Rafferty's house.

The drive to the cousin's house took about five minutes and as far as I could tell, Emily didn't tail me. LouAnn Rafferty lived on a narrow, winding gravel road not far from the lake. With all the rain we'd had in the early days of summer, trees lush with nourishment lined the way down the hill to the address Tom gave me. Wild turkeys walked along the side of the road, and this glimpse at Mercy's natural beauty gave me a peaceful feeling. After a visit from Emily and Lydia together, I needed a few moments of tranquility.

Tom was leaning against his Prius parked in Mrs. Rafferty's cracked concrete drive when I pulled in. His arms were folded, his annoyance evident.

I greeted him with a kiss and his features relaxed.

"I am determined to get inside and talk to that woman. I hope you can help me out."

"Maybe I should have brought Clyde along. She probably knows him since Dirk mentioned she visited Mr. Jeffrey at times."

We'd been walking toward the front door and Tom stopped. "Why didn't I think of that? Good idea to mention Mr. Jeffrey's cat."

"Wait a minute." I pulled my phone from my pocket. "I *did* bring Clyde along. Let's go."

The house needed some serious TLC. The front lawn could have used mowing, weeds had taken hold in many spots, and as we climbed the five steps to the sun-bleached front door, I noticed mortar missing between many of the bricks.

Tom rapped on the door, using the tarnished brass knocker. "Mrs. Rafferty? I've brought someone I think you'll want to meet."

I whispered, "Really? That's how you plan to get her to come out here? She doesn't know either of us and—"

The door cracked open and I could see the chain still attached. A pale and drawn face appeared through the small opening. Her iron gray hair hung limp below her ears and the profound sadness in her expression was almost palpable. I felt a tug at my heart.

"Mrs. Rafferty, my name is Jillian Hart. First of all, I am so sorry for your loss." I wished I could reach through the crack, grab her hand and squeeze it.

But then I saw a flicker of interest light her muddy brown eyes. "You're the cat lady. The one who makes the quilts. I've seen your picture in the newspaper."

I smiled. "That's right. I do adore cats and would love to meet yours in person."

"I have some, you know. Your quilts. Bought them from Martha at the Cotton Company."

The Cotton Company was the local quilt store and the owner took my kitty quilts on consignment when I had a few to spare.

I glanced at the window to the right of the front door where a chubby calico cat had just jumped between the shade and the window to check us out.

"You bought them for your fur babies. How many cats do you have?"

"Four. But I can't talk to you about Norman. Sorry." She started to close the door.

"Wait." I brought up the cat cam display on my phone and held it up so she could see. "Would you like to see Clyde?"

She lifted a hand and started to reach through the small opening in the door.

I pulled back the phone a tad. I didn't want to deny her a peek at Clyde, but we needed to get inside and talk to LouAnn and this seemed the best way to accomplish that. "Let us in and I can show you better."

"Is Clyde on TV again?" She squinted at the phone I now held at my side.

Tom spoke and I was glad he sounded gentle, because this woman could use a giant dose of kindness. "He's at Jillian's house right now. She can tell you all about him."

The door closed with a thwack and my stomach sank. But then I heard her fumbling with the chain. Seconds later, LouAnn Rafferty let us into her dark, cramped living room.

Cats owned this house. The giant kitty condo in one corner took up a generous amount of space. Four cat beds neatly lined the wall beneath a mounted large-screen TV. LouAnn may have been a recluse, but I'd noticed the satellite dish outside. She wasn't completely cut off from the world.

The kitty quilts she'd mentioned sat folded on the two wing chairs facing a worn and claw-tattered chenille sofa.

"I told you I bought your quilts," LouAnn said. "Problem is, I have only two and my children fight over who gets to sit on them. When the Cotton Company has others for sale, I plan to buy two more."

I could fix that problem immediately—I always carried a few extra in my minivan—but for now, I wanted to meet her cats. "Where are the rest of your fur friends?"

"You saw Cinderella in the window. Snow White is under the couch, but she'll come out in a minute. Curious girl, that one. Hansel and Peter Pan were eating when you knocked and those boys do not give up their meals for anyone or anything." LouAnn carefully removed the quilts from the two chairs and gestured at them. "Sit down, Jillian. You being a cat person, you understand they will come to meet you in their own good time."

Tom took the other wing chair, and as LouAnn sat across from us on the sofa, she clutched the quilts to herself like security blankets. Fairy-tale names? Security blankets? Trying hard to stay positive, I was encouraged that this dejected-looking woman had her cats for company. By the looks of her—a housedress that hung on her skinny frame, the unwashed hair, the dull eyes—I was certain LouAnn suffered from depression.

"Thank you so much for letting us in, Mrs. Rafferty," Tom said.

"You're welcome. Don't much like people coming around—and I'm smart enough not to trust a strange man at my door, no matter what tale he tells me. But if you're a friend of Jillian's, that means you're okay. Just don't expect to haul me downtown to be questioned by the police lady that keeps callin'. Norman is dead and there's nothing left to be done for him."

"You don't like to get out and about?" I was glancing around and began to notice hints of her probably once-happy life. Several pictures of her and, I assumed, her deceased husband hung on the wall above the sofa. I recognized the London skyline in the background of one photo. They'd traveled. They looked like a loving couple. They'd had a life.

"I do my errands once a week," LouAnn said. "I often visited Norman on errand day—but as you know, I won't be visiting him anymore. Of course he was sick. Real sick. His skin was all yellow the last time I saw him. Plus he missed his Clyde. Don't understand why he let go of his cat and it took me a while to figure out where Norman sent him. He wouldn't tell me."

Her tone was flat, her demeanor the same, as if she feared to care about this man's death, even if she'd visited him once a week for a long time.

"Sounds like he was a secretive man," Tom said. "Did you notice anything unusual about him other than signs of his illness the last time you saw him?"

But before she could answer, two cats came wandering into the room, tails up. They couldn't ignore the sound of strange human voices—or, they'd simply finished their food. One was a tuxedo cat, his coat shiny, his mittens whiter than white. The other was long-haired and sandy colored with dark brown stripes on his legs and tail. They walked right up to our chairs and the tuxedo jumped into my lap.

LouAnn almost smiled. "That's Hansel. He's my smartest cat—but then, he's a tuxedo."

I stroked his silky back and he began to purr. Not to be outdone, Peter Pan soon rubbed against Tom's leg. He bent and petted him, saying, "I appreciate your choice of companions."

"You like cats?" LouAnn sounded surprised.

"I have a big tabby named Dashiell. He's diabetic and I've gotten rather handy with an insulin syringe."

LouAnn finally released a smile and it was such a transformation. I could tell she'd once been a beautiful woman—and could be again if she gained a little weight and began to care about her appearance.

"You named him for Dashiell Hammett. You were saying earlier through the door that you're a private investigator, so I guess that's a great name for your cat. Personally, I am a fan of fairy tales, not detective stories—but you probably figured that out. I like happy endings." Her smile disappeared. "Why is it so important to talk to me? I'm nobody. I don't know why a man who's dead from cancer has the police so interested."

"Because he didn't die from cancer," Tom said solemnly.

LouAnn's already pasty skin paled further. "Whatever are you talking about?"

"He died from an overdose of his heart medicine," I said.

She was shaking her head and clutching the quilts tighter. Snow White, probably sensing her owner's distress, quickly appeared from beneath the sofa and jumped into LouAnn's lap. She was a white domestic shorthair with green eyes—a gorgeous animal.

LouAnn lifted her and spread one quilt over her lap

so Snow White could curl up on it. She laid the other quilt next to her and Cinderella bounded from her window seat and settled on it immediately. After stroking them both for what seemed an eternity—but was probably more like thirty seconds—LouAnn recovered her composure and looked at Tom. "Norman would never take his own life. He was fighting the cancer hard. It was that shifty young man who came to care for him, wasn't it? He did something to my cousin."

"Are you talking about Buford Miller?" I asked.

LouAnn seemed to have completely returned to the land of the living if her facial expression was any clue. Those tight jaw muscles indicated her anger. "The boy never introduced himself to me when I was there and doesn't that tell you something? I suppose this is about Norman's money. This charlatan inserted himself into Norman's life, probably got him to change his will and there you go. You hear about such things all the time on the TV. He killed my cousin because he couldn't wait for him to die of natural causes."

I said, "Actually, Buford was hired through a home health care service, so he probably had a background check and—"

"Sorry to interrupt." Tom glanced apologetically at me before facing LouAnn again. "But how much money in Mr. Jeffrey's will are we talking about, Mrs. Rafferty?"

She thought for a second before saying, "Why, I don't know the exact number. I'd guess at least a million dollars."

My eyes widened in surprise.

Whoa. Now there's a motive for murder.

Twelve

After LouAnn mentioned Norman Jeffrey's small fortune, Tom began to ask where all this money came from. But she seemed so flustered by the news that he hadn't died of cancer that Tom backtracked and decided to ease her toward those questions. He switched his focus to the family. She said their relationships were a little complicated and even an explanation about this seemed difficult. "I am rather parched, not to mention troubled by this news. And I'm not used to talking to anyone but my cats. Can I get you and Mr. Stewart some iced tea? I think a glass of tea might settle my mind."

After we accepted her offer, LouAnn wandered into the kitchen, all four cats following behind, no doubt certain their mistress in the kitchen meant good things for them.

Tom whispered, "I guess before we leave I should tell her about Buford's death, but I didn't want her to get sidetracked. We need to know more about her family."

"That's what I was thinking, too, but we *should* tell her. Otherwise she'll find out and wonder why we withheld an important piece of information like that. Do you want me to break the news?"

"I was hoping you'd say that. She did buy two of your

quilts, so she obviously felt connected to you even before you showed up."

LouAnn called from the kitchen, saying, "My children are begging for treats. I'll be a minute."

"Perfect," I said quietly. "I'll be right back." I tiptoed out the front door and went to the back of my minivan. Now seemed like a perfect time to pull out a couple of the quilts I kept packed in the back. I knew LouAnn and her cats would appreciate them.

I returned to the house at the same moment LouAnn walked back into the living room carrying two glasses of tea. She immediately saw what I was holding and her eyes grew wide. I caught a glimmer of life once again.

"Four cats and two quilts will never do." I held the quilts out to her. "One of these is a nine patch and the other is a log cabin."

Good thing Tom stood and grabbed the tea glasses from her because LouAnn appeared so surprised, I feared she might drop them.

She pressed her hands to her cheeks. "I couldn't possibly accept such a valuable gift from a stranger." But her gaze never left the quilts.

"Of course you can—because we are no longer strangers." I walked closer to her.

She kept staring at the quilts. "You have no idea what this means to me." She took them as if someone had offered her spun gold. When she looked up to thank me, her eyes filled. Then she actually laughed. "I won't be crying. I don't want to shed any tears on these. Thank you, sweet lady."

She spent the next few moments examining each quilt and then took all four and covered the cat beds one by one. It didn't take long for her fur friends to waltz in from the kitchen and sniff at the new additions to their future comfort. LouAnn slowly eased to the floor, knelt and watched them.

Tom set his glass on the old maple lamp table between the wing chairs. He put an arm around me, pulled me close and whispered, "Another reason to love you more."

After a few minutes, Tom helped up LouAnn so she could return to the kitchen and fetch her own tea. We then sat down again. Meanwhile, the cats continued to test out their quilts. Cinderella and Snow White actually ended up in the same bed and seemed proud they'd both won the "Who gets a new quilt?" game.

With LouAnn seemingly less distracted, Tom decided to start over about the money issue. "From what I hear, Mr. Jeffrey lived a quiet life in a small house. Where did his wealth come from? An inheritance?"

"Oh no. None of us comes from money." She went on to explain that Mr. Jeffrey had been a CPA and financial adviser. We learned through her halting narrative that he'd lived alone and worked from home, crunching numbers and investing for others. He kept one cat after another as his sole companion—but never more than one at a time—and all of them named Clyde. I learned that the current Clyde visiting my home was number seven.

She went on. "He helped us, or rather I should say, helped Oliver, my dear husband, make wise investments. We paid off our mortgage and I still watch my spending as he taught me to do. I have enough for me and my kitties for as long as I live. And it would have been plenty to take care of Oliver, too. Until he . . . left me. It's been the longest five years of my life." She began twisting the simple gold band on her ring finger.

"I lost my husband several years ago, Mrs. Rafferty. I understand what you're going through." I peeked at Tom. He knew how I felt about John, how much I'd loved him. I worried Tom would take what I said the wrong way, that I wasn't ready to marry him. And that begged the question. *Was I?* I swallowed hard. This wasn't the time to be thinking about my love life.

Tom cleared his throat, eager, no doubt, to get back on track. "If your cousin didn't take his own life—and I believe you when you say he wouldn't do that—can you think of anyone besides Buford Miller who might want to harm him?"

"No. Norman and I are a lot alike—we keep to our-selves—but he is . . . *was* a good man." She shook her head and I saw tears welling again. "Someone hurt him, stole what little time he had left on Earth. That's plain evil."

"I agree," Tom said. "That's why anything you can tell us about your cousin is important. We can't understand a crime until we know the murder victim."

She nodded slowly, her eyes thoughtful slits. "That seems right. I've just never known anyone who was *mur-dered* before."

Tom clasped his hands between his knees and leaned toward LouAnn. "Can we talk about the rest of the family now? Your cousin Millicent has a son and you have other cousins, correct?"

"Yes."

"Can you explain the relationships for me?" Tom took out his notebook and pen.

"My cousins Norman and Millicent were brother and sister, and my two other cousins, Wayne Jeffrey and Ida Lynn Ford, are also brother and sister. I was an only child. Ida Lynn and Wayne both live in Woodcrest, and Millicent and Dirk live in the low country."

"What can you tell me about Mr. Jeffrey's sister, Mil-licent?" Tom said.

"She is full of herself—that's for sure. Been married more than once. Dirk visits me when he's in town and he said she's not with anyone now. She kept the Boatman name because that was Dirk's daddy. After her last wed-ding, she and her husband went off to live near the ocean. I hear tell the man left her. He had a bunch of money, but along with the money came a roving eye. She lives in some big fancy house on Hilton Head Island now, but I've never been invited there."

"I understand that Mr. Jeffrey decided Clyde should live elsewhere," I said. "Why?"

"Guess he figured he was too sick to care for Clyde properly—that's the only thing I can come up with. When I went over to his place—I went to do some tidying up every now and then—I saw Clyde was gone. I asked what happened and he wouldn't say except to tell me Clyde needed better care than he could give him at the time. He was getting the chemo and it made him plenty sick."

This puzzled me. "But you obviously love cats. Why couldn't Clyde stay here with you?"

"Norman believed Clyde needed to be the one and only cat. As you can see, that wouldn't happen here. Dirk finally told me about Clyde disappearing, but I don't think either he or Millicent ever did tell Norman when his cat up and ran off."

"Really?" Tom said.

"Norman kept saying how good Clyde was doing, how happy he was. He would have been devastated if he knew what happened."

Hansel jumped into my lap again, apparently tired of attempting to share a new quilt with a stubborn Peter Pan. "Did you find out about Clyde's journey from watching the news?"

"Yes, ma'am. I knew Dirk had to be relieved because he was pretty upset about Clyde's disappearance. He was hoping against hope the cat would come back when he was ready. Cats are known to do such things, so I didn't worry too much about it. Dirk told me not to bother Norman with it since he was so unwell, and I agreed. I'm just glad that wandering boy showed up back in town."

Since Dirk had come here *after* the cat disappeared, maybe he'd known Clyde would return to Mr. Jeffrey's home and hoped to catch him before his uncle saw him and got upset. No, that didn't make sense. How could Dirk know a cat would make a two-hundred-mile journey? I had a feeling there was more to the story. "Dirk came here often, did he?"

She nodded. "He cared for his uncle Norman more than Millicent ever did. Visited quite a bit. Norman and Dirk had some kinda business going on, if you ask me. But I wasn't privy to whatever it was."

Tom gave me a sideways glance that indicated this was good information. Then he said, "Did Dirk visit the other cousins while he was here? Woodcrest isn't that far away, after all."

"I wouldn't know. They don't care much for me and"— she glanced upward—"may the good Lord forgive me, the feeling is mutual."

I decided that if this had been another time in her life, LouAnn might have been the one to find her cousin's body. And perhaps she would have convinced him not to give his beloved cat away in the first place. Now that she had engaged in our conversation and trusted us, it seemed the right time to let her know about the other murder.

"Before we leave," I said, "there's something you should know. We don't want you to learn about it on television or read about it in the *Messenger*."

She seemed to withdraw almost at once, shook her head slightly. "I don't like the sound of this."

"It's about Buford Miller," Tom said softly.

For the first time since we'd arrived, her cheeks took on color. "He *did* hurt my cousin. Why didn't you tell me the minute—"

I held up a hand. "No. It's not that. He was murdered, too. In your cousin's house."

Her hand covered her heart and she closed her tired eyes. "Oh sweet Jesus." She looked upward again. "Forgive me, Lord, for speaking ill of the dead."

Thirteen

We left LouAnn Rafferty's house about thirty minutes later. Tom had explained the circumstances of Buford's death and told her as much as he felt necessary—which wasn't a whole lot. He didn't mention how Buford died, just that he must have had a key to Mr. Jeffrey's house since there was no forced entry.

LouAnn, not used to talking to anyone for this length of time—never mind strangers bearing stressful news—seemed to shut down as the discussion went on. Tom and I both realized it was time to leave. At least if he had to return for more questions, she would willingly open the door.

Tom headed to Woodcrest in search of the other cousins, but he planned on returning to Mercy in time for Millicent's three o'clock interview at the police station. Before I started for home, I checked my cat cam first. I saw four sleeping cats. Obviously everything was fine in their world. As I backed out of LouAnn's driveway, I swore I saw Emily Nguyen's car speeding away in the opposite direction, but I couldn't be certain. If she was following me, I had no control over it.

After traveling the few miles back to my house, I was

surprised to see an ancient-looking but gleaming navy blue Ford sedan waiting in my driveway. When I pulled up, I saw Birdie, Buford's landlady, clutching the steering wheel. I left my car at the end of the driveway and got out to meet her as she struggled out of the old Ford.

"Good thing it only takes five minutes to get from here to there in Mercy," she said as she greeted me. "I don't much like driving. People are in such a hurry these days."

I gave her a hug and took her hand. "Come on in. Have you been waiting here long?"

"Nope. Brought along a soda pop and sipped on it. I do allow myself one Pepsi a week. I know the stuff's not good for me, but it sure does taste good."

We went around to the back door, but before we climbed the steps to the house, she stopped and looked out on Mercy Lake. "Sure is a fine view you have here, Miss Jillian. This lake's always been pretty. And I know for a fact the fishing is good."

I disarmed the security system, turned back from the door and offered my hand to help Birdie up the steps. She accepted gratefully.

"I hope you don't mind cats. There will be four of them awaiting our arrival inside."

"My son has a lovely cat and everyone in town knows about yours. No secrets in Mercy, but then, you understand that since you've lived here a spell. As long as the cats don't bite or scratch, I'll be fine."

A few minutes later, we sat in my living room, me on the couch and Birdie in the chair across from me. She wore a bright floral skirt and a pale yellow shirt with ironed creases in the sleeves. Her flat-soled leather shoes were definitely made for walking. She'd been sniffed by the kitty residents and rubbed on by at least two of them—in other words, she'd passed the test. I noticed something different about Birdie as I studied her nearly ageless, round face. It wasn't only that she refused my offer of tea or water or coffee and seemed anxious to get on with why she'd come to visit. She seemed . . . troubled.

"I'm guessing this is about Buford, right?" I smiled, hoping to ease whatever was worrying her.

"Yes, little lady. Needless to say, you know the police have been to my home. Or rather the county sheriff deputies have. Came with their official papers and their guns and badges. Half scared me to death."

"You're saying Candace wasn't the one to come and tell you about his death?"

She shook her head, her lips tight. "I wish she had, but I guess she has other things on her plate. But see, I'd never in my life seen these gentlemen who barged in and searched Buford's room—and callin' them gentlemen is a kindness they don't much deserve. Mean faces, rough voices. I understand a murder is serious business, but what did I ever do to deserve such rude behavior?"

On rare occasions I knew that Mercy PD called on the County Sheriff's Department for assistance. "I'm sure Candace would have come herself if she could. A search warrant is a little frightening, I'm sure."

"Child, you have no idea. They tore that boy's room apart. And did they put his things back the way they found them? You can rest assured they did no such thing. So I called around and found Buford's daddy—Buford only had his daddy left and the man's a poor excuse for a father. Been an alcoholic for years. Anyways, I found him at one of the homeless shelters and told him to come by and take whatever he wants of Buford's belongings. The rest is headed straight to Goodwill. Not quite sure if what I said registered. The man sounded drunk."

"I am so sorry you had to deal with that situation. Is there anything I can do to help?" Chablis jumped into my lap and curled up for a snooze.

But Clyde must have heard something in Birdie's

voice that bothered him, because he now sat at her feet, looking up at her expectantly.

She stared down at him, her head tilted. "Is that cat smiling or is my imagination getting the better of me?"

"He does seem to wear a constant smile. I can see why Mr. Jeffrey was so attached to him."

"Not attached enough to keep him," she said. "You're sure he doesn't bite?"

"He hasn't bitten anyone since he's been with me. He seems like a friendly guy."

Birdie reached a tentative, gnarled hand to Clyde's head and touched him. He stretched to enjoy more pressure from her outstretched hand and soon she was stroking his head. "Nice boy, this one."

My tone gentle, I said, "Birdie, I don't believe you drove over here to meet Clyde or mention that search warrant. Tell me more."

"You're just like a rooster that never misses the dawn—I can't get nothing by you. It's what those deputies found in Buford's room that has me concerned. I'm hoping you'll talk to Candace for me—because I could tell you two are like sisters."

"Of course I'll relay anything you want me to—or make sure you can tell her yourself."

"She doesn't need me bothering her right now. All I can say is, I have never in all my seventy years had something like this happen in my home—and once these crimes are solved, it's my sincere wish that the police keep a close eye on my neighborhood."

"What did the deputies find?" I couldn't hide the concern in my voice. Birdie was definitely scared.

"A gun and drugs is what they found."

"What?" I was astonished.

"And you know if that boy had a gun and drugs, other people with guns and drugs can't be far away."

"Oh boy. You have every right to be concerned," I said.

"The way those deputies looked at me, you'd a thought I was the one that gave those bad things to Buford." Her fear had given way to indignation. "A drug dealer? At my age?"

"I'm sure they told Candace what they found during the search. She won't let you down, Birdie. She'll make sure you're protected." My mind began to whirl with possibilities. What if Buford had returned to Mr. Jeffrey's house to steal whatever he could to buy more drugs or to pay off his dealer? He probably knew everything of value that Mr. Jeffrey owned and what items would net him the most cash. Dirk had mentioned no valuables were kept in the house, but maybe they were hidden away. Had Buford found watches or cash or jewelry that Dirk knew nothing about?

Birdie's voice interrupted my thoughts. "Protect me? Maybe they'll drive through the neighborhood once or twice, but the police have their hands full right now. They don't have time for the likes of me. I've been afraid in my own home, Miss Jillian. I never in my life have felt such worry."

"I understand. I'd feel the same way. You never saw anyone suspicious hanging around your place? Never saw Buford bring people inside, people who seemed . . . less than upstanding?"

"Not one of his friends seemed upstanding, but I never imagined they were criminals. What if he owed some terrible person money?" she asked, echoing my earlier thoughts. "Maybe they'll decide to do their own kinda search—one that might include my whole house— with me tied up or even dead."

She was right to be concerned. "Listen, I'm sure you're aware that my friend Tom does security work. He installed all the cameras for my house after I had a break-in here. He would love to help you feel safe in your home."

"How can cameras do that? By the time I see who-ever is hanging around, it could be too late."

"Tom monitors his clients with technology—even when he's away from his office. He can get the police out to your house fast—or he'll come himself."

"I don't know, Jillian. Things like that cost money and—"

"We can work something out. You need to feel safe. That's what's important right now." But I was concerned that Tom might not have time for a new job right now. I'd have to convince him this was important.

"If you believe this can help, I trust you. I got an emergency fund. I suppose this is one of those times I should use the money." She rose slowly, using the arms of the chair for support. "I knew you were the right per-son to come to. Even if Tom can't help right away, I feel better having talked to you. Now I gotta get back. My son's on the way. He took a few days off from his job at the university and said he'd stay with me until I got over my little *fright* as he called it."

"I'm relieved you'll have someone there with you, Birdie. Meanwhile, I'll talk to Tom and Candace about making sure you stay safe after your son leaves."

As I helped Birdie out to her car, she said, "Do they know what happened to poor Mr. Jeffrey? It's a terrible thing for a man to die alone like that." I heard a tremor in her voice and the hand gripping my arm tightened.

"Not yet, but they will. Candace won't rest until she knows everything."

She nodded, her eyes red-rimmed behind her glasses. "That's good. The man deserved better than to die alone."

I opened her car door and stayed close as she slowly edged behind the wheel. After she drove away, I tried to reach Tom, but my call went straight to voice mail. I left a message, but he was probably too busy tracking down

Mr. Jeffrey's other cousins to answer calls. Then I remembered he'd be at the police station at three when Millicent arrived for her *appointment* with the police. I could catch him before he sat in on the interview with Candace. Maybe he could find a way to fit in an assessment of Birdie's house while her son was in town—because she was right about the drug dealers. She needed security and her son couldn't hang around forever.

First, however, I had to catch some nourishment. I'd had nothing to eat since that delicious Danish at Belle's Beans. I decided to microwave a frozen organic-beans-and-rice burrito. Healthy canceled out Danish, I decided—but it could never cancel out how yummy that pastry had been.

Fourteen

The Mercy police station is in the back portion of the city courthouse. The building sits in the town square and is old and beautiful, with pillars and marble steps. Walking into the lobby, I never failed to appreciate the elegance of a time long past and the craftsmanship that went into construction in that bygone era. The tile gleamed, the oak doors and banisters smelled of lemon oil and the plaster walls had recently been painted a creamy white. One of the reasons this lobby was shining walked toward me, a broad smile on her face, her broom and dustpan at the ready.

Audrey had worked in the courthouse for most of her adult life—probably for fifty years. She swept up any scrap of paper or piece of dust that a visitor shed so it was immediately out of sight. We exchanged a hug—Audrey loved hugs—and she immediately checked the floor at my feet for cat hair. It was her routine. I was guilty of bringing in fur from time to time.

Finding nothing, she looked at me with brown eyes growing cloudy with age. "You use that sticky roller thing before you came today?"

"I didn't, but I guess the cats decided you had plenty of work to do without my offering a contribution."

She laughed. "Deputy Candace is busy, busy, busy. She call you to come in 'cause you got that cat who's been all over the TV?"

Everyone knew about Clyde, it would seem. "Candace didn't call me. I was hoping to catch Tom. Did you see him come through?"

Audrey shook her head. "Nope—not unless he came in the jail entrance downstairs."

"Good. I haven't missed him, then. I'll head on to the police station."

"You take care, Miss. Good seeing you."

Though the hallways, courtrooms, judge's chambers and clerk offices were well maintained, it was a different story where the police offices were housed. A trek to the left down a long corridor led to the police station. Here lay the shabby side of the building—and *not* shabby chic. Discomfort never failed to gnaw at my gut when I saw the row of old benches where people waited to speak with the police or to pick up a relative released on bail.

But when I entered through the police office's scarred door, Dispatcher B.J. greeted me with a cheery, "Hey there, Jillian," and the small knot in my stomach eased.

"Is Tom here yet?" He *could* have come in through the basement and up the stairs as Audrey mentioned, though I doubted it.

"Nope. Is he supposed to be?"

"He said he'd be here to meet with Candace and Millicent Boatman."

A female cleared her throat. A person I hadn't even noticed sat in one of the chairs that lined the wall in the small waiting area.

I turned to see a woman in her late sixties or early seventies with florid red hair and wearing a bright pink Jackie O–type suit. From the furrow of down-turned lines near her mouth, I decided this person had done plenty of frowning in her time. She wore a fuchsia hat, cream-tinted panty hose and what were probably vintage pink leather heels. Had I walked into the 1960s version of *The Twilight Zone*?

I smiled and she repaid me with a stone-cold glare. "What's your business with Millicent? I know for a fact that you are not a police *person*." She raised her dark penciled brows at B.J. "Would that be the correct terminology, young man?"

"I'm definitely not a police officer," I told her, and quickly sidestepped to block her view of B.J. I had the feeling she'd talk right past me to him if I didn't make that move. "I hoped to meet up with a friend who is supposed to be here when Millicent arrives and—I'm Jillian Hart, by the way." I walked the few steps to where she sat and offered my hand.

She ignored the gesture but in her thick South Carolina drawl said, "Oh, I know who you are. My name is Ida Lynn Ford and I am wondering what you or your friend wants with Millicent."

I dropped my hand to my side. So this was Ida Lynn—one of Mr. Jeffrey's cousins from Woodcrest. "My friend is—" I turned to B.J., who gave me the "Don't say anything else" stare. "My friend has business here, is all. But it can wait." I pivoted toward the exit, only to have the door open before I could take a step.

Tom walked in and held the door for a woman about Ida Lynn's age, who had straight white hair cut in a stylish bob. They seemed to be sharing a joke because they were both laughing. She was dressed in an expensive-looking baby blue linen outfit.

The resemblance between this woman who now clung to Tom's arm and Ida Lynn Ford was remarkable; the two had to be related. They could have been sisters except for Ida Lynn's frown lines. Millicent's flawless pale skin shone through even under the room's harsh lights. Her expertly applied light pink blush, rose-colored lipstick and sculptured brows accentuated her features.

A surprised Tom said, "Hey, Jillian. What are you doing here?"

I glanced at Ida Lynn. She stood, her eyes wide. The expression she now wore made the look she gave me earlier seem downright friendly. Millicent, however, seemed too wrapped up in Tom to even notice her.

Ida Lynn spoke, her tone stiletto sharp. "What did you do to your brother that has brought you under suspicion, Millicent?"

Millicent blinked and had to crane her neck to look past me at Ida Lynn.

The waiting area was so small, I had to move back against B.J.'s desk so they could greet each other—but *greet* was obviously too kind a word. The room swirled with unspoken wrath. The reasons Mr. Jeffrey's family didn't communicate much were written all over the ensuing silence. Too bad I couldn't read the words.

"Suspicion?" Millicent said in a whispery voice that reminded me of Marilyn Monroe. "Whatever are you talking about, Ida Lynn? I am under no suspicion."

Ida Lynn smiled the most spiteful smile I'd ever seen. "Perhaps they'll change their minds once they talk to *me*." She looked at Tom then. "I see we meet again, Mr. Stewart."

Millicent glanced up at Tom, her scrutiny offering much less enthusiasm than before. "You know my cousin?"

Tom's ears reddened, a sign I understood. He was embarrassed. "I did speak with Mrs. Ford earlier in the day," he said hesitantly. "But I had no idea she'd be coming here."

Ida Lynn clutched her pink leather bag tightly to her abdomen. "You come to my home, question my loyalty to my family and don't expect me to march directly to the source? To this disgusting little hole in the wall they call a police station?"

I glanced at B.J. and saw a smile playing on his lips. It was a good thing Ida Lynn couldn't see his face or she might go off on him. He was rather enjoying the verbal onslaught. Not me. I thought the experience of sharing a tiny space with these two women was rather like chewing on glass.

Thank goodness I caught a glimpse of Candace from the corner of my eye. She strode down the hallway toward the low swinging gate that separated the waiting area from the rest of the police offices.

I read the surprise on her face when she saw me, but she immediately addressed Tom and the two women. "Sorry to keep you waiting. Mr. Stewart, I didn't expect you." She glanced between the cousins. "Which one of you is—"

"I'm Ida Lynn Ford, Norm Jeffrey's cousin. I need a word, Officer. Or is it Captain, or Chief or—"

"It's *Deputy* Carson. Actually, I'll be speaking with Mrs. Boatman first. We had an interview already scheduled." Candace looked at Tom, who still had Millicent hanging on his arm. "I see you've already met Mrs. Boatman."

Tom said, "I've had the pleasure of meeting all of Mr. Jeffrey's female cousins, though Mrs. Ford's brother has been difficult to track down. I ran into Mrs. Boatman in the hallway and introduced myself. She'd like me to accompany her into the interview."

Ida Lynn pointed at Candace. "You hold on just one minute, *young lady.* I have been waiting patiently for more than thirty minutes to have a word with you."

I felt the icicles in her voice stab at me. What was wrong with this woman? Why was she so angry?

Candace smiled. "I understand how that would be upsetting, but I will speak with you *after* I talk to your cousin and Mr. Stewart. As I said, I already scheduled a talk with Mrs. Boatman. Come on in, you two." She opened the gate and extended her arm in the direction of the hall.

After Tom and Millicent passed Candace, she looked at me. "Would you mind staying here with Mrs. Ford, Jillian? Looks like you have questions for me, too."

"I actually came to—"

"Thanks." She turned and hurried after the other two, calling to Tom to head for the chief's office.

"Talk to Tom," I finished under my breath. I closed my eyes and inhaled deeply before daring a glance at Ida Lynn. Her cheeks almost matched her red hair.

She plopped down on the chair she'd vacated earlier, reminding me of a toddler put in a time-out after a temper tantrum. I wasn't sure if the tantrum was over or just beginning.

Fifteen

I guessed B.J. understood that redirecting Ida Lynn's negative energy might be needed, because he smiled and said, "Would either of you like a soft drink or a bottled water?"

Ida Lynn turned her head away from him and refused to acknowledge the offer, but I asked for water. Actually, I would have preferred a giant tumbler of white wine.

I took a seat kitty-corner to the unhappiest of cousins. "I'm sorry you have to wait, but it's great you came down here. You must have cared a lot about Mr. Jeffrey." This was an assumption and perhaps wishful thinking on my part, but I hoped to start a conversation with the woman. As much as her demeanor made me uncomfortable, I couldn't help being curious about why she was so upset.

"You know nothing about me or my family. All you know about are cats, including the one that ended up at the center of this nasty business."

"So you know about Clyde."

"I've known about Clyde a lot longer than you have. I saw your little interview on TV. Hardly a mention of Norm. It was all about the cat."

"You are absolutely right and I felt terrible about—"

"Terrible?" Ida Lynn said. "Not terrible enough to mention my family."

"True, but I have met LouAnn since that interview. She seems like such a nice person. I am so sorry for your family's loss." And I was. But was Ida Lynn sorry? I couldn't tell.

A tiny slackening of the muscles around her neon pink lips told me, however, that I might be on the right track. She still hadn't made eye contact with me, but she didn't seem as intense and I'd apparently piqued her interest. She said, "LouAnn talked to you?"

"She did. She seemed to think highly of Mr. Jeffrey."

"But not highly of *me*." Now her cold gray eyes met mine.

"She said nothing unkind about you, if that's what you mean." *At least not directly,* I thought. I remembered LouAnn saying that the cousins didn't care for her and the feeling was mutual. But perception was reality to many people and perhaps a mere lack of communication had these relatives at odds with one another.

"Did she even mention me at all?" Ida Lynn's forehead creased as she raised her dark penciled eyebrows.

Ah. So perhaps I had hit on an issue that mattered to Ida Lynn. "She did. I got the sense she feels as if all of you have drifted apart." Okay, this was pure conjecture, but my instincts told me to keep her talking.

"Drifted apart? That's putting it mildly. She didn't come down here to this godforsaken police station, did she? I mean, the poor woman is a hermit. Talks to cats all day. So what if her husband died and left her in perpetual grief? Mine's dead, too, and I say good riddance to bad rubbish."

"She does seem to miss her husband, but certainly not all widows react to their loss the same way."

Renewed anger flared Ida Lynn's cheeks with color. "What do you know about me and my husband?"

"I'm sorry," I said quickly. "I know nothing about him. It's just that you . . ." I let my words trail off. I'd driven this off in the ditch and to get information flowing again, perhaps I needed to be quiet and let her calm down.

She sat taller and reminded me of Syrah when he's doing his "I am the king of the mountain" pose. She said, "I am allowed to say anything I want about my dead husband. That is not a privilege *you* possess."

"You are absolutely right. I am so sorry."

She smiled almost congenially and gave a slight nod. "I accept your apology. I suppose you and LouAnn have much in common. Speaking of which, you helped another cat lover I happen to know. Ritaestelle Longworth—you do remember her?"

Since Ritaestelle and her cat Isis lived in Woodcrest and so did Ida Lynn, I supposed it was no surprise they knew each another. "Ms. Longworth is a wonderful person."

"Well, the dear soul happens to be a friend of mine. She spoke quite highly of you. But I must always judge for myself. You were quick to apologize when you were wrong, and that shows me at least one admirable character trait."

I could feel my tight neck muscles loosen a tad. Apologies, even if rendered without the greatest sincerity, can work miracles. She no longer seemed angry, but I had the feeling anything I said might set her off again, so I had to be careful.

"LouAnn, I take it, wasn't as reclusive before her husband died?"

"She and Norm always had that tendency to shut themselves off when they got their feelings hurt. I've been known to have a sharp tongue and they'd go crying in their milk when I supposedly offended them. But, hear me, young woman." She pointed a finger at me. I noticed for the first time that she was wearing gloves that matched her outfit and it was all I could do to keep my eyes off them. "I loved Norm even if we didn't have regular visits. These police officers have no right to question my loyalty to my family."

She was getting worked up again and I was beginning to wonder what Tom had said to her—so I decided to ask. "Did your interview with Mr. Stewart upset you?"

She sat back, seeming to contemplate the question. "He's a nice-enough gentleman. Very polite. It's just all these insinuations that my cousin died an unnatural death and that somehow I might be involved have me flustered. I have to set these people straight, but they are too busy to talk to me. It is *most* infuriating."

B.J. reappeared with a chilled bottled water and I took it from him gratefully. But when I saw Ida Lynn eye the water thirstily, I offered it to her.

"Why, thank you, Jillian. I suppose I am a bit parched after the drive here and the long wait."

"And while you wait, why not tell me what you loved about Mr. Jeffrey? I'd really like to learn more about him—especially since his cat is staying with me."

She unscrewed the bottle cap and took a long sip. It smeared her lipstick and made her appear even more unbalanced than the odd hair and the outfit did. "Norm. Such a good man. He would never take his own life and I am quite upset when I hear such rumors."

"You heard that?" I asked.

"From that strange woman who spoke with me about Norm's death. Miss Monk, I believe? At first, she said it was the cancer, but then when I spoke to her again, she said they delayed the release of the death certificates because they needed to correct their statement regarding the manner in which he died. Overdose of medication? I seriously doubt that." She shook her head and screwed the cap back on the water bottle. "Norman would never take his own life and I am certain that *der-*

elict who was supposed to care for him probably killed him."

Could be true, I thought. *But then, who killed Buford?* But I wanted to get back to what Ida Lynn had just told me. Lydia made two calls to her—and yet this woman wasn't the nearest relative. Millicent was. That seemed odd. So, hoping to sound only mildly curious, I said, "The coroner's investigator called you?"

"Oh no. I called her. Until there's a cause of death and all the paperwork is done, probate cannot begin. My husband was a lawyer and I am fully aware of the process."

"The death certificates go to Millicent, right?" I said.

"Well, I'm not sure, but I could not be certain she'd even show up here to take care of a funeral. I decided to start the process of caring for the dead. You see, Millicent thinks she's too good for us with her big house on Hilton Head Island. Too good for Norm, as well."

"But Mr. Jeffrey took his cat to live with her, didn't he? So he must have placed some trust in her. He must have even seen her as recently as two months ago."

"Dirk came and *got* that cat. Norm was in no shape to be driving anywhere. I would have taken in Clyde myself, but I travel. I have no time for pets. I told him I couldn't give Clyde a proper home."

So the story was a little different from what I'd heard from Dirk. But before I could contemplate this further or even ask Ida Lynn any more questions, my personal stalker walked through the door and into the waiting area.

It was all I could do to stay quiet.

Sixteen

Emily Nguyen made her entrance into the station and said, "My gut told me all the action was going on down here — and I was right."

B.J. stood, perhaps hoping to act like this was indeed a police station and not Emily's TV set in Asheville. "How can I help you, Miss Nguyen?"

She eyed Ida Lynn as if she were a marlin she'd landed on a deep-sea fishing excursion. "Tell me who you've got here, besides Jillian? A suspect, maybe?"

Uh-oh. But before I could stop the confrontation, Ida Lynn shot back. "Who are you to call me a *suspect*, young woman?"

"Emily Nguyen, Channel Five News, Asheville. Your name, ma'am?" She looked like she would have shoved a mic in Ida Lynn's face if she had one with her.

"I am no suspect and I will *not* give you my name." Ida Lynn glowered over at B.J. "Is this *your* doing? Did you invite this . . . this *media person* here?"

"I would never do that, Mrs. Ford — " B.J. stopped, realizing his mistake too late.

Emily jumped on it. "Ford? As in Ida Lynn Ford? Mr. Jeffrey's cousin?"

Her triumphant smile made me a little sick to my stomach. Emily wanted more than a story about a cat, and she fully understood she was onto something now.

Ida Lynn pursed her lips and said nothing as she appraised Emily, her stare hot enough to roast marshmallows. She clutched her bag, and her gloved fingers drummed the gold clasp.

Emily turned to me. "Jillian? Why is Mrs. Ford here?"

I closed my eyes and pinched the bridge of my nose, trying to think of a way to defuse this situation. The swollen silence that ensued was too much for me to stand. "Emily, I am not your source for everything you want to report on in our town. I will not answer your questions, and that interview I promised featuring Clyde? If you persist in bothering this woman, it's off the table."

Emily turned one hand palm up. "We have a cat story over here." She turned the other palm up. "And we have a major-crime piece over here. Hmm. Which story do you think I care about more right now?"

"There are good people who could be hurt by your prematurely reporting on the . . . the *problems* in Mercy." I dared a glimpse at Ida Lynn. She was livid and I didn't blame her.

"The problems? Don't you mean the unexplained deaths?" Emily pulled a cell phone from her trouser pocket. "I need a news team down here right now."

I stood and stepped toward her. "*Wait.* Please don't bring the media circus back here. Think about this. You won't get the story—because . . . because they'll give it to someone who isn't a weather girl." If Emily wanted to coerce me or Ida Lynn or anyone else into revealing information by threatening us this way, she had another thing coming. Didn't she realize her ego was far bigger than her actual ability to nab this story alone?

It was Emily's turn to contemplate her next move. I could tell from the way her shoulders sagged that she quickly understood she wouldn't get the story. It would go to a more experienced reporter.

Ida Lynn finally spoke to Emily, derision dripping from each word. "You do the *weather*? My, my. Why am I not surprised at your lack of professionalism, barging in here and acting like you are entitled to intimate knowledge of my family?"

But Emily apparently wasn't the least bit intimidated. "I *will* get a news-anchor position one day, and it won't be in Asheville. This story could be my ticket out of that market and on to a big city." She turned to me. "If I promise to keep this on the down low for now, do I get access to inside information?"

"That isn't up to me." I looked at Ida Lynn. "I respect your privacy, Mrs. Ford—as well as that of your cousins. But this story *will* get out eventually. There have been crews from major news stations down here already. A whole bunch of them parked on my front lawn because they were covering the story of Clyde's journey home. Now, things have turned ugly. Between my stepdaughter, who is the editor of our local newspaper, and Miss Nguyen here, perhaps we can control the sensationalism. What do you say?"

"Can you control *her*?" Ida Lynn waved a hand at Emily.

The phone rang and I don't believe I have ever seen B.J. more grateful to get back to the business of being a dispatcher. He sat and took the call.

About now, I wished *I* were the dispatcher. But I couldn't give up on trying to mediate this mess now. "I'll talk to Miss Nguyen and help her understand that your family should be treated with respect. I have had several conversations with her already. She *is* capable of doing this the right way—with a little guidance from my stepdaughter."

Emily cocked her head and looked at me with an expression of surprise combined with a hint of gratitude. There was hope for this girl yet. She said, "I can be respectful—if I know what I need to be respectful of."

Ida Lynn sighed. "I suppose you're correct about the press inserting themselves into our lives." She leaned toward me and whispered, "But before I talk to this young woman, I need to speak with LouAnn, Wayne and Millicent. We cannot be at odds with one another while a spotlight shines on us."

I was sure Emily had heard every word, but I pretended she hadn't. "Good idea." I looked up at the eager face of the wannabe reporter. "Can you sit tight and let me get back to you? I'll be like a liaison between you and the family." As soon as I used the word *liaison*, I felt ill all over again. What had I just gotten myself into?

Emily pivoted to leave, but then over her shoulder she addressed Ida Lynn. "Love the suit. Vintage is so *now*."

She left, thank goodness, and as soon as the door closed behind her, Candace appeared. Could that be just a lucky break or had she been around a corner listening and waiting until the coast was clear?

Candace said, "Mrs. Ford, if you could join the interview now?"

Ida Lynn stood. "It's about time. But I want you to include Jillian. Seems we have a problem with this little weather girl hanging around your town and—"

"Emily Nguyen?" Candace's frustration was evident. "That young woman reminds me of a fruit fly hovering around rotting bananas."

"Jillian has kindly offered to deal with her so my family doesn't have to. I have accepted this solution." Ida Lynn smiled, her smeared lipstick looking almost comical. "If you are about to inform me exactly what is happening concerning the death of my cousin, I want Jillian to know so she can filter out anything that might be, well, *embarrassing* to us. We don't want unpleasant details passed along to Miss Nguyen."

Candace looked at me with questioning eyes.

"Is this arrangement okay, Deputy Carson?" I asked, nodding slightly to affirm this was what Ida Lynn and I had discussed.

She took a few seconds to consider her answer before saying, "Anything to keep from having to deal with Emily Nguyen myself sounds like a good plan. Now, y'all come on back."

Ida Lynn stood. "At the very least, Millicent should have a say before we firm up our agreement."

"You can ask her yourself." Candace started down the hall, fully expecting us to follow her.

Ida Lynn hesitated. "I have to speak to her *now*? We'll be in the same room?"

Candace turned. "Is that a problem?"

"Um, no. Absolutely not. I was hoping to have a few hours to consider exactly what to say to someone I haven't seen in years. But carry on, Deputy Carson. A Southern woman such as myself can handle anything." Ida Lynn lifted her chin and moved forward, wavering on her pink heels.

I wanted to grab her elbow to keep her from falling, but I had a feeling any goodwill I'd managed to manufacture between us would disappear in an instant if I touched her.

Tom and Millicent sat chatting and smiling when we entered the chief's office. The woman didn't seem the least bit distraught about her brother's death as far as I could tell.

But she stood and held her arms wide in greeting when we stepped into the room. "Why, Ida Lynn. I am so glad you decided to join us. I have truly missed your company. Why is it that tragedy so often rebuilds bridges we thought we'd burned forever?"

Candace walked over to the wall where Chief Baca's framed credentials and commendations hung and dragged over two straight-back chairs. Tom stood and offered Ida Lynn the more comfortable, padded seat next to her cousin, and though she looked up at Tom with suspicion, she did accept the spot.

Millicent grabbed Ida's hands in hers and stared into her eyes. "Can we put the past behind us, Ida Lynn? Please?"

What past? I wondered.

"As long as I get to say what's been on my mind for several years," came Ida Lynn's taciturn reply.

Candace took the chief's leather chair behind his polished mahogany desk. "Unless the past has something to do with the death of Mr. Jeffrey, can we please leave the reunion for later?"

Millicent laughed. "It has nothing to do with the present. Please ask your questions, Deputy Carson. Ida Lynn and I will have a nice dinner together and work out our troubles."

I now realized her distinctive laugh, the odd smiles, her clinging to a stranger as she had with Tom earlier, meant that Millicent dealt with uncomfortable situations by appearing cheerful and sociable. Why she hid behind this mask of affability, I didn't know, but I had complete confidence in both Candace and Tom. They'd figure it out.

Candace folded her hands on the desk, a yellow legal pad beneath them. She didn't pick up the pencil that was lying there to take notes. Instead, she focused completely on Ida Lynn. "Mrs. Ford, first of all, I am sorry for your loss. I also apologize for the wait. I have to sort through the facts in a precise way so I can gather information about the deaths of both your cousin and Buford Miller."

Ida Lynn started to speak, but Millicent broke in. "Can we wait for one second, Deputy?" A box of tissues sat on the chief's desk and Millicent pulled one out. "Ida

Lynn has had a bit of a makeup malfunction. Look at me, sweetheart." She gripped Ida Lynn's chin and turned her face so she could correct the smeared lipstick.

I watched this small scenario, observing Ida Lynn's compliance, and decided there had been a time when these two had probably been close.

Candace, however, showed no interest in this renewed bonding between the two elderly women. "Moving right along, when was the last time you spoke in person with Mr. Jeffrey?"

The question seemed to transport Ida Lynn back to the here and now—and reminded her she was none too happy with her cousin. She pulled away from Millicent. "Did you ask Millicent when *she* last visited with Norm?"

Candace smiled stiffly and I could tell her patience tank was running on empty. "I did. And now I am asking you."

She sat straighter, clutching her precious pink purse tightly in her lap. "Actually, I am a bit challenged with short-term memory. I can't tell you the precise date. He was missing his cat and—" She turned to Millicent. "He apparently had no idea the creature had disappeared from your house. Dirk lied and told him the animal was fine—but from the news reports, we know he'd been gone from Hilton Head for months."

"Why, Ida Lynn, do you think I wanted to tear a dying man's heart out by telling him about that horrible mistake? I am not that cold."

"She is making herself sound so innocent, so caring," Ida Lynn said. "Ask her son how many times she's been to town to visit with Norm."

Candace's gaze fell on Millicent. "Did you lie to me not fifteen minutes ago about the last time you visited your brother in person, Mrs. Boatman?"

Millicent sighed heavily. "It just sounded better if I

said I came here. We talked on the phone. It's the same thing."

"It makes a difference," Candace said slowly, "because that means you did *not* have a face-to-face conversation with Mr. Jeffrey at the time you claimed you did. You told me he said he only had a few months to live when you came to see him—in fact you related this story in great detail."

"The conversation took place, simply not here in Mercy." Millicent let out another nervous laugh. "I am still not sure what the difference is."

Tom cleared his throat. "Lying to the police about even the smallest detail is never a good idea, Millicent." He probably hoped to give Candace a moment to regroup, because she looked downright exasperated.

Millicent leaned around Ida Lynn and smiled at him. "When you put it like that, Tom, I fully understand. I am so very sorry for the confusion." But her apology seemed only directed at him and not at anyone else in the room.

Candace turned her attention back to Ida Lynn. "When you last spoke to your cousin, did Mr. Jeffrey tell you he only had a few months to live?"

"He *never* said a thing about that." Ida Lynn cast a sideways glance at Millicent. "He was quite optimistic about his treatment. I must say, he appeared unwell during the chemo. Very thin, very weak. That is why when Mr. Stewart came to my home and started questioning me about whether Norm would ever take his own life, well, I had to come here immediately and set the police straight. He would never do such a thing."

Millicent nodded her agreement. "Norm was always an optimist. Ida Lynn, however, did not grow up in the same house with my brother, and I saw him often when I was living here in Mercy. He did have his dark moments. Cancer is such a difficult thing and—"

"But here's what's bothering me right now," Candace said in a firm tone I understood to be her cop mode. "Even though Norman Jeffrey's fingerprints were all over every other bottle of medicine in his cabinet, the heart pill container had been wiped clean. No prints. Not one. Can either of you ladies make sense of that?"

Seventeen

Ida Lynn paled and seemed at a loss for words.

Millicent gripped the arms of the chair tightly. "Are you saying someone gave him too many pills *on purpose*?"

"That's exactly what I'm saying," Candace said.

"It had to be that awful boy who supposedly cared for Norm," Ida Lynn said. "No one else visited except for LouAnn, Dirk and on occasion myself—and *we'd* never harm him." Her eyes shifted in Millicent's direction as if to point out that her name had not been mentioned on this *harmless* list.

Millicent, however, seemed oblivious. "Yes. It had to be that Miller boy."

"Mr. Miller might have been the logical suspect before yesterday," Candace said. "But like I said, he's dead, too. Someone bashed him over the head in Mr. Jeffrey's kitchen yesterday."

Millicent winced and Ida Lynn clutched her purse so tightly, her knuckles whitened.

I understood why Candace was being so blunt. She wanted to gauge their reactions and by my estimate, the ladies seemed equally shocked by the jolt she delivered.

Ida Lynn found her voice first. "Whatever was Buford Miller doing in Norm's home after the poor man had been dead for a week?"

Candace leaned back in the chair. "Information we obtained through a search of Mr. Miller's rented room indicates he might have gone to your cousin's home to steal items that could be sold."

"But he was being paid by the agency Norman contracted with, wasn't he? He had an income." Ida Lynn no longer had an abrasive edge to her voice. Instead, she was subdued and even curious.

Tom said, "Some folks never have enough cash for whatever reason. Was there anything of value in the house, something Buford Miller might have believed he could sell or pawn? Or perhaps he kept cash hidden somewhere? A secret safe, maybe?"

Millicent shook her head. "Norm would *never* keep cash in the house. His job for the better part of his life was to take care of money—other people's and his own."

"Besides, he was a frugal man," Ida Lynn added. "He had no use for expensive items. And no use for those who might believe objects equal happiness." She glimpsed at Millicent, but again, her cousin seemed oblivious to what Ida Lynn might be trying to imply with her suggestive looks.

Ida Lynn's expressions weren't lost on Candace, however. For the first time, she picked up the pen and jotted down a few words on the legal pad. She then looked up and glanced back and forth between Millicent and Ida Lynn. "Did Mr. Jeffrey play any part in why your family seems so . . . fractured?"

Millicent blinked several times and remained silent.

Ida Lynn stared down at her purse and mumbled, "Fractured. That does sound appropriate."

Candace said, "I'd like to eliminate family members as suspects since there *is* another angle I can pursue, but unless you ladies are more forthcoming, I'll have to start talking to your acquaintances to get to the truth."

"What other angle?" Ida Lynn said quickly.

"Sorry. In any murder investigation, the police keep certain facts to themselves." Candace rested her folded arms on the desk and leaned toward Ida Lynn. "Why are you so upset with your cousin, Mrs. Ford?" She nodded at Millicent.

"You've just informed me Norm was most likely murdered. Why wouldn't I be upset?" Ida Lynn's hostile attitude was back in full force.

"But I'm guessing you somehow blame Millicent. You two obviously haven't spoken about Mr. Jeffrey's death before today. Why is that?"

Millicent cleared her throat. "It's my fault, Deputy Carson. I should have telephoned Ida Lynn, LouAnn and Wayne the minute I learned of Norm's passing. They have every right to be angry with my lack of communication."

Ida Lynn shifted in her chair so she could look at Millicent directly. "And what about the *years* of your lack of communication, Millicent? You certainly can't blame Norm's death for that."

"Sometimes it takes a tragedy like this to bring family back together. I am so sorry, Ida Lynn." Millicent took one of Ida Lynn's gloved hands in both her own. "I have missed you so."

"This is all very touching," Candace said evenly. "But I am not Dr. Phil. We are investigating two murders and I need answers."

Tom said, "Maybe all that money Norman saved over the years will bring you ladies together if he's decided to leave it to family members who seem to have had a few differences."

Millicent seemed pensive. "Why, he probably did leave us all a little something, I'm sure. My brother wasn't a vindictive man. And there are a few photographs I would love to have."

Ida Lynn forcefully withdrew her hand from Millicent's grasp. "Oh, for heaven's sake. How do we know if he had any money left? That Miller boy could have stolen from him or the cancer could have used up everything. Cancer is an expensive disease."

Millicent gasped. "Why, I never thought of that, Ida Lynn." She turned to Candace. "But despite all our family issues, I loved my brother. Money is the last thing on my mind right now."

"I am assuming Mr. Jeffrey left a will. Either of you know where it might be?" Before they could answer, I recognized the familiar sound of Candace's text message signal. "Excuse me." She pulled the phone from her pocket, read the text and set her cell down on the desk. I heard frustration in her voice when she said, "I have a couple more interviews scheduled and both folks arrived at the same time." She glanced back and forth between Ida Lynn and Millicent. "The will? Where can we find it?"

Millicent and Ida Lynn exchanged glances that indicated they were clueless and Millicent confirmed this by saying, "Why, I have no idea. A bank? Or perhaps with his attorney, whoever that might be."

Candace sighed heavily. "Find out if you can and we'll do the same. But you two ladies need to realize murder is far more serious than any family feud or dispute over money. I expect you both back here tomorrow, ready to tell me the truth about why you've been estranged from each other, and why you've had so little contact over the years with Mr. Jeffrey. I have to rule out family hostility as a motive. And just so you know, you won't be together when you talk to me."

I wondered why Candace said this last part, but decided maybe she expected these two women to talk and get their stories straight, that perhaps this estrangement had been an act and these two had something to do with the murders. If their stories tomorrow matched up *too* perfectly—or not at all—Candace would be more suspicious than she was right now.

She stood and the rest of us did as well. Ida Lynn, who I guessed was the older, rose with the most difficulty, but she swatted away Millicent's attempt to help her. She certainly was feisty and her behavior had me withholding a smile.

"Tom, could you stay, please?" Candace asked.

"Sure." He touched my arm. "See you later, okay?"

I glanced between Candace and Tom. "There're a couple things I need to tell you both, but I can text you."

I followed the cousins down the hall, feeling like a border collie herding reluctant cattle back to the barn.

Millicent led the way, but she stopped dead in the hallway on seeing the two men in the waiting area. One was her son, Dirk, and the other had enough of a family resemblance—same nose as Ida Lynn and small blue eyes similar to Millicent's—that I figured this was the last of the cousins.

Ida Lynn confirmed this by saying, "Why, Wayne, you dragged yourself away from the television long enough to come down here?"

"*Not* good to see you, either, Ida Lynn," the man replied, sounding as testy as his sister. "The fashion police finally arrested you, I see."

Wayne was tall and lean. A gray fringe of hair surrounded his balding head and I surmised he was the youngest of the family—excluding Dirk. Wayne was maybe in his early sixties, perhaps five or ten years younger than his sister, Ida Lynn.

Dirk offered me a nervous smile. I wondered if he was downright frightened to see the majority of his family all in one place. From what I'd witnessed and listened to over the last hour between the two women, I couldn't blame him. What would Mr. Jeffrey's funeral be like if everyone—including LouAnn—got together? That was, if they could sit down and actually plan a funeral without Ida Lynn being, well, *Ida Lynn*, and Millicent putting on the "I'm a Southern lady" act. Because clearly it was an act, which only made me wonder what she was really like.

Millicent walked through the gate and held her arms out to Wayne as she had done with Ida Lynn. He actually embraced her, though their exchange seemed brief and tense. No love lost there, either, I decided.

B.J., who had been on the phone, said, "Deputy Carson says you two gentlemen can go on back. Last door on the left."

Dirk kissed his mother on the cheek and actually smiled at Ida Lynn as he passed her. She didn't return the warmth—but then, I wondered if Ida Lynn was capable of warmth. Perhaps she was more capable of evil.

Wayne walked by me without a glance. The sight of Ida Lynn and Millicent together may have grabbed all his attention.

Now what? I wondered once the men were gone and the three of us stood in front of B.J.'s desk. My hand immediately went to my pocket and the comfort I knew I would find there. I took out my phone. "Would you two like to see Clyde?"

Ida Lynn glanced at her watch. "Not really. It's nearly suppertime. What I *would* like, young lady, is an early meal before I return home. Where should we go to eat?"

We? As in the three of us? Wow. This ought to be almost as fun as the last couple hours. These two were perhaps the strangest people I'd ever met, and now one of them was inviting me to socialize with her and a cousin she obviously couldn't stand. Or did she want to gain something from our sitting down together? For instance, more information than had been provided about Mr. Jeffrey's death.

"We could all go back to the Pink House," Millicent suggested. "They have excellent food where we're staying." She looked at me. "And you can show us your pictures of Clyde. I am so happy he is unharmed, and I would love to make arrangements to take him with me when we are ready to leave town."

As if Shawn would allow *that* to happen. How I wanted to bail on this offer and go home to the comfort of the cats. But if these two women got together without a third party present, what would happen? We *might* have another murder.

On the other hand, I thought, *perhaps all of their bickering is an act.* If I didn't go with them, these ladies would have a chance to get their stories straight for the next interview. Or maybe they'd already been in contact and had agreed to avoid any questions from the police that pointed a guilty finger at either of them. As weary of them as I was, I could learn plenty if I asked the right questions.

Reluctantly I said, "The Pink House seems like a fine choice to me."

But Ida Lynn was a "last word" person and having the last word in choosing a restaurant was no different. "Since I have to travel the farthest home, I believe we should go to McCluskey's. It's between here and Woodcrest. They open early for supper to accommodate seniors. I'll lead the way."

And with that, she walked out the office door, her gait still unsteady thanks to her ridiculous shoes.

Following behind the two older women, I took the opportunity to text both Candace and Tom before we left the courthouse parking lot, since both women definitely needed extra time getting into their vehicles. I asked Tom to call Birdie about setting up security at her house and mentioned Birdie's concerns about the sheriff's finding a gun and drugs in Buford's room to both Tom and Candace. Why hadn't I thought to text Tom in the first place? But I knew the answer. Any moment I could steal with him, any conversation, no matter how small, made me feel more confident that I could help find out who killed the two men. Despite the difficulties Ida Lynn and Millicent presented, I felt capable of dealing with them. In fact, I was probably the right person for the job. I'd been raised by my grandparents and knew that seniors are wise. These two, though contentious, were no different. Yes, I could handle them and hopefully learn useful information to help solve these crimes.

I followed their two cars as we made the slow drive down the highway leading to McCluskey's. Once we arrived, I saw wooden rocking chairs lining a long front porch, giving the rustic-looking restaurant an inviting warmth. The place was known for Southern-style food and enormous portions. The smell of yeast rolls and fried chicken made my mouth water before we'd even been seated. I hadn't realized how hungry I was.

Red-checkered cloths covered each table and country sayings were painted on square wooden planks that hung on the walls—things like, "You have two choices for dinner—take it or leave it," and "I was weaned on cornbread and iced tea." The waiters and waitresses wore old-time country outfits—waitresses with white aprons over brown dresses, and waiters in brown vests and cowboy boots. The place had a perfect down-home Southern ambiance. Although both my dinner companions were definitely oddballs, the restaurant's atmosphere settled me. Thank goodness Ida Lynn left her hat and gloves in her ancient Lincoln; maybe that meant I wouldn't need to be on my toes hunting for any other clues she was off her rocker. I could concentrate instead on the conversation and what I might glean to pass on to Candace and Tom.

After we ordered and the waitress placed huge glasses of sweet tea in front of us, Millicent said, "I'd love to see your photo of Clyde. I do miss that boy."

At least she's interested in him, I thought. But when I showed her my phone, she seemed surprised when she saw Clyde and Chablis cuddled together.

"You recorded this?" she asked.

"No, that's live," I replied. "I have cameras so I can check up on my feline friends when I'm not home."

Ida Lynn, who was sitting next to Millicent, pulled the phone in her direction so she could see, too. She squinted at the screen. "How absurd. Why would you need to see them? They're animals. They do what animals do when you're not around. Sleep and eat."

I decided no answer was the best answer. She'd never understand how upset I'd been when Syrah had been abducted nor how much comfort these live pictures offered me.

Millicent tugged the phone away from Ida Lynn and stared at the screen. "When I return home, I will most certainly take Clyde with me."

I sure didn't want to get into that right now. She'd lost him once, and unless Mr. Jeffrey had left specific instructions in his will about his cat, I was certain Shawn would fight to keep Clyde in Mercy. If she was determined to have him, though, it might be a losing battle—Mr. Jeffrey had sent the big kitty to live with her once already.

When I didn't respond to Millicent, she handed my phone back and voiced my thoughts. "Norm *did* want him to be with me, after all."

"And," Ida Lynn said haughtily, "you allowed the cat to get out the door, only to be found months later. Your negligence was shown to the rest of the world on national television and I can only take comfort that Norm was not alive to see that spectacle."

"I will be *so* careful next time. He is a very quick cat, you know."

Since Clyde had escaped from my house as well, I decided I shouldn't judge what had happened on Hilton Head. He *was* one speedy and determined feline. Still, I wondered if Millicent had it in her to be careful. She seemed so . . . disengaged. Even now, in this off-the-beaten-path restaurant, her eyes moved around the room as if someone more important might show up who would require her full attention.

"We'll see what happens with the cat. I doubt you can hang on to him, and if Clyde gets lost again, Norm will turn over in his grave." Seemed Ida Lynn was even more skeptical than I was about Millicent. They'd known each other for years and had probably been childhood friends—childhood friends who knew many secrets about each other.

It was time to find out why everyone in this family was so at odds. After I took one last look at my kitties on the phone, I set it facedown on the table. "Back at the police station, I heard plenty of innuendo about family problems. What was Mr. Jeffrey's part in all that?"

Of course Ida Lynn spoke first. "He tried to make peace between us and finally he just gave up." She looked into Millicent's eyes. "You know he'd be quite happy to see us breaking bread together."

Millicent smiled. "He would, indeed." She switched her dreamy gaze to me. "It all happened so many years ago."

I smiled at her. "What happened, Mrs. Boatman?"

"Oh, please call me Millicent, dear. And you truly are a dear."

"Thank you, but—"

Ida Lynn broke in with, "Get on with it, Millicent. The police girl will be asking you the same thing tomorrow, so why not practice your storytelling skills? Tell her how LouAnn stole Oliver away from you."

Millicent blinked several times and returned my smile. "It's true. She stole the love of my life."

I tried not to seem surprised, though I was. "And she ended up marrying Oliver?"

"Yes indeed. Sweet, handsome Oliver." She gazed past me as if staring back into the past.

"And you never forgave LouAnn?"

"The whole thing divided us, you see." For the first time since I'd met Millicent, I could tell she was being sincere.

"Divided you and LouAnn?" I asked.

"At first. But then Norm supported LouAnn rather than me, and Wayne was so busy using drugs and getting arrested, we were all fed up with him. Only Ida Lynn stood by me . . . for a while." She glanced at Ida Lynn and then quickly looked away.

What else happened? Still, this news about LouAnn astounded me and it was all I could focus on. Sad, lonely LouAnn was at the center of these family woes? And her dead husband, whom she mourned so utterly, was the love of Millicent's life? This sounded like they'd watched one too many episodes of *The Guiding Light* when they were young. "Sounds like plenty of trouble. Tell me more about what happened."

But before either of them could answer, my worst nightmare plopped into the empty chair beside me. "I got lost. Unfamiliar territory, but I guess I stayed on the right road because I spotted Jillian's minivan in the parking lot." Emily smiled. "So, here I am."

Eighteen

"And exactly who are you?" Millicent said—sounding much less haughty than Ida Lynn had when she'd asked the same question earlier.

But Ida Lynn practically dissected Emily with her scowl. "Keep your mouth shut, Millicent. She's the *press*." The amount of loathing she added to that last word was remarkable. I wondered if Ida Lynn had done any acting.

"Do Wayne and LouAnn know the three of you are talking about them behind their backs? Because I couldn't help but overhear." Emily's tone sounded innocent enough, sweet almost, but there was no doubt in my mind she wanted to stir the pot by mentioning the relatives.

I stood, lifting Emily by her elbow. "You promised to wait on this and let me be the go-between. Now, stand behind your word and please leave these ladies alone."

Emily shrugged off my grip and nodded at Millicent. "I didn't promise *her* anything."

"Do I have to call Deputy Carson to send an officer?" I hadn't intended to raise my voice, but Emily Nguyen was wearing on my last nerve. She kept showing up everywhere I went.

A restaurant employee with the name tag PAUL had

apparently been hovering nearby and overheard me say the word *officer.* He rushed to our table. "Is there a problem?"

"Nope," Emily said quickly. "I was just leaving. But I'll be seeing all three of you soon, I'm sure." She pointed at Millicent. "Especially *you.* Love that color dress with your eyes, by the way."

She hurried out the door with Paul making certain she got to her car. I eased back into my chair.

Turned out the restaurant gave us a free cheesecake dessert for the "upset" Emily caused. The food was delicious—I had chicken and dumplings—but Emily's unexpected arrival shut both women down. I didn't learn another thing about anyone in the family, including Mr. Jeffrey. Millicent and Ida Lynn created tag-team deflection of my every question.

When dinner ended and I was finally on my way home, I reflected on my earlier thought that once upon a time those two had been as close as sisters. Yup, decades ago, they'd no doubt survived interrogation by suspicious parents on more than one occasion.

This conclusion made me more determined to find out just what other events might have happened over the years—espccially Ida Lynn and Millicent's estrangement— and why the disruption in their relationships lasted so long. Two men were dead, after all—and one or all of these relatives knew things they weren't saying.

Three happy kitties greeted me when I arrived home, putting my thoughts of family secrets aside. But when I realized I didn't see Clyde sitting at the back door waiting along with Syrah, Merlot and Chablis, I panicked.

I ran into the living room and switched the television screen to my monitoring channel. Clyde wore his GPS collar. I could find him. After all, he hadn't been gone that long and—

I felt a nudge against my calf and a sleepy-eyed Clyde

offered up one of his deep-throated meows. I knelt and petted both his cheeks with the backs of my hands, and he began to purr. "You scared me, buddy."

Soon I was surrounded by my three jealous cats, all vying for attention—and of course for a meal. As soon as all of them were happily enjoying their individual bowls of Fancy Feast, I realized I was exhausted. Ida Lynn and Millicent were a challenge and I needed to recharge if I planned to throw more questions about the family at the two of them.

I'd texted Tom with my whereabouts earlier and he'd replied with one word: *interesting*. But dinner with the two women turned out to be a bit of a disappointment thanks to Emily Nguyen. Something *had* to be done about her unexpectedly showing up and inserting herself into this investigation. I was beginning to think we had the GPS collar on the wrong mammal.

When Tom arrived at my house close to nine p.m., my first question after he kissed me in greeting was, "Can you put a GPS tracker on Emily Nguyen's car? Or is that illegal?"

Tom settled next to me on the couch; I'd been watching a rerun of *Seinfeld* so I could revive myself with a few laughs. But now he was the one who laughed.

"Are you serious?"

"She keeps popping up." I went on to explain about the dinner I'd shared with the cousins. "When I thought about Clyde's collar, I wanted to buy one for *her*."

He grinned. "Putting a collar on her would be a little obvious, Jilly, don't you think?"

"It's just unnerving to know that someone is following me and can surprise me at any moment. So, I guess I *am* serious about the GPS tracking."

"In South Carolina, I can legally put a slap-and-go type of GPS locator under her bumper if you want me to. Who knows? Maybe she's already tracking *you*, so turnabout is fair play."

My hand went to my mouth and I spoke through my fingers. "Do you think that's how she always knows where I am?"

"Wouldn't surprise me. I can check right now."

He left and came back to the living room in less than five minutes. He held a small black device that fit in the palm of his hand. He sat next to me again. "Here you go. I won't have to buy one, which is nice, since this model costs around three hundred bucks. I can just download the instruction manual, reconfigure it and slap it on *her* car first chance I get."

I leaned back against the cushions, still stunned by what he was showing me. "Why, that little sneak. Yes, maybe turnabout *is* fair play."

"Right now this thing is telling her that you're home. I may be able to jury-rig the GPS to make her believe you're home even after I stick it on her car."

I said, "You could take it to the motel where she's staying and—"

"And get caught on a surveillance camera? No way. Tomorrow morning, meet me at Belle's Beans and bring the tracker with you. I'll drive my work van over there with my equipment and wait outside. When she shows up—and I'm sure she will—you keep her occupied and I'll do the deed. Last I knew, the town of Mercy hasn't taken to the notion of CCTV on every street—except around the banks. And those cameras aren't anywhere near Belle's place."

I paused, considering what we were about to do. "Should I really stoop to her level, Tom? It seems like a child's game."

He held out the device. "With this on her car, at least she can't ambush you. You'll know when she's coming because I'll set up a screen on your phone to track her vehicle."

I nodded. "So I'm not actually keeping her away from me. I'll just have fair warning if she's right on my tail."

"Right. If you change your mind, say the word and I'll remove it. Deal?" His brows rose in inquiry.

"Deal." Chablis jumped into my lap, ready to cuddle after watching fireflies from the cat perch with the rest of her crew. I let her get comfortable before I spoke. "Now, tell me about Wayne and Dirk. What did the guys have to say to Candace?"

"I wasn't there. Candace gave me a new assignment right before she spoke to them. I did meet Wayne—he's a blue-collar guy, electrician, I think—and I only said a few words to Dirk."

"Darn. I wish we knew more. I know of at least one event in the family's past that triggered a lot of bad feelings, but I believe there's more. Millicent was just a little too forthcoming about issues from long, long ago. That could mean she's hiding more important information about the present, perhaps concerning the family money issues. The two women certainly avoided talking about money at dinner. I sure hoped you'd hear more from those guys."

"Me, too. I'm certain Candace explored that territory."

I stroked Chablis and related the details of Millicent and Ida Lynn's decades-long episode of *Family Feud* that began after LouAnn stole Millicent's boyfriend—the now-deceased husband Oliver. I finished by saying, "But I still have no clue why Millicent and Ida Lynn turned on each other."

"It's hard to imagine LouAnn stealing *anything*. What did Millicent have to say about that?" Tom patted the spot next to him—Merlot waited eagerly on the floor next to the couch, hoping for an invite. Of course, if the invitation hadn't been quick, he would have jumped up anyway.

"Now that I think about it, Millicent and Ida Lynn carefully controlled what information they offered up about the past. They even deflected my attempt to get them to elaborate by mentioning that Wayne once had a drug problem. Those two ladies can dodge questions better than any two people I've met."

"Hmm. Maybe I should do a thorough background check on him. They mentioned Wayne had drug problems and that leads to money problems and money problems lead to desperation."

"You believe Wayne was desperate enough to murder a dying man because he'll inherit some of Mr. Jeffrey's fortune?"

"I believe that hunger for money makes people do awful things. Wayne didn't appear to be impaired when I met him, but he could still be in debt, depending on how long he's been sober." Tom put his arm around me and pulled me closer.

"Any other vibe from Wayne when you met him?"

"He seemed like a regular guy. Not talkative. I kind of like Dirk—but that doesn't mean he couldn't be our killer. Dirk went in and out of town a lot, checking on Mr. Jeffrey before he died. As for Millicent, LouAnn and Ida Lynn, well, they just seem . . . batty. It's what's behind the facades that bothers me. Sometimes, we don't know whom we're talking to."

I nodded thoughtfully. "After time spent with those ladies today, you are so right."

Tom said, "Maybe we'll get a clue from the financial information Candace wants me to hunt down. That's what I've been trying to gather all afternoon—stuff on bank accounts, investments, property ownership for all these family members—in other words, I'm wearing my PI hat. I learned Norm Jeffrey handled much of the financial business for the entire family, not just LouAnn, at one time or another. As for property ownership? It's public record. No problem there, though I haven't pulled up the info from Hilton Head yet. Candace will be subpoenaing bank, phone bills and credit card statements for the victims, but I have ways of getting a peek at the rest of the family's finances. Just a glimpse so I can steer Candace in the right direction and she can then legally gather pertinent information. I haven't even run Buford Miller's name through any of my databases yet. Maybe his chirping to Candace about Mr. Jeffrey led to his murder."

"Oh no." The thought that our visit to Buford may have caused his death made me sick to my stomach.

"Jilly, I know what you're thinking. But Miller must have been up to no good. We just don't know what he was doing yet. We didn't create his problems, so don't go blaming yourself for his death. It's my job to help find out what turned him from a small-town badass into a victim."

"This is complicated, isn't it?" I was unable to shake the guilty feelings brought on by what Tom had said.

"Yes, but tomorrow I should know a whole lot more. Candace's subpoenas should be ready by then. When it comes to financial issues, those requests to banks and credit agencies have to be very specific. She has her hands full putting what few clues she has together concerning the murders, but if I figure out exactly how she should word her official requests to a judge, it will make her job a whole lot easier."

I leaned against Tom's shoulder. His strength, the way he looked at the world, helped me challenge my belief that I carried any responsibility for the terrible thing that happened to Buford Miller. "You'll be a great help to the investigation, Tom." I gave him a quick kiss. "I just wish I could have been a fly on the wall when Candace talked to Wayne and Dirk. As normal as they seem, could they be as ... *odd* as the female cousins?"

"What little I did learn about Wayne is that he's put two kids through college. Doesn't mean he's a nice guy, but that shows responsibility. And despite my gut instincts, Dirk could be hiding something."

I said, "He's pretty protective of his mother—came here to check on Norm Jeffrey every so often and—"

"Or check on Mr. Jeffrey's money." Tom stroked Merlot, who promptly turned on his back for a belly rub.

"Love of money really is the root of all evil—probably for as long as there's been money," I said, feeling sad.

He turned and kissed my temple. "That's exactly right."

"I'm too tired to think about all this serious stuff," I said. "Except for one more thing. Can you help Birdie feel safer in her home? The woman seemed freaked-out when she drove here."

"Oh yeah, I saw your text. I couldn't find a phone number for her, and when I stopped by her house, she wasn't home."

"Good for her," I replied. "Maybe she was out with her son. She said she expected him to visit."

"Good. We can leave the protection up to him for now."

I yawned. "I have got to get some sleep. What time should I be at Belle's tomorrow?"

"Nine a.m. sound good?"

"Nine it is."

Nineteen

The next morning, I left the GPS device on the front seat of my minivan beneath a box of tissues so Tom could find it easily. I was glad we'd decided on Belle's Beans for our attempt to turn the tables on Emily Nguyen. I smelled the coffee as soon as I slid from behind the wheel and I sure needed a jump start after a restless night. Though Emily had tricked me, followed me and annoyed me, I still kind of liked her spunk. Still, I felt a tad guilty about what Tom was about to do.

I ordered my usual vanilla latte and skipped the pastries that tempted me. For this very reason I'd eaten yogurt and fruit at home before driving here. Belle baked many of the cakes, cookies, scones and pastries herself and she could have opened a bakery alongside her coffeehouse if she had the time. Personally, I wanted her to stick with what she did—provide Mercy with the best coffee in the world.

As I waited by the counter, Belle came through the door, smiling as usual. She was carrying two white boxes that I assumed were full of more delicious baked goods.

"Why, Jillian Hart, I am so glad to see you." She offered the boxes to the Belle of the Day behind the counter who in return gave her my coffee. Belle handed it to me.

"Thanks," I said. "You have time for a visit?"

"For you? I do indeed." She glanced at the Belle of the Day whose real name I didn't know. "Could I have a mocha java, medium size, sweetie?"

The young girl nodded and looked eager to get busy with her boss's order. We sat at a middle table in the busy café and Belle greeted many of the customers by name. Her snow-white hair, constant smile and sincerity were just as much a part of this place as the coffee.

Belle didn't waste any time getting into what had to be the talk of the town—two deaths. "Sad thing about Mr. Jeffrey. And then Buford Miller a few days later in the same house? That place must be cursed."

"I'm thinking it's no coincidence both men died in there." I sipped my latte and looked over the rim of my cup at her misapplied coral lipstick. Belle had put it on, as usual, in a straight line across her bottom lip and it had spread nearly to the crease in her chin this morning.

"You're smack in the middle of it, aren't you? Saw you on the cable news yesterday doing an interview with the famous Clyde. You looked so pretty and composed on TV. Love the new short haircut and those auburn highlights. Of course, that interview was probably recorded before they found Buford, so you had reason to seem poised." She looked at me slyly. "You don't seem that way now."

"You know everything, don't you, Belle?" I knew the piece had aired already, and was glad I missed it. "Do you know anything about Mr. Jeffrey?"

"He used to come in pretty regular before he got the cancer. Hot chocolate man. After he took sick, Buford came in every once in a while to pick up hot chocolate for him." Belle shook her head sadly. "I shoulda made sure he got some every day—taken it to him myself. He was a good man."

Had word leaked out yet that Mr. Jeffrey was murdered? If anyone knew, Belle would. I had to test her. "Cancer is a terrible thing."

"It is indeed, so why'd someone have to go and murder the man when his days were running short anyways?"

I had my answer. "I know. Who do you think might be involved?"

Belle offered a sly smile. "Jillian, you are not fooling me for one minute. You know more than I do, so come right out and ask me about those crazy cousins and about Buford. You know I always want to help."

It felt like a weight had been lifted. Leave it to Belle to always be straightforward. "I wasn't sure if folks knew about Mr. Jeffrey being murdered and I didn't want to be the one to disclose that information. So do tell me about these people. The cousins are especially difficult to deal with."

"Don't I know it?" she said. "Except for LouAnn. Sweet as a grandma's kiss, that one. Before she lost Oliver, her husband, about four or five years ago, those two came in here every Tuesday. They ordered the same thing—two big coffees and one piece of my carrot cake to share. Tuesday *is* carrot cake day."

"Good to have your take on LouAnn. I had a difficult time getting her to talk to us—to Tom and me. He's helping with the investigation into the murders. Anyway, she seems so sad. I'm guessing she and her husband were very close."

"Oh, they were. Never could have kids—wanted 'em bad, too. But they had each other for more than forty years. Inseparable, those two. No surprise she hasn't gotten over his death."

I took another sip of coffee, already feeling a caffeine spark in my brain. "I heard from Ida Lynn that LouAnn stole Millicent's boyfriend way back when. What do you know about it?"

Belle smiled knowingly. "Now, there's a story that's been twisted every which way. Oliver was LouAnn's man first and last. Millicent came in between."

"I'm not sure I understand."

The Belle of the Day came to the table with the mocha java and Belle thanked her. After she sipped, she said, "Let me explain it, then. My memories of those days are strong, even if I can't recall where I put the pen I just used a minute ago." Belle took another careful taste of her steaming drink.

"Come on. You're still sharp as a tack, Belle."

"Some days." She smiled lopsidedly, thanks to the errantly applied lipstick. "Anyways, I was there at the beginning of the whole mess—LouAnn, Ida Lynn, Millicent and I all went to the same high school. Ida Lynn and LouAnn are a couple years older than me and Millicent. She's my age—though you'd never know it from looking at her." Belle lowered her voice. "She's seen a scalpel more than once, if you catch my drift."

I smiled, nodding my understanding. "Tell me more about this mess, as you called it. Was there a love triangle?"

Belle shook her head no. "LouAnn and Oliver were high school sweethearts. But when LouAnn went away to college, Oliver stayed here to work for his daddy. Millicent made a move on Oliver the minute LouAnn left town. He may have dallied with her, but not for long. LouAnn only made it through one semester before she came running back here, she missed him so much. She and Oliver married that spring. My daddy was a preacher— don't know if I ever told you that—and he did their wedding, so I was there. I got to see Millicent pout through the whole ceremony and all through the reception, too."

"So LouAnn didn't steal the love of Millicent's life?" I said.

"Who told you that?"

"Ida Lynn—and Millicent agreed."

"Consider the source. That sourpuss Ida Lynn and her cousin Millicent were thick as thieves back then—I'm sure she only ever heard Millicent's side of the story. Ida Lynn and Millicent's separate feud didn't begin until years later when Millicent started chasing after men twice her age who could give her pretty things. I don't believe Ida Lynn ever forgave Millicent for abandoning her for one man after another." Belle stared down at her drink with troubled eyes. "I gotta teach that new girl a few things about coffee, I see. Yours okay?"

"Tastes perfect. So tell me. Why would Millicent's hunt for romance matter to Ida Lynn? I mean, Ida Lynn got married, too."

"But much later. You want *all* the details, don't you?"

"If you have them. It might help us all understand what seems like a *very* divided family. If Candace and Tom know them better, there may be a trail of betrayal or anger that could have led to murder."

"I believe Candace and Tom should focus on the money, my sweet Jillian. 'Cause Norm Jeffrey had a bunch and after how they treated him—the way his own sister and two of his cousins ignored him all those years—I doubt his money will be handed out to any except maybe LouAnn or Dirk. Ironic, though, because she's the only one who couldn't care less about money. And then there's Wayne. He's a whole other story. Lots of trouble in his younger days, but word is he's settled down."

"What kind of trouble?" I asked.

"Let's say he hung around with the wrong people. Found himself in jail with his drug buddies more than once."

"The cousins mentioned that. But he's fine now?"

"Honey, all I know is what I hear—that he's been clean for a good number of years."

Belle was a gold mine of information. Tom and I should have come to her first rather than try to pry information out of the cousins. "Why do you believe most of the family ignored Mr. Jeffrey? You said yourself he was a good person."

"Pettiness, no doubt. He was a fine gentleman, and I understand that despite how the relatives acted, he still took care of their money, did their taxes—in other words, he worked for them for free."

"Hmm. There's probably more to that story. But let's get back to the rift between Millicent, LouAnn and Ida Lynn."

"Here's what I know. When LouAnn came back to town and straight into Oliver's arms, Ida Lynn took up for Millicent. She told off LouAnn right before the wedding—right when LouAnn's momma was putting on the veil. We all heard it, and we all saw Ida Lynn stomp out of the church. There's poor LouAnn crying on her big day and who of all people comforted her? *Millicent*."

"But I'm still hazy on how this became Ida Lynn's issue. Was it the episode at the church that started the rift between Ida Lynn and Millicent, then? Or did they become enemies simply because Millicent was a little too sociable with the older men in town?"

"Who knows? Ida Lynn probably felt left out of both her cousins' lives. Like I said, Millicent and Ida Lynn had been inseparable for years—and the friendship probably meant more to Ida Lynn since she didn't have any other friends. I was busy with college and didn't keep up with the gossip as well as I did in high school. Whatever happened to completely upset the applecart probably involved a man."

"When Ida Lynn said that LouAnn stole the love of Millicent's life, maybe she was *really* talking about Millicent stealing the love of *her* life. Was there a spark there? Could they have even dated?"

"Could be, though I'd never heard such a thing. Dig a little deeper. Talk to LouAnn—in fact, I have carrot cake in the fridge here. You take a piece of that over to her house and she might open up a little. The woman needs help, you ask me. I've seen her in the BI-LO supermarket and she's one unhappy lady. Looks nothing like the LouAnn I once knew."

"Taking cake over to LouAnn is a great idea."

She smiled. "Nothing like a sweet memory to get a person talking. You think of anything else, you come find me. I'll tell you anything I can remember. But for now I have work waiting in the office. Invoices, payroll—all my favorite stuff." She laughed.

The minute Belle stood, I saw Emily Nguyen walk up to the counter and order. Of course, that meant Tom was busy outside putting the GPS device on her car. I should have been happy. But I couldn't shake the feeling we were doing something wrong. Her following me and now our turning the tables seemed . . . *dishonest*.

Belle turned to see what I was staring at. "Then there's *that* girl. Fancies herself some kind of reporter. Saw her here talking to Dirk, Millicent's son, yesterday."

"Really?" Maybe Emily was digging around in the family treasure trove of secrets herself. "Did you speak with her at all?"

"Enough to offer a 'hey there' and be polite. Jillian, I keep Mercy's secrets in town—don't ever share them with strangers. I noticed Dirk seemed quite interested in her. But he's probably your age and she can't be more than twenty-two years old. I don't like seeing a man flirting with someone young enough to be his daughter."

"Was she interested in him?" I asked.

"Don't know. I got distracted. I suppose she knows who he is and wants to grill him about the murders."

I nodded. "No doubt she recognized him from the interview he did about Clyde. I believe it aired right after the cat was discovered hanging around Mr. Jeffrey's house and the body was found."

"Just 'cause the girl works in the TV business doesn't mean she *watches* TV," Belle said. "Oops, she's headed our way. Let me get you that piece of cake."

Off Belle went, leaving me to deal with Emily, who approached with a wide smile as if we were long lost friends.

Twenty

"Jillian, I'm surprised to run into you again." Emily took Belle's vacated seat.

Not too surprised, since she tracked me, I thought. "I'm here a lot. It's a busy place. No hard feelings about yesterday, I hope." I wasn't sure how long Tom needed to switch the GPS locator to her car, so I figured I should make peace between us and keep her talking for a minute or two, though I surely didn't want to.

"No hard feelings. I'm doing my job, and you're apparently making friends. Why's that?"

I dodged her question by asking one of my own. "What's on your agenda today?"

"Why, that's up to you. You said something about meeting your stepdaughter, I believe."

I'd forgotten about that. "You're right, I did. Why don't I give her a call later today?"

"Later? What's wrong with now?" Emily continued to smile and I wondered if she put Vaseline on her teeth like pageant contestants since she felt the need to smile so darn much this morning.

"She's a busy person, what with running a newspaper and all, so—"

"Call her. I'm sure she'd love to visit with a colleague." More smiling.

Thank goodness Belle appeared with a small pastry box and rescued me. "Here you go, Jillian. I believe this will do the trick." She gave me a knowing look before patting Emily on the arm. "Why, hey there, little lady. So glad to see you came back to visit us. Where did you say you're from, again?"

The intuitive Belle kept Emily busy with questions long enough for me to make my escape. I was only sad that I had to leave the remainder of my latte behind.

Tom's van was parked across the street and he'd apparently been waiting for me to appear. He saluted as if to say I was good to go and drove off, probably to meet up with Candace.

I wasted no time, worried Emily would follow whether or not she had a working GPS to track me. My phone rang the minute I turned off Main Street as I headed for LouAnn's house. Tom told me he rigged things so Emily would get an error message when she pulled up the tracker on her phone or tablet. Mission accomplished—at least for now.

I pulled into LouAnn's driveway a few minutes later, hoping this wasn't her errand day. The first thing I noticed was that the lawn had been weeded and the grass cut. Just those two small changes seemed to brighten up the little brick house.

Cinderella sat in the window as before, but this time when I knocked, LouAnn answered immediately. Though she still seemed down in the mouth, her body language was more welcoming than before. "Hello, Jillian. Nice of you to drop by."

"I should have called, but I was having coffee at Belle's Beans this morning and brought you a little something."

She showed me in and I noted that unlike last time,

when her home had felt like a prison cell, the blinds were all open, shedding much-needed light into the living room.

LouAnn gestured toward the kitchen entrance. "If you've already had your coffee, I suppose you might not want another cup—but I do have some made. Oliver and I always started the day with coffee and I have kept on doing that because—" She cut the sentence short and I could see she was fighting tears.

"Do you know I still have my late husband's recliner? It's ugly and my cats have torn it up, but I can't seem to let go of the old thing. Whenever I feel low, I sit in that chair and I can almost feel his arms around me."

She nodded in understanding. "Some days I picture Oliver sitting at the table across from me, working on his crossword, his mug of coffee right by his hand."

I sat on the edge of the wing chair across from the couch, clutching the small box. LouAnn still hadn't sat down. I wasn't sure if that meant she expected me to depart quickly or if her depression had made her indecisive. I recalled the days after my husband passed. Back then, figuring out what to eat was the biggest decision of my day.

Cinderella jumped on the arm of the chair with some difficulty given her size and she sniffed at what I held. The other cats slept soundly on their quilts—no surprise, considering the average cat sleeps about eighteen hours a day.

I said, "Would Oliver want you to go on like you have been? You seem so unhappy. I ask because when I'm down and out, I say to myself, 'If John reappeared for even one second, what would he say about the way you're living? Would he be glad you've chosen to move on?' The answer these days is always yes."

She sat on the sofa. "Since you were last here and were so kind to me, I've been asking myself questions like that. I even thought about learning how to make those little quilts myself. I still have my sewing machine in the attic somewhere. I do care about living well. Deep down, I do."

"If you didn't, these four fur friends of yours wouldn't be so well cared for. And I would absolutely *love* to teach you to quilt—but you'd have to come to my house for lessons, Mrs. Rafferty. That way you could meet *my* cats, too."

I saw her expression perk up as she warmed to the idea. "I would like that. I'll bet they're wonderful kitties. And please call me LouAnn. Now, what's brought you here today?"

I opened the box and tilted it to show her. "Belle wanted you to have this."

LouAnn gasped and pressed trembling fingers to her lips. "Oh my. That Belle is such a sweet woman."

"Since I left half my coffee behind, I would love to have a cup, if the offer's still open."

Soon, LouAnn and I were sharing carrot cake and dark roast coffee in her kitchen. She liked hers black, but she had brought out cream and sugar for me—cream that no doubt helped Cinderella get to be the size she was now. The chubby calico wound around and around my ankles in anticipation once she smelled that cream.

Cinderella's purrs brought the others into the room soon enough and I was surprised none of them jumped on the table. Mine would have, but her four seemed to realize the small oak table was off limits. That didn't keep them from sitting and watching our every move as we ate the delicious carrot cake dripping with cream cheese frosting. So much for my yogurt and fruit breakfast.

LouAnn never uttered a word as she ate. No doubt she was reliving the times she'd shared carrot cake with Oliver, but I could tell her thoughts were peaceful—that Belle had sent over a miniature box of comfort.

After I drained my mug, I said, "I've met your cousins and shared time with Millicent and Ida Lynn. They seem so rooted in the past and I was wondering if you could tell me more about your relationship with them. It would help the police if you shared more about your family."

LouAnn pushed away the now-empty pastry box and took our forks to the sink. She didn't seem all that eager to talk about her cousins. All four cats followed her, hoping for a taste of the cream cheese they smelled.

Without turning around, she said, "Millicent finally came to town, then. I was afraid she wouldn't."

"Why is that, LouAnn?" Maybe more specific questions would help her get started.

She turned, her face creased with sorrow again. "Because she hates me. They all do—even Wayne."

I gestured at her abandoned chair. "Please sit and talk to me."

"What's the use of talking about the past? They won't ever change their minds." She went to the pantry and took out a jar of cat treats. She doled out a few to each cat. As they gobbled them up, she petted each one on the head. "Cats don't mind if you make a mistake or two. They go on with their day-to-day existence and love you just as much as when you came into their lives."

I nodded. "They do. But what if your cousins could change their minds? Would you welcome that?"

She reclaimed her seat, considering the question for several seconds. "Maybe so. Our trouble started so long ago, I don't even know for sure why they're so upset with me."

"Could it have had something to do with Oliver?" I prompted.

"Ah, so they told you. You're talking about Oliver and Millicent some forty-five years ago. About Ida Lynn being so silly."

"I'd love to hear your side," I said.

"Those two are good at twisting things—and at poisoning Wayne's mind. They convinced him I'm some evildoer, that I stole Oliver away from Millicent, which isn't true. Good thing Norman never bought into their stories." She paused and looked down. "But now he's gone."

"What else happened besides Ida Lynn being what seemed to me to be overly dramatic?" I asked. "Because I sense there's something more going on."

"Why, it's about Norman, of course."

Yes. It must be about Norman, I thought. I'd gotten sidetracked, it would seem. Maybe we all had. "Tell me about his relationship with you first. You said you visited him the week before he died. Was he worried about anything?"

LouAnn rotated her wedding ring as she thought about the question for several seconds. "A dying man is always worried, I suppose. I know he was unhappy with Buford, but it was over minor things." She paused. "But you have to understand—Norman was a quiet man. You could say that for him to even tell me about Buford was unusual."

"What *did* Mr. Jeffrey say about him?" Now we were getting somewhere.

"He thought Buford was taking things—just small things, really. A few old coins, gold cuff links that had belonged to Norman's father. He even asked me to hunt around for them, hoping he'd just forgotten where he'd put them. Most of Norman's valuables—like his mother's jewelry, his stock certificates and who knows what else—he kept in a safe-deposit box."

"Was he thinking about filing a police report? Or complaining to the home health care agency that Buford worked for?"

LouAnn shook her head. "Oh, Norman would never do that, not over material things."

"But he spoke with you about this situation, LouAnn. Why exactly did he tell you?"

"Jillian, you know how we do things in the South. Norman tells me and then I talk to Buford and say something like, 'How's things with you? You doing okay?' You know—get to the root of the problem without saying exactly what the problem is."

"And *did* you talk to Buford?" I refilled my coffee cup from the pot sitting on a trivet between us.

"No, but I called Birdie. I asked her if Buford was having troubles—you know, money troubles."

"You know Birdie well enough to call her?" LouAnn certainly was full of surprises. She seemed to know important information, information that she didn't realize the police should know.

"Birdie and I have been friends for years. Even before she went to work cleaning Millicent's house. It was a big place on the hill here in Mercy. Millicent and Dirk's father lived there before their divorce—oh, had to be more than thirty years ago."

"Millicent knows Birdie, too?" Why hadn't Birdie mentioned this connection to the family? Was she embarrassed about having been a housekeeper?

"Why, of course she knows Birdie." LouAnn looked at me as if I hadn't been listening.

But I was still trying to process this information. Birdie was much more involved in all this than I'd realized. "Sorry I got distracted. How long did Birdie work for Millicent?"

"Oh, not long. Soon as Norman found out Birdie was polishing silver and had her knees on a marble foyer erasing every streak and scuff, he made sure that assignment came to a swift end."

Did I need to shake the cobwebs out of my head or was I missing something? "Norman got Birdie fired?

And I suppose that means Norman knew Birdie back then, too?"

LouAnn laughed for the first time, a pretty, gentle, "you do not understand" laugh. It transformed her features. A sparkle shone in her eyes for the first time. "Fired? Of course not. See, Birdie only started working to put her son through college. Soon as Norman heard about that, he made sure that problem went away."

"He helped Birdie out with her son's schooling? What a kind thing to do."

"Responsible, you mean. We all knew that boy was Norman's son."

What? I sat back, stunned. This was huge. But I stayed quiet so LouAnn could continue uninterrupted.

"When we heard that Birdie didn't have to work anymore because her son's education was paid for, well, that's when everyone got up on their high horses. Argued with Norman about it and when he wouldn't budge about his decision, they stopped talking to him."

I blinked, still shocked by this news. When I found my voice, I said, "Did anyone outside the family realize Birdie and Norman had a child together?"

LouAnn's brow wrinkled as she considered the question. "I don't rightly know. We didn't talk about such things back then. We did plenty of assuming, though."

"Was that when family ties started to fray? After Norman helped Birdie out with their son's education?"

"They got worse at that time, but they were fraying well beforehand. See, Norman helped build everyone's investments and though Oliver and I were grateful and followed his advice, the others took pleasure in argument for argument's sake. That bunch isn't fond of being told what to do."

I set my coffee mug down. "They lost money because they made investments Mr. Jeffrey hadn't approved of?"

"I believe so, but of course I heard this from Norman, not from them. He said he told them he was done helping if they wouldn't do what was sound, said he couldn't be responsible if they all lost their savings."

"None of them told you directly they'd lost money because they didn't follow Norman's advice?" I asked.

"Oh, none of them would admit to such a thing. Plus there was already bad blood when my marrying Oliver had Ida Lynn so irate. She seems to delight in carrying grudges—even ones that don't involve her directly. She probably turned the others against me—except for Norman, that is."

This confirmed what I'd already been told by Millicent and Ida Lynn. "So, you were considered an outsider as far as your family was concerned even before this incident involving Birdie?"

"In a way, though we still talked in a polite manner, met up at church, pretended we were a close family. Back when the rumors started about Norman and Birdie being romantically involved, Ida Lynn came to me for confirmation. I refused to discuss it, told her to talk to Norman about his life, not to me. She may have walked into my house purring that day, hoping I'd talk behind Norman's back, but she left growling and hasn't stopped since."

"Did you know about Birdie and Norman's relationship from the beginning?"

"I was sure he loved someone, but like I said, he wasn't much for sharing his private business. When Birdie went to work for Millicent and he stepped in, it all started to make sense."

"You figured out he would only pay for this boy's education if he had a strong connection to Birdie and to him?"

"Norman never came right out and told me, but he had a picture of the boy in his room. He was wearing a cap and gown with all these gold braids on his shoulders—and the young man had a hint of Norman in his eyes. See, I used to go over and dust a bit, straighten up for Norman, him being a bachelor and all and none too tidy. The picture was put away in a drawer near his bed."

I wondered if it was still there. "Put away? You mean hidden?"

"Not hidden, just private. Norman had a few quarters on this little table by the bed and I opened the drawer to sweep them in. That's when I saw the picture."

"Neither Norman nor Birdie seemed to have anyone in their lives. Why weren't they together?"

"Knowing Birdie, I believe she rejected him. She's a careful, thoughtful soul. Norman would have married her despite what the folks in Mercy might have thought about him settling down with a black woman. Still, he protected their secret, supported his son, but he couldn't hide his sadness. He went on and led a life that included a cat, his love of numbers and not much else." She nodded, her mouth a grim line. "I do believe he was devastated. Why else would he shut himself off like he did?"

I hoped the silence that ensued would allow LouAnn to consider what she'd just said. It didn't take long.

"Oh my," she said. "I'm exactly like Norman, aren't I? Why, I could die alone in my house and not be found for days because I've shunned the world." She twisted her ring more forcefully. "Oh my."

"I don't believe you'll let that happen," I said quietly.

"You're right. I won't." She emphasized her words with a nod. "I don't expect too much to change as far as my cousins go, though. None of my family except Dirk ever talked to me much over the years except when they wanted something." She halted, apparently considering this. "Except when Norman took sick. Then all of a sudden, Millicent started calling for updates about Norman's health and so did Ida Lynn. Wayne even stopped by. I hadn't seen him in maybe ten years."

"Why do you think that is?" But I had a good idea why.

LouAnn's eyes slowly widened in understanding. "I have been so wrapped up in my own grief, I never thought about it until now. Why, it's all about Norman's money, isn't it?"

Twenty-one

I couldn't wait to get to the police station to tell Candace all I'd learned about the family's history, but before I left LouAnn's driveway, I pulled up my cat cam feed. All four cats slept in various places. Late-morning siestas were a necessity if they wanted to be ready to race after one another at dusk. I switched to the GPS app that Tom put on my phone last night, hoping it was active and I could see exactly where Emily Nguyen was right now.

The round, shiny red dot on the map of Mercy told me exactly where—and I didn't like what I saw. Despite what I'd said about our talking to Kara *together*, Emily was at the newspaper office. I hadn't even had a chance to phone Kara and tell her much of anything about Emily. This could spell disaster if Kara didn't want to cooperate with an out-of-town media person—and I wouldn't blame her if she refused to help Emily.

I hit the speed dial number for the *Mercy Messenger*. Kara answered on the first ring and thank goodness she didn't say my name.

Sounding breathless and anxious, I said, "Kara, I know Emily Nguyen is there and why. I am so sorry I didn't let you know sooner about her wanting to talk to you, but if she's there, please don't say my name. I'm on my way."

"Sure," Kara replied coolly. "I'm here all day. *All* day."

I assumed that meant Emily had been pestering her for probably as long as I'd been talking with LouAnn. I pulled out of the driveway, and though I kept to the speed limit, I found it hard not to press down on the gas pedal and drive like Candace usually does—way too fast.

The *Messenger* office is on Main Street less than a block from Belle's Beans. When Kara took over the newspaper, she rented out the two floors above the original offices. They'd sat long empty in the three-story, hundred-year-old building. Now, an interior designer occupied floor two, and a tax preparer, who only used the space a few months a year, rented the third floor.

The *Mercy Messenger* printed papers three days a week, but Kara had hired an eager young man in the last few months to make sure the paper's Web site had news content, obituaries and advertising every day. I was so frantic to get to Kara's small office at the back of the building, I blanked out when he greeted me and couldn't remember his name.

"Hey there, um . . . um . . ." I stood there, staring at his handsome young face, still at a loss. What *was* his name?

"It's Andy," he replied to my unspoken question. "You look upset, Jillian. Can I help?"

"Kara's expecting me." I rushed past his desk, now remembering his entire name. Duh. Andy McMahon, fresh out of college and glad to have found any job in journalism to start building his résumé.

The building was long and narrow, with the largest room still housing an old and now-unused printing press. Kara outsourced the print edition of the *Messenger* since a web printer would have been bigger than the entire building and, well, unnecessary for the small number of print editions the town needed.

I usually loved walking down this hallway, which Kara had refinished while retaining the nineteenth-century details, like the original transoms, and the wood floor that creaked with age. But today the beauty of the newspaper offices didn't have their usual soothing effect. Why was I so nervous? What did I think Emily had been saying to Kara?

What bothered me, I decided, was that Emily was such a wild card, she might do anything—even get Kara to reveal things about the investigation that Emily knew nothing about. After all, Kara's longtime boyfriend, Liam, was an assistant county DA, so she probably had knowledge beyond what she'd reported in her newspaper. I reassured myself that Kara was too smart to ever do that, but Emily was, if nothing else, persistent.

Kara's office door had a battered metal sign—EDITOR-IN-CHIEF—hung from the transom with a cord. She had found it at an antique mall and loved it. The door was closed, but I heard muted female voices beyond.

I knocked and heard Kara call, "Come on in."

I couldn't detect the earlier irritation I sensed on the phone and perhaps my showing up was enough to make her happy she didn't have to deal with Emily alone.

I tried to seem surprised when Emily turned around in the chair that faced Kara's desk. "We keep running into each other today, Emily, but . . . didn't I say we'd speak with my stepdaughter *together*?"

"I am a little impatient," Emily said with a laugh.

Kara walked around her desk and hugged me, whispering in my ear, "I could have used a heads-up."

Her hair was fastened in a loose ponytail and she was wearing comfy clothes—a tunic-type cotton shirt and blue jeans—the stuff she wore on her "writing days."

She'd been interrupted, and hopefully it was just this disruption in her routine rather than Emily herself that had produced her annoyance.

Kara returned to her desk and I pulled a metal folding chair over to sit beside Emily.

"What did I miss?" I tried to sound as cheerful as possible.

"Nothing," Emily said. "I haven't been here all that long. You slipped out of that coffee place before we finished our conversation. Urgent business, Jillian?"

I supposed that since Emily couldn't track me, she'd decided to take the direct approach and simply ask me where I'd been.

"Errands," I offered, and looked at Kara. "So, I mentioned to Emily that since the events here are becoming much more about murder than about Clyde, maybe you could help her navigate how best to get her story out there first."

"Emily and I were discussing that. I explained what I've learned about reporting the news in a small town—how different it is than in a bigger city. It's not as *in your face* as she's used to." Kara smiled at Emily with more patience than I could have mustered—because I'm sure Emily had been badgering her with questions.

"But," Emily said, "I pointed out that I have to get this story to my producer with the angle about the cat still prominent. Something like 'Cat Returns Home Only to Discover Horrific Crime.'"

"*Horrific*? Really?" Kara said. "When did you last see that in a headline other than in a tabloid? And would you want to pair that word with *cat*?"

Emily sat back. "Hmm. You're right."

"The reason I wanted Emily to talk to you," I said to Kara, "is because this investigation shouldn't focus on Clyde right now. Two men have been murdered."

"But that's my only in, Jillian." Emily's voice had taken on a whiny tone.

"No, it's not the only way you can report on this," Kara said. "If you bring people a compelling, interesting story with the correct emphasis, you will sell it. I assume you want to freelance this?"

"You mean go solo on this?"

"Yes—that is, if your contract with Channel Five allows it." Kara raised her brows in inquiry.

"Since I am not a full-time news reporter—just weather and traffic—there is nothing in my contract that says I can't freelance."

"Okay, then." Kara folded her hands on the desk. "This story is complicated. There are things we don't know yet, things the police are still investigating. You wouldn't want to offer this as an incomplete piece to your station or as a freelance article. Your news station would certainly want to investigate it themselves. I don't believe that will get you where you want to be in your career. Does that make sense?"

Emily nodded her agreement, and for once, she didn't talk back.

I breathed a sigh of relief, felt the muscles in my tight neck relax. *Thank you for speaking her language, Kara.*

Kara went on. "Here in Mercy, I may know certain facts about an ongoing police investigation, but I've learned that law enforcement is my best friend. They understand my job and I understand theirs. If I jump the gun, report half-truths, get people stirred up, well, next time when I show up at a crime scene, no one will give me the time of day."

Unfortunately, Emily didn't quite understand what Kara was trying to teach her. She said, "But on CNN they—"

"We don't have CNN here," Kara cut in. "And in my

opinion, the big news outlets blur the lines between fact and fiction in their rush to be the first ones to report. I don't operate like that."

"But my station in Asheville—"

"You sat here and told me your story before Jillian arrived. You quit meteorology school because you want to be an on-air news reporter and you believe Clyde is your ticket. You're misguided. They'll take this story and they'll hand it to someone with more experience. You're still *the weather girl*."

Emily slumped in her chair. She'd heard this from me, but coming from Kara, it seemed finally to sink in. "I can't give up," she muttered.

"I am not about stomping on anyone's dreams, Emily. Here's the deal. You go back to your motel room and Google my name—Kara H-A-R-T. You'll get a lot of hits. I've sold freelance pieces about crimes in both the big cities and here in Mercy. If you want to become a true journalist, not merely a town crier who shrieks out the latest rumor, we can work together. I'm willing to share a byline with you on this serious crime piece. I can open a few doors you have no access to, but I'll only do that if you agree to start acting like a responsible reporter."

I almost stood and applauded. Kara was an amazing person. She'd taken Andy under her wing and now she was doing the same for Emily. Part of this was because she understood the skill needed to break in to the crowded news arena. But she cared about the victims here in Mercy and perhaps wanted to instill some much-needed compassion in Emily.

Kara stood. "You go do your research on me. Meanwhile, Andy has been assigned to do the legwork on this story. He's got a degree in journalism—something you really should think about pursuing yourself, even if it's broadcast journalism. But for now, you can learn a lot from Andy. I'll ask him if he's willing to show you a few steps you seemed to have skipped in your desire to report on these murders." She reached out her hand. "Okay?"

They shook hands and Emily offered Kara an enthusiastic "Yes."

She turned and hurried out of the office but a few seconds later stuck her head back in. "Thank you so much, Jillian." Then she was gone.

I released an even bigger sigh than earlier. "Thank *you*, Kara."

"No problem." She took her seat behind her beloved gouged and scratched desk, one she'd rescued from a neighbor's curbside trash when she worked as an investigative journalist in Houston. "Emily has decent instincts but absolutely no clue how to play nice with others. She wants to be a reporter and somehow has confused that concept with becoming a news *reader* on TV. If she's as smart as I think she is, it would serve her to set reachable career goals."

"I completely agree. And now, I have to admit to something that has me feeling a little guilty—how I knew Emily was here with you." I went on to explain about the slap-and-go GPS device that Tom had transferred to Emily's car.

Kara shook her head in amazement. "Wow. Does Emily want to be a journalist or a private investigator?"

"I can only hope Lydia Monk doesn't get wind of how easily she could stalk me. Anyway, I'm on my way to talk to Candace about information I've learned from LouAnn Rafferty and   "

"One of the cousins?"

"Yes. Since I'm here, I thought I'd fill you in on what I've just learned about that family."

"But this isn't for public consumption, I assume?" Kara said.

"Right, but you can use it later, I'm sure—maybe just for background." I went on to explain what I'd learned about the love of Norman Jeffrey's life and about his son.

"Wow," she said when I'd finished. "So many questions are bombarding my brain cells right now."

"Yes," I replied, glad she understood. "But a few words are front and center in my thoughts—*Last Will and Testament*. I mean, there's big money involved here. Did Norman Jeffrey reveal his deepest secret when he wrote his will and decided who he'd leave his money to?"

"I've got to write notes, think about all these family connections. If I don't write it down, it won't make sense to me later. Meanwhile, you need to go straight to Candace with this information."

I stood. "I'm on my way—but I am so sorry about Emily showing up here. Thanks for understanding."

"No problem, Jillian. I understand people like her. In this business, you run into them all the time."

We hugged good-bye, but as I walked down the hall ready to leave, I heard male voices in the office. When I made it to the end of the hall, I found Dirk Boatman and Wayne Jeffrey standing in front of Andy's desk.

Dirk smiled in greeting and Wayne nodded, his expression inscrutable. I felt uncomfortable in Wayne's presence, though I wasn't sure why. Maybe it was because I couldn't get a read on him.

Andy said, "Nice seeing you again, Jillian," before looking up at Wayne again. "So you want the obituary to run a day or two before the funeral. And when *is* the funeral?" He poised his fingers over his laptop keyboard.

Dirk said, "We thought my uncle would be given to us earlier, but because of the autopsy, the body will be released to us today—so we're thinking in about three days?" He glanced at Wayne as if for confirmation.

I was almost out the door when I heard Wayne's answer. "Norm left you in charge, Dirk. *You* decide. But if

I were making the call, I'd say put a rush on all this death business so we can get on with our daily stuff."

I walked out, wondering what Wayne meant about Dirk *being in charge*. I thought I understood, but perhaps I could get clarification from a certain someone. Considering how she felt about me, I figured Tom might be able to get her to open right up.

Twenty-two

As I walked into the courthouse building and headed toward the police station, I called Tom's cell. He said he and Candace were meeting to compare notes on both cases, and I should join them.

When I entered the office, B.J., who had a phone to his ear, waved me toward the break room down the hall. Tom and Candace were eating takeout from the Main Street Diner and my mouth started watering immediately. One of those famous chili dogs could sure provide a nice, if short, distraction from what had certainly been a stressful day. I sure hoped they'd over-ordered.

As if reading my mind, Tom reached in the open box between them on the table and held up a dog wrapped in white paper.

"Bless your heart, Tom Stewart." I sat in the one remaining chair after greeting Candace with a small hug and Tom with a kiss. Home fries and a glob of ketchup filled the box, along with two more wrapped hot dogs.

We all ate in silence for a minute or two, and finally I spoke. "I have a lot to tell you, but first, Tom, I need a favor."

"Give a woman a free chili dog and see what happens? A to-do list." He winked at Candace and smiled at me. "Oh, all right. Go ahead and ask."

I grinned but then grew serious. "Can you call Lydia Monk and find out who is the executor of Mr. Jeffrey's will? She might know since she handles the death certificates at the coroner's office."

"Why did this show up on your radar right now, Jillian?" Candace asked. "Do you know something I don't?"

I told them about seeing Wayne and Dirk at the newspaper office and how their conversation about Dirk being in charge had me wondering. "Did Mr. Jeffrey appoint Dirk executor? Certainly a will would tell you and Tom more about who would benefit most from Mr. Jeffrey's death."

Candace nodded. "We didn't find a will in the house, so I already called probate court, hoping the will had been filed and we could have a look. It hasn't, and really, we don't even know if there is one."

Tom balled up his now-empty hot dog wrapper. "A man like Jeffrey? There's a will. But why call Lydia? Why not ask Dirk straight away?"

"I intend to—especially if it means we can limit Lydia's involvement in the case," Candace said. "We've been in fact-finding mode from the get-go, but once I start asking questions about inheritance, that could send a message to the entire family that we consider all of them suspects. And I do, by the way. Even the ones who seem like sweet or maybe *not so sweet* old ladies."

Tom looked between Candace and me. "If Dirk's the executor, as Jillian suspects, you'll be asking him questions anyway."

Candace sighed and I could tell she was frustrated. "Duh, yeah. I sure have plenty of them. I simply hope we could find the will and read it first. A money angle, when we have reason to believe the victim was wealthy, is definitely important."

I said, "LouAnn told me Mr. Jeffrey kept most of his valuables in a safe-deposit box. Seems like a likely place to keep a will."

Candace shook her head at me, still irritated. "Don't you think I *know*? Unfortunately I can't just take the word of what one relative said to you about a million-dollar motive, Jillian. I need a look at the financials—at the facts. And the bank isn't exactly bending over backward to rush over information concerning Mr. Jeffrey's accounts. No one knows better than I do that serious money equals serious motive, but I need evidence first."

"Could the executor get you into that box without a subpoena?" I asked.

"Yes," she said, "and if Dirk's the executor, I hope he'll cooperate. Once I read the will, we'll know who benefits most."

"Maybe money's not the *only* motive," I said.

Both Candace and Tom looked puzzled, and Tom said, "What are you thinking, Jilly?"

"When I spoke with LouAnn, she told me something you might not know—and it's important." I related the details of Mr. Jeffrey's relationship with Birdie and that they had a son. After relating what I knew, I asked, "Do you think Birdie might be named in that will? And maybe even their child?"

Candace said, "I never met Birdie's son—he's a professor I think—but you're saying he's also Norm Jeffrey's child? Unbelievable."

Tom said, "Hold on. Are you sure LouAnn is right about all this?"

"I don't know it for a fact but believe it's true. He supported that child—probably supported Birdie. What I found odd is that although LouAnn was much sharper

than when you and I visited her, she seemed to have no clue that this information about Mr. Jeffrey and Birdie was important."

Candace finally spoke. "This entire family wants us to believe they're clueless. I'm not buying it." She shook her head, still seeming astonished by what I'd told her. "This could take the case in a completely new direction. I'd never suspect Birdie of harming anyone, especially for money—before today, that is."

"Why do you know so little about her son?" I asked. "I mean, you and Birdie seemed close when we went to her house."

"First off, Birdie's son is not in my generation. He's much older than me, so I wasn't around him at school or anything."

"Okay, Birdie had a kid, yet you never saw him, never met him," Tom said. "Was he sent off to boarding school or raised by another family?"

"Absolutely not. At least I don't think so. When she'd come over to visit with my granny, she just seemed . . . hesitant to speak about him. Much later, when I was old enough to understand, I learned that Birdie wasn't married—can't remember who told me—and I decided she was ashamed. This is Mercy, remember, not the big city. Heck, this town runs on gossip and as a police officer, I do listen. But as far as the father of Birdie's son? Never heard a word. Or maybe I wasn't paying attention. No, obviously I wasn't paying attention. Sheesh." She thunked her forehead with her palm.

"Don't beat yourself up," I said. "Folks here may not believe everything they hear, but they sure like to repeat tidbits—and apparently those tidbits didn't include anything about Birdie and Mr. Jeffrey."

Candace squinted as if she were looking into her past to see what else she could remember. "Once, I recall asking after Birdie's son—you know, just being polite. She changed the subject. Later, Granny told me not to ever question Birdie about her life—that she was a private person and I should respect that."

"In other words," Tom said, "you already had a little anecdotal proof that what LouAnn told Jillian is true, but you just didn't know it. If this son is named in the will, he's got motive, too. Even without adding money to the equation, he could have been harboring bad feelings about his absent father for his entire life."

Candace gripped the back of her neck and began massaging it. "And I don't even know the man's name. Birdie just always called him her boy."

"She mentioned to me that he was coming to town. After they found the drugs and the gun in Buford's room, she was frightened and wanted his support. You can talk to him face-to-face," I said.

"Oh, you can bet that's gonna happen," Candace said. "My problem is, what if Birdie never told him who his father was?"

"You should talk to Birdie first," I suggested. "She is worried about Buford's criminal friends coming around. That would be a good excuse to bring her here and have that conversation."

Candace sighed. "Chief Baca sure picked a perfect time to go to that convention. He's not close to Birdie like I am. He could handle this with tact and gentleness, but still keep it professional. Of all the people on this growing suspect list, I'd cut her first—but her son? No way can I eliminate him right off the bat. I don't know him from Adam. So, besides Dirk and the group of seniors who either border on crazy or are as mean as snakes, I've got a stranger to contend with."

Candace's jaw clenched and I decided this new information was a little overwhelming. Police work in a small town was nothing like in the city. She knew most people she arrested by name—might even know their dog's name. I said, "You've got so much on your plate. Can someone else talk to Birdie?"

"No," came her abrupt reply. "No way."

"Okay," I said quietly. "I get it. Birdie is your friend. What about Buford's murder? Who's handling that investigation?"

"Morris and the new officer, Lois . . . Lois . . ." Tom drummed his fingers on the table, trying to remember.

"Jewel," Candace said.

"That's right. Anyway, they found Buford's father in a church-sponsored homeless shelter way over in Faith's Path. Lois told me she learned a lot watching Morris work the grapevine to find the guy. The man was in such bad shape, they took him to the county hospital for detox. That's all I know."

"He won't be any help," Candace said. "All I know is Buford's murder is obviously connected in some way to Mr. Jeffrey's murder—first by Buford having been ever-present in the man's life, but second by his landlady Birdie knowing both victims so well."

"The Buford case is complex," Tom said. "He had criminal ties that could have gotten him killed, but you're right. His connection to the murdered man is no coincidence."

"We need to know what's in that will." Candace looked at Tom. "Change of plans. Can you talk to Dirk Boatman? This whole Birdie thing has thrown me off my game. I have to figure out exactly how to approach her."

"Sure. Need me to do anything else?"

"No . . . not that I can think of." Candace sounded as if she hadn't been paying attention.

No doubt her thoughts were with Birdie and a long-kept secret Candace believed she should have known about.

I stood, gathered the trash on the table and walked to the wastebasket. "I'll help you both any way I can."

But Tom and Candace seemed miles away, their thoughts on a complicated double murder with little evidence and too many suspects.

Twenty-three

I slid behind the wheel of my minivan and decided to check the GPS tracking app, hoping to find Emily far, far away. Where had this day gone? And how long had it been since I'd checked my phone? I wanted to go home and take a late-afternoon nap, but first I had to make sure Emily wasn't waiting down the street for a chance to talk to me again.

But when I took out my phone, I was stunned to see a half dozen alerts generated by Clyde's GPS system on the password log-in screen.

My pounding heart threatened to burst through my chest as I read through the messages. The first said *Exit through back entrance*. The second was *Tracking established*. What followed were several GPS coordinates that I didn't understand.

Clyde had escaped again.

I got out of the van and raced up the courthouse steps to find Tom. We nearly collided in the lobby and apparently one look at my face told him something was wrong.

"What's the matter, Jilly? You're white as a sheet."

I handed him the phone with a shaky hand. "Clyde got out. He's gone again. But how?"

Tom stared at the screen and began tapping buttons and swiping through screens.

But I couldn't stand around while Clyde was out there again. He might not survive this latest escape. I tugged on Tom's shirtsleeve. "What are you waiting for? We have to find him before he gets hurt." I grabbed his free hand and tried to pull him toward the exit.

He held me back. "Jilly, did you lock up the house? Set your security alarm when you left?"

"Of course, but we have to go and—" Then it dawned on me. "Are you saying someone broke in? That a stranger might be in my house this minute?" I dropped my hand from his arm and ran for the door, panic constricting my throat.

But Tom came up behind to grip both my shoulders and stop me. He put an arm around me and held the phone in front of my face. "The feed to your cat cam has been cut and I got no alert on my phone about your system being compromised. I should have. So yes, something is wrong."

"You mean Syrah, Merlot and Chablis could have gotten outside, too? Please tell me that's not true."

He held my face in his hands, forcing eye contact. "It's okay. We have Clyde's location right here." He held up the phone again. "I know your house's coordinates by heart and he's right nearby. If the other cats got out, they're probably with him. But we need Candace's help on this one. A crime has been committed. Someone or something compromised your security system and cameras."

"Candace. Yes. Get her. But I have to go." I took off again, not responding to Tom's call for me to stop.

When he caught up with me, he was on the phone, talking to Candace. I was already behind the wheel when he hung up.

"I'll be right behind you." He handed me my phone. "Promise you won't go near your back door without me?"

"Promise. Now come on. We're wasting time."

But though I drove like a maniac, I was no match for the green-and-white squad car with Candace behind the wheel. She'd responded to Tom's call for help immediately. I felt immense relief when she passed me. Thank goodness she was the one to lead our little convoy to my house.

But as I pulled in front and parked—Candace had driven straight up the driveway to the back entrance—I realized I was trembling all over. Those cats had to be all right. What would I do if anything happened to them?

Tom's van pulled in behind the squad car and when I started hurrying up the driveway, he held his hand up like a traffic cop to stop me.

I was about to ignore his silent plea for me to stay back, but when I saw his big black automatic weapon in his other hand, I complied. Shifting my weight from one foot to the other, I stared at my phone screen and saw the numbered coordinates for Clyde suddenly change. He was on the move. My hands shook and my thoughts were scattered—I wished I could connect to a screen with a map, but I couldn't recall how. By comparing the numbers, I could tell his GPS coordinates hadn't changed *that* much. Tom said Clyde was close. Surely we could find him. But first I had to know about my other fur kids. Were they all right?

Please let them be all right.

What seemed like an eternity later, Tom came walking toward me, his expression calm.

"Are they okay?" I asked.

"They're fine, Jilly. Whoever did this is gone. Come see for yourself."

I ran to him and he took my hand. We jogged toward the back door.

He said, "Someone destroyed your security system—and they knew what they were doing. They cut wires and cables. They disabled cameras inside and out. Don't touch anything but your cats when you get inside. Candace already has her evidence kit out. She's dusting for prints and checking for clues to figure out what happened."

We went up the back steps and Tom pushed open the door with his elbow so as not to put his prints over fresh ones made by the intruder. I could see that the lock had been completely removed and when we entered the mudroom, I saw it lying on the tile.

I had a million questions, but first I had to see Syrah, Merlot and Chablis. Only then would I be able to think straight again.

Candace was in the walk-in pantry, checking the control panel for the security system. I glanced in as I passed and saw she had a flashlight focused on the buttons and switches, examining them closely.

Merlot and Syrah sat in the middle of the kitchen, taking in the action with curious stares. Chablis had chosen what I supposed she considered a safer position. There are "bush cats" who go low when threatened and "tree cats" who move to high ground when they're in trouble. Chablis was a "bush cat" and she crouched under the table in the breakfast nook, her fur so puffed out she looked like a stuffed animal.

I squatted in front of Merlot and Syrah. "How are my boys? You okay?"

But they seemed absolutely unbothered and fascinated by Candace's activities. After petting them both, I walked over to the table where Chablis had taken refuge. As soon as I knelt down, she came to me and rubbed against my knees, back arched. If whoever had broken in had dandruff, she might have a problem. Chablis is allergic to human dander—or dandruff, as most people call it. But after I examined her thoroughly, I could tell that her fluffed-out appearance was probably due to fear and not an allergy attack.

I picked her up and cradled her like a baby, and the minute I did, I felt my jangled nerves quiet. Time to find Clyde.

Tom was watching Candace work and I held my phone out to him. "Tom, could you take my phone and tell me where to locate Clyde? I can't remember how this thing works."

"Sure." He spoke to Candace then. "Is it okay to check the perimeter of the house? I'll make sure to watch for footprints around the places where Jillian has cameras."

"You know better than I do where those are, but I could use some help with this panel. Where would the intruder have touched this thing to disable it?"

Chablis purred contentedly. I swayed with her in my arms while I waited for Tom to point out the places Candace should focus on in the pantry. Didn't they understand that Clyde was more important? I needed to find him *now*. But not many people, even my two best friends in the world, could ever completely comprehend how much the safety of my animals mattered to me.

Tom finished his instructions, and I set Chablis next to Syrah and Merlot on the kitchen floor before we carefully stepped over the damaged lock and out onto the deck. He took my phone, tapped a few buttons and found the map with ease.

I waited impatiently while he switched his gaze between the screen and the landscape a couple of times. Finally he pointed to the empty lot next to my house. "He's over there and right now, he's not moving."

I hurried down the deck steps that led to the backyard

and the lake. Tom was on my heels. He said, "There might be footprint impressions close to the house, so let's avoid going near there."

But my mind was on Clyde. I had no idea if he was a bush cat or a tree cat since I'd never seen him frightened, but I soon found out. His orange body stood out in the lush green foliage and leaves of summer. He was sitting on a low branch of an ancient hickory, looking like Alice's Cheshire cat.

I approached slowly, murmuring softly that he was going to be okay. He didn't move, just blinked several times, his beautiful smile the best thing I'd seen all day.

"He's within my grabbing distance. I can take him down if you think he'll let me touch him," Tom said.

"It might be better if I climb up and get him. Give me a boost?" I asked.

"Oh, I want to see this. I might even take a picture and give it to Kara. The headline will read, 'Jillian Hart Saves Another Cat in Trouble.'" He cupped his hands low so I could use his intertwined fingers as a step.

He gave me enough of a boost to grab the limb Clyde sat on, but as soon as I wrangled my way onto the branch, the cat jumped down and made straight for Tom.

"How ungrateful is that?" I said with a laugh.

"You need help getting down?"

"As Clyde just showed us, down is easier than up." I gripped the limb, dropped to the ground and picked up Clyde. "I wish you could tell us what this was all about, fella."

"He didn't even give me a chance to snap that picture." Tom laughed. "You looked pretty good up there."

"The last thing I need is any more publicity concerning this cat. Please do not mention his little tree-climbing adventure to anyone." But I had to smile. All the cats were now safe and sound.

While I went back to the house, Tom told me he would

be checking around the house to see what damage had been done to the cameras and to look for any evidence that might help us figure out who did this.

When I got back to the house, Clyde content in my arms, I saw Candace bag the door-lock assembly as evidence. Her camera was on the floor nearby and fingerprint dust marked the paint on my back door. She said, "So you found the wandering cat. That's a relief. But now it's time for you to take an inventory."

"Inventory?" I lifted my chin as Clyde rubbed my face.

"Your house was broken into, Jillian. That suggests a burglary, don't you think?"

"Oh. Gosh, yes. I was so worried about the cats, I hadn't even considered that anything might have been taken."

I set Clyde down and he bounded through the mudroom, straight for the water dish. He didn't turn and run to escape again. He was settling in. Then I wondered how long he'd been outside and felt terrible I hadn't checked his GPS sooner. But Tom could probably tell when he did an autopsy on my poor, dead security system.

Candace placed the bagged lock and door handles in her evidence kit and picked up her camera. "I'm done with the door. We'll take a look room by room. It helps that I'm almost as familiar with your house as you are."

The kitchen, aside from what had been damaged in the pantry, appeared as I had left it. But once we walked into the living area, I noticed immediately that the TV remote was not where I usually kept it on the end table. It sat on the couch. I pointed this out and Candace picked up the remote with a gloved hand.

She punched the power button. "You use your TV as a computer screen, right?"

I nodded. "Since we know the live feed to the cat cam and security system was lost, I don't expect you'll see anything on the screen. It will have to be repaired as soon as possible so I can check on my fur friends when I'm gone—more now than ever."

We both stared at the blank screen with its two words: *No Signal*. Candace switched the signal input on the remote and Animal Planet lit up the screen. At least my satellite TV was still working.

Candace's eyes narrowed, her mind in gear. "So our intruder probably turned on the TV to see if he or she had cut everything off. But the hub of this network is your desktop computer, right?"

"Yes." It was Tom who answered for me and we both turned at the sound of his voice. "I doubt that will help us since wires were cut outside. But we still might be able to see who did all this damage."

"How?" Candace got busy dusting the remote. But even I could tell there were so many prints on it, it was an exercise in futility.

"I have surveillance videos backed up to remote storage. The system is programmed to save everything from the minute an alarm is engaged. Even if this person disabled the cameras and cables, the cameras would have caught something beforehand." He held up his tablet computer. "Good thing I've got my work van with my equipment. We can see what was happening right before the feed was lost."

We stood on either side of Tom as he went through several steps accessing a server that had multiple security layers. But the intruder seemed to have scoped out where every camera was. We saw no car in my driveway, and we saw no one approach my house. We only had the image of a pair of what looked like long-handled wire cutters right before we lost the feed.

"Whoever it was, they knew exactly where to find the lines that needed to be disconnected step-by-step to keep them from showing up on camera." Tom gripped my shoulder and massaged the muscles gently. "Sorry, Jillian. I'll make sure that doesn't happen if there's a next time. I should have updated your system with newer products as soon as they came on the market. Clyde's GPS is completely WiFi and connected directly to your phone, and it's a good thing. I can make those changes to the house so you won't lose feed again."

"Hey," I said. "Aren't you the one who told me that if someone wants to get past a security system, they'll find a way?"

"Yes, but—"

Candace cut in. "She's right. You can't blame yourself when you're dealing with someone this determined. Let's keep looking for evidence. Did you see anything outside I can use?"

He shook his head. "Nothing."

All three of us searched the rest of the house, but it was my knowledge of cats that gave us the few clues that might explain why someone had entered my home. Under my bed, I found clumps of short orange cat hair. I followed wisps of similar hair down the hall and through the kitchen leading to the back door. This was definitely Clyde's fur.

We stood in the kitchen, staring at the damaged back door. Candace had to put her evidence kit up against the door to keep it closed, which meant it had probably been left ajar while the intruder invaded my home.

"Whoever came in here was after Clyde," I said. "Cats will shed like crazy if they're stressed and it looks like that's what happened."

Candace said, "Certainly all your cats would have been spooked by a stranger coming in here unannounced."

"Trust me," I said. "Clyde hid under my bed, was chased out and escaped through a door you can clearly see would have been ajar after the lock was removed."

"I wouldn't argue with the cat expert, Candace," Tom said. "I think she's right."

All four cats had followed us as we'd traipsed around hunting for evidence and now sat behind us watching. They were probably thinking, *Now they get it. Took them long enough.*

"Thank goodness for Clyde's collar, is all I can say."

Candace appeared puzzled as she stared at the handful of orange cat hair in my fist. "This keeps coming back to the cat. Why?"

"All I know is, you'll figure it out." I glanced at the door. "Meanwhile, Tom, I hate to ask, but can you fix this before it gets dark?"

"You plan to stay here?" Candace said. "I don't think that's a good idea."

Tom put his arm around me. "More than the door has to be fixed. I'll put a temporary lock on the back. But your system has to be completely redone—and this time, no one will break in without me knowing the second it happens. My place is cramped—Finn sure likes to spread out—but you know you're welcome there."

I smiled up at him. "Too cramped with five cats, including Dashiell. If you add that temporary knob and locks, maybe it will be okay. And you could stay with me, Tom." But who was I kidding? I was shaken to my core by this brazen attempt to steal Clyde.

"No way are you staying here." Candace was emphatic. "Your door is damaged and Tom has a lot of work to do here. Besides, if someone wants this cat, we need to make it more difficult to find him."

I was too spooked to argue, even though transporting four cats to a temporary home would place even more stress on them.

"Kara has plenty of room in her new house—even with two cats of her own. I'm sure I can stay with her." I looked at Tom. "That means you can continue the investigation. And by the way, could you please help Birdie feel more secure in her house before you start work here? I'm worried for her."

"Wait a minute. You want me to put your job on hold so I can—" He stared down at me. "Yes, of course that's what you want."

Twenty-four

By early evening, the cats and I arrived at Kara's place. Her two kitties, a calico female and an orange-and-white male, were sister and brother. Thank goodness they were mellow, but that didn't keep the cats from engaging in plenty of hissing—all except Chablis. I'd brought my brood to Kara's house before and Chablis went straight to the pantry where the treats were kept. She sat at the door and meowed.

Kara laughed and accommodated her with a handful of treats while the other cats scoped one another out. A breakfast bar overlooked Kara's gourmet kitchen and I slid onto one of the high-backed stools. She'd moved in a few months ago. If there's a new-house smell—a freshness that comes from uncluttered space and beautiful fixtures—then this place had it.

"Have you eaten?" she asked.

"No time. I had to gather up clothes and cat quilts and food and get the crates ready and—"

"I get it. That works out because Liam is on his way and we're barbecuing skewered veggies for supper. I've made a quinoa salad and sliced up fresh peaches, too."

Kara, a recent convert to vegetarianism, had been

finding ways to embrace her new and amazing kitchen. "Sounds delicious. Beneath this frazzled exterior lies a hungry woman."

"Good. Would you like wine? Tea? The hard stuff? Because after what happened at your house, you might need a finger or two of Jack Daniel's."

"Wine would be great. Did I sound off my rocker when I called and asked to stay here?"

Kara placed a glass of chilled white wine in front of me. "No more than usual."

I smiled wearily. "I'm convinced someone came to take Clyde. I only hope that person didn't follow me here."

"You do know that you were tailed to my house, right?" She sounded so lighthearted that what she said made me think she was joking.

"What are you talking about?" I sipped my wine, the Biltmore House White I loved.

"Tom called. He told me he made certain no one followed you here—except for him, of course. Apparently you didn't even notice he was behind you."

"You're kidding." I had to laugh. "I guess I'm worse than terrible at spotting a tail. And here I thought he went back to the police station to work with Candace."

"He texted me that he's on his way there since he knows you arrived safely. That man loves you so much." Kara poured herself a glass of red wine. "When *are* you two getting married?"

"What are you talking about?" I tried to sound shocked, but I wasn't fooling her for a minute.

"You are such a lousy liar, Jillian. I wasn't an investigative journalist for years without trusting my instincts, and my instincts tell me he's asked and you've said yes. Which is wonderful, by the way."

I felt as if a two-ton weight had fallen from my shoulders. Since Kara was John's daughter, I'd been worried the most about her reaction to my saying yes to Tom's proposal. I should have known she'd be happy for us. "Thank you. I didn't want to upset you or—"

"Don't be silly. My dad would have wanted this for you. And Tom is the best. I used to work with him before I bought the paper, if you've forgotten. I know his character and looking at the two of you together makes me feel warm all over."

"I guess we can tell the rest of the family now—well, *his* family since I have no one but you. I wanted you to hear before I told anyone else."

"Any plans yet?" She swirled her wine before tasting it.

"I've been procrastinating. I guess I wanted to make sure this was the right thing for both of us. How lucky can a woman be to have two such fine men end up loving her? I've been wondering if I truly deserve it."

"You most certainly do. Think about it, Jillian. You lost your parents before you even knew them, and while you were raised by loving grandparents, they passed away, too, while you were still pretty much a kid. How old were you when they died?"

"I was in my early twenties." I felt a lump in my throat thinking of them. They'd sure taught me how to love unconditionally.

"That's what I'm talking about. You were a kid. So the fact that you're surrounded now by people in this town who love and care about you? Well, I say you deserve Tom's love and so much more. It's about time you shouted from the rooftops about your engagement."

I smiled, fighting back emotion. "I know that's what Tom wants."

But Kara had grown serious. "Are you hesitant to remarry?"

"I'll admit I'm a little scared. It seems like when I love people with all my heart, they go away. I couldn't bear it if Tom went away." The tears I'd been fighting spilled down my cheeks. It suddenly dawned on me that this was what I'd been fearing since Tom asked me to marry him. This was why I'd been holding back, questioning my decision. But until this moment, it had been hidden in my subconscious.

Kara set down her glass, came around the bar and hugged me. "No one is going anywhere. You are cherished by Tom, by me, by Candace. You've helped me settle into this town. You deserve every good thing that comes your way."

I drew back and wiped away the tears with the heel of my hand. "Thank you so much."

Clyde cut short any further conversation by chasing Kara's orange and white boy Pulitzer around the kitchen. No surprise her calico was named Prize. Clyde, although fast, was no match for the much smaller Pulitzer's speed. The race around the kitchen island continued through the open living area and up the stairs to the second floor.

"Friends already," I said. "Maybe everyone should hiss at each other first, get it over with and move on to playtime."

"It would be a better world." Kara picked up her glass and motioned me toward the patio off the kitchen. "Let's catch the sunset."

We were joined about fifteen minutes later by Liam Brennan, Kara's boyfriend – although there had to be a better word than *boyfriend* since they were both in their thirties. Liam, with blond hair and an Irish twinkle in his blue eyes, greeted me with a hug and then wasted no time quizzing me about the recent crimes in Mercy. After all, he could end up prosecuting this case in the future.

"What insights do you have into these two murders, Jillian?" He'd chosen whiskey for his drink, and the amber liquid glittered like jewels in his glass as it reflected the setting sun.

"You probably know more than I do. Candace and

Tom are working hard trying to come up with answers. Mr. Jeffrey had plenty of money, which as you know, means plenty of motive for the relatives. But Buford Miller? I'm not sure why he was killed, except he must have made someone pretty darn angry."

"Why's that?" Kara asked. She'd moved her patio chair close to Liam's and their hands were locked. I wondered if her interest in weddings went beyond her questions about my relationship with Tom.

"Because it was a brutal murder," Liam answered. "It takes a lot of power to hit someone hard enough to fracture their skull. Still, adrenaline will give even the frail a surprising amount of strength."

"True." Kara nodded. "So we have Mr. Jeffrey's death—a sneaky crime made to look like an accident or possible suicide—and Buford's vicious murder with little or no evidence left behind. At least that's what I took away from my conversation with Candace about the crimes. She told me they had no murder weapon in the Miller death and very few clues."

"Two killers, then?" I wondered aloud.

"That would be my guess," Liam said. "Candace said you know about Miller's drug connection. Since this county has a big drug problem, I—"

"A drug problem?" This surprised me.

"Don't you read the Crime Beat section of my newspaper, Jillian?" Kara said with mock surprise. "Half the problems in the area are related to makeshift meth labs, homeless alcoholics robbing convenience stores and stolen prescription drugs."

I sighed. "I skim that section. Too depressing."

"But Kara and I have to pay attention. It's part of our jobs. She reports; I prosecute." Liam drained the inch of whiskey in his glass. "Buford Miller had access to both illegal and legal drugs, though none of his legitimate patients ever voiced a complaint about missing their medicine. That's how I've been trying to help Mercy PD—by checking on this home health care agency he worked for. Looks like their licensing is all in order."

"You found nothing suspicious?" I asked.

"Not yet," he said, "but I have a stack of background checks I plan to go through. This whole thing has made me realize how these private agencies are popping up to give in-home health care, and we haven't been paying as much attention as maybe we should. The elderly can be taken advantage of so easily. Unfortunately, older people are not quick to complain when they suspect a caregiver isn't on the up-and-up."

I nodded. "You're right. That generation was taught not to complain and to believe health care providers shouldn't be questioned. If my grandparents were still alive, that's what they'd tell you."

Both Liam and Kara nodded in agreement.

Kara said, "That's not to say Buford's agency did anything wrong aside from hiring a not so upstanding employee."

"Did Buford have a record?" I asked.

"One DUI," Liam replied. "The drugs the sheriff's deputies found in his room were significant—several grams of cocaine and a bunch of meth. No wonder he needed a high-powered automatic handgun."

Kara responded immediately. "I moved here to a small town from the fourth largest city in the United States and this area probably has more guns than I could have ever imagined. It's no surprise to me."

"Most of the weapons in this area are used for hunting," Liam said. "A Sig Sauer isn't exactly something you take out to the deer lease. He needed protection."

"When Candace figures out who his drug connections are, she'll know plenty more than she does now about Buford's death—though it could be unrelated to Mr. Jeffrey's murder."

I sat back in my chair, thinking more about the idea of two killers. "Buford had the most access to Mr. Jeffrey's medication. Could he have been hired to murder Mr. Jeffrey? And then whoever hired him decided Buford needed to be silenced?"

Liam smiled. "You and Candace are on the same page. No wonder you're such good friends. She's been thinking along those lines, but says she wants to rule out any drug connection—someone Buford might have owed money to. We have a CI in the area that I've hooked her up with."

I was a tad confused. "CI?"

"Confidential informant," Kara said. "We have them in the newspaper business, and the police use them all the time—especially to hunt down leads in drug-related crimes."

"I get it. I'm just not up on all the lingo. So first she rules out a drug-related murder and only then she can move on to explore other motives?"

"She's prioritizing, but she's probably exploring every possibility as she gathers the evidence," Liam said. "Investigations like this don't always lead straight to one suspect. Sometimes the evidence lines right up, but with this many family members? Not easy. She told me about the cousins, the sister and of course Dirk, the nephew. I believe her words were 'the family is a *hot mess*.'"

"She's right. Everyone seems to hold grudges, keep secrets and refuse to speak to any of their relatives for years at a time." I shook my head. "I've met them all and Dirk seems to be the only sane one."

"Good thing he's the executor of the will." Liam said this so casually, like this was known to the world, I couldn't speak for a few seconds.

Finally I said, "You understand Candace was looking to confirm that piece of information? I had my suspicions, but she told me they couldn't be sure until she found the will."

"Wait a minute." Liam dropped Kara's hand and leaned toward me. "Dirk said he told Candace he was the executor. The guy called me right after his uncle's death, asked me what steps he had to take for probate. If I remember right, he said his uncle didn't have a lawyer, that he had this do-it-yourself will stashed somewhere and wondered if I could help him find it since I was a county attorney."

I blinked several times. Maybe Dirk carried the secretive family gene after all. "I can assure you he never told her. Do you know if he found the will?"

"Nope. That's the only conversation I've had with the man. I did mention if the will was in a safe-deposit box, he could get access as the executor and file it for probate." He paused. "And I remember telling him that once that will was filed in court, it would become public knowledge. Anyone could find out how Mr. Jeffrey divided his estate. That piece of information seemed to surprise him."

"When exactly did you talk to Dirk?" I asked.

"The day after Mr. Jeffrey's body was discovered. I remember because that's the same time all the cameras came to Mercy to cover Clyde the cat."

I reached into the pocket of my khakis for my phone. "I have to call Candace. She needs to know about Dirk."

Liam stood. "I'll make that call. You need to relax, Jillian. Trust Candace to get her hands on that will as soon as she can."

While Liam made the call, Kara refilled my wineglass. "He's right. You should use your visit with me as a minivacation. Recharge, forget about the case."

"You're probably right. It's so hard to leave it behind after meeting the family—especially LouAnn. Then there's

Birdie, who seems like such a fine person. But if she's protecting her son—"

"Jillian, stop. Drink your wine and chill out." She walked across the patio and lit the barbecue. Moments later she brought out a platter of kebab sticks skewered with mushrooms, tomatoes, chunks of summer squash, onions and green peppers. Clyde tried to escape through the French doors when she made her first trip back outside from the kitchen, but Kara was wise to him and aborted his attempt. Old habits die hard. New place, new exit strategy.

While she basted the veggies with olive oil mixed with herbs, Liam returned.

"Candace sends her love and says she'll take care of everything. She'll find Dirk and bring him in. She's glad you helped uncover what may turn out to be a true attempt to deceive . . . or maybe just a white lie."

I didn't buy the white lie idea. "Surely he didn't forget he was the executor of that will."

"No. But it's only one piece of information—information she needs, of course."

"My impression was he cared about his uncle. But this seems odd. Or maybe it's just typical for this family." I explained what I knew about the sister, the cousins, the nephew and even Birdie and her son. Meanwhile, Clyde and Pulitzer, his new best friend, sat and stared through the lowest panes of glass. You'd have thought Kara had just thrown fresh tuna on the barbecue.

When we sat down inside to eat, I said, "I promise no more talk of murder. I want to enjoy every bite of this meal. Not only does it smell delicious; it looks pretty enough to be on the cover of *Bon Appétit*."

Kara blushed. "Simple food *can* look pretty."

Liam insisted on cleaning up after we were finished eating. I was too exhausted to argue. I curled up on one end of Kara's taupe-colored velvet sectional and Chablis immediately joined me. Prize, a sweet, quiet calico girl, found Kara's lap while the boy cats chased a moth that had flown inside when we came in for dinner.

"They won't stop until they catch that thing," I said.

"You got that right," Kara replied. "They do tickle me with their stalking instincts. You'd think they were chasing dragons."

I laughed. Instincts were as important to animals as they were to folks like Tom and Candace and Kara. No, they were more important, more deeply imbedded, more pure. Maybe we should all be as watchful, playful and fierce as cats.

Twenty-five

I awoke the next morning crowded to the edge of Kara's queen-size guest bed by four cats. This was why I had a king-size bed at my house. And Clyde? He took up almost as much space as a large child. I peeked over the comforter toward the end of the bed, knowing what I would see.

Sure enough, Syrah sat staring at me with a look that conveyed I had fallen short of his expectations. Didn't I realize it was time for his breakfast? I grabbed my phone from the bedside table and checked the time. Wow. Well past his mealtime. I'd been tired, but I hadn't realized just how tired until now.

After slipping into the flip-flops by the bedside, I made my way downstairs to the kitchen. Kara was dressed and about ready to leave—or I assumed as much since she had her car keys in her hand.

"Morning, Jillian. Coffee's made, I have bagels, yogurt, and there are leftover peaches from last night. Help yourself." Then she focused her gaze behind me and grinned. "Your entourage, I see."

I turned to see four cats sitting in a row, silently encouraging me to serve them their breakfast before I made another move or spoke a word. I opened the pantry where I'd stowed their food last evening. Kara had already set four small glass bowls on the counter.

"You put out a paper tomorrow, right?" I poured kibble into each bowl.

"Yes, and I wish I could headline the edition with 'Murders Solved,' but I can't. I won't even offer speculation. Anything we discussed last night is strictly off-limits for my paper. I print facts and leave the conjecture to the readers."

"Not many in your field do that anymore." I set the dishes on the floor and watched four cats decide which bowl belonged to whom. Because I'd overslept, they didn't squabble too much. They were hungry.

Kara said, "I have to go. I told Emily she could come by the office and watch us put the edition together. She seemed excited about a lesson in journalism, small-town style."

"Thank you for taking her on. Maybe I won't even see her today." I gave Kara a hug, her damp hair smelling like lavender. "Anything I can do around the house to help out? I don't want to be a freeloader."

"Um, how many quilts have you made not only for cats, but for soldiers' children? How many hours have you given to helping the animals at Shawn and Allison's shelter? How much time have you spent helping Candace? You couldn't be a freeloader if you tried."

Minutes later, she was gone. I wondered where her cats were and found them, curled together, in Kara's home office, enjoying the heat of the morning sun penetrating the window. Bet they were worn out after last night's playdate with my crew.

But if I thought I could spend the day reading or watching movies on Kara's Blu-ray player, I was wrong. After my breakfast and shower, I felt antsy—so out of the loop here on the outskirts of town. I wanted to know if Candace talked to Dirk about Mr. Jeffrey's will. I also wanted to know if either she or Tom had made contact with the CI. In other words, I wanted to know everything.

Birdie worried me, too. She'd been so upset about what the police found in Buford's room. And then there was the issue of her son. Did he even know the identity of his father? Did any of us *really* know besides Birdie? The cousins were speculating—or perhaps making an educated guess once the son's photograph had been found in Mr. Jeffrey's nightstand drawer.

I decided to call Tom, hoping he'd at least spoken with Birdie this morning.

"You sleep well?" Tom asked when he answered my call.

"Better than I have in a week. Did you talk to Birdie yet?"

"Sorry, no. After Liam called Candace last night with confirmation that Dirk is the executor, we've been scrambling to gather his information. We're about to interview him, but first, with Liam's help, we pulled phone records proving he did call the county DA's office the day after Mr. Jeffrey turned up dead. We're going to ask Dirk to explain his lie and I'm guessing Candace won't be as nice as the last time they spoke."

"I hope you get the truth and finally have a look at the will." I almost asked him to please phone Birdie but decided he was far too busy. Instead, I told him I loved him and disconnected.

Maybe I could call Birdie and explain that Tom was tied up, but that he promised to get busy on helping protect her house as soon as he could. I liked that lady and didn't want her to think I hadn't come through on a promise.

After I had no luck finding Birdie's phone number, I decided to visit her. The cats, now grooming themselves after their meal, could occupy one another. I turned Kara's TV on to Animal Planet as I often did at home. Maybe I'd return here and see that nothing had been broken, scratched or toppled in my absence.

I already had a key to Kara's house and knew her security code—a system similar to mine that her former employer, my Tom, had installed just last month. *My Tom.* Gosh, that sounded so good, especially now that Kara knew we planned to marry.

I left, feeling anxious about not having the assurance my cat cam offered. But as soon as I drove back to Mercy, the gorgeous foliage lining the narrow country road distracted me. This was truly a beautiful part of the county. The weather app on my phone indicated rain headed our way, probably as soon as tonight, so I rolled down the van window and took in the fresh, warm air while I had the chance. But dust and pollen always lingered in the air on this side of town and an open window might not have been the best idea.

Sure enough, I spent the last five minutes of my drive sneezing, and by the time I pulled in front of Birdie's house, my eyes burned. So much for the beautiful outdoors. Several cars lined the street in front of her house and I realized I might get to meet Birdie's son—or rather Birdie and Mr. Jeffrey's son.

I knocked and soon her round face peeked from behind the lace curtain on the door. The stress I'd seen in her eyes gave way to relief and she quickly opened the door.

"So glad you dropped by, Miss Jillian. Come on in."

"I hope this isn't a bad time." But by the look on her face, I could tell I was welcome and that lessened the uneasiness I'd felt building all morning.

"Perfect time." She took my hand and led me down the hall toward her living room. "You been cryin'?"

"No. I am allergic to something that blooms in the summer."

"I'm so glad you're not troubled." She gripped my hand tighter and I noticed her fingers were ice-cold despite the warmth of her home.

We walked into the living room and I saw Wayne Jeffrey sitting on Birdie's Victorian sofa, his arms spread along the scrolled wood of the sofa back. "Fancy seeing you here, Ms. Hart."

"I—I could say the same." What was *he* doing here?

Birdie, intuitive as always, said, "I haven't seen Wayne here in a very long time. He still hasn't stated his business."

"My business?" he replied. "Did you ask Jillian what *her* business is? I mean, I am an old friend. But her?" He pointed at me. "How long you known her?"

Birdie raised her chin. "Long enough. Why you here, Wayne?"

"Got my reasons. You said something about coffee right before the town snoop showed up. How about it?"

The chill I felt in Birdie's hands now seemed to envelop the room.

"I'll get right on that, Wayne." Birdie's tone was even harsher than when I'd heard her speak to Buford the first time I met her.

When she started for the kitchen, I said, "Let me help you."

"What?" Wayne said. "She can handle coffee. Meanwhile, I'd like to get to know you better, Ms. Hart. My cousins have been yakking on and on about you."

A smart comeback would have been nice, but I wasn't the person to make it. Instead, I decided that if he wanted to know me better, I sure as heck wanted to know more about him, too. But first, he had to understand that he wasn't running the show. I repeated my offer to help Birdie out.

"No, dear. You visit with Wayne, keep him company now that he's setting there like a potted plant on my sofa.

Just make sure he keeps his feet off the coffee table." She left the room slowly, her arthritic walk seeming more pronounced than the other times we'd met.

At least someone was good at comebacks and I smiled inwardly at Birdie's spunk. Easing into a brocade wing chair across from Wayne, I came up with the only thing I could think of to say. "I'm sorry for your loss, Mr. Jeffrey."

"Is that so? That's why you've been talking to my family? 'Cause you're sorry? Or is it more about you worming your way into their affection so you can end up with my cousin's cat now that he's passed on?"

I blinked several times, trying to figure this out. "You believe I want to keep Clyde?"

"You seem to collect cats like some folks collect stamps. That animal meant a lot to my cousin and he's going back with Millicent as soon as the funeral's over. He stays in the family. You hear me?"

Did he really care about Clyde? I wasn't convinced. "If you believe I ever intended to keep Clyde as my own, well—where did you get such an idea?"

"I saw you on the news with him, all prettied up and makin' the world believe you're the savior of all cats." He leaned forward. "He doesn't belong to you. You got that?"

The menace in his tone was obviously intended to frighten me. But why? Keeping my voice even, I quietly said, "I have no intention of keeping Clyde."

Thank goodness Birdie appeared with a tray holding three mugs, spoons and a sugar bowl and creamer. I quickly stood and took it from her. She thanked me as I set it on the coffee table.

Wayne leaned in and doctored one mug with cream and sugar. "Now here's what I'm talkin' about. My cousin Norm always did say you made the best coffee." He sipped the coffee and smiled with satisfaction.

Birdie glanced at me and I read the apology in her eyes. My guess was that she was sorry she hadn't been straightforward about her relationship to Norman Jeffrey when Candace and I first came to visit.

Hoping to rescue her from self-admonishment, I smiled at her before I addressed Wayne. "Mr. Jeffrey talked to you about Birdie, did he?"

"No. My cousin didn't much care for me. As for his private business, we were left to figure the whole mess out. Norm never said who his woman was, but once he decided this one here was too good to sweep my cousin's floor, we understood. We aren't a stupid family, are we, Birdie?"

Birdie sat on a padded straight-back chair next to me, her hands grasped together in her lap. "*Stupid* is not a word in my vocabulary, Wayne."

The coffee on the tray tempted me. I wanted a cup just so I'd have something to hang on to as the tension in the room crept ever higher. But if Birdie wasn't having coffee, I wasn't, either.

Before another word was spoken, I heard a door open in the kitchen. We all looked in that direction and Birdie's eyes widened, her expression bordering on terror. She offered Wayne a pleading look and shook her head ever so slightly.

A male voice called, "Mama, why are all those cars out front?" A thin, light-skinned black man with a receding hairline and the most beautiful golden eyes walked into the room. "Oh, I didn't know we were expecting company."

He walked over to Wayne and extended his hand. "Theo Roberts."

Wayne didn't stand, but he did shake Theo's hand. "And I'm Wayne."

I noticed Birdie take a deep breath and quietly blow it out, her eyes fixed on Wayne. He hadn't mentioned his last name—at least not yet. If he'd said Jeffrey, Theo might start asking questions Birdie wasn't ready to answer since that name had been in the news.

I rose and Theo took my extended hand in both of his. "And you are . . . ?"

"This is a new friend of mine," Birdie said. "Nice lady named Jillian Hart."

Theo smiled broadly. "I thought I recognized you. You're the one who has poor Mr. Jeffrey's wandering cat."

Wayne mumbled, "For now."

Theo turned. "I'm sorry. I didn't hear you."

"Nothing." Wayne stood, his gaze on Birdie. "Time for me to head out. Didn't know you'd invited Ms. Hart over. We'll talk again, though." He raised one bushy gray eyebrow, his blue eyes stone cold.

He left without any further acknowledgment of Theo or me.

"Who was that man?" Theo asked. "He seems to have upset you, Mama."

"He's nobody. Sit down and have coffee. Have a proper talk with Miss Jillian. I'll get another cup for myself." She started to get up.

Theo stopped her, saying, "Please stay where you are. I can at least save you a few steps."

Five minutes later, we all held mugs of the delicious coffee Birdie made so proudly from beans her son sent to her from New York. We made small talk about my brief television appearance, I asked about Theo's job—he was a professor of economics—and Birdie seemed to slowly calm down as the conversation went on. Especially since we never returned to questions about Wayne's visit.

From the nonverbal cues I picked up on, I surmised that Theo knew little or nothing about Birdie's relationship with Mr. Jeffrey or with extended family members like Wayne. She'd probably never told her son who his father was and the thought that he might learn this from someone as nasty as Wayne Jeffrey must have horrified her.

It struck me then that I shouldn't know who Theo's father was when he did not. It seemed wrong. I hoped Birdie would sit down with him before Wayne came back—because I had the feeling he would return. The man looked ready to splay open Birdie's old wounds in front of her son. Tom's first impression of Wayne had been that he was "okay." I now begged to differ.

"How did you meet my mother?" Theo asked.

I told him about my earlier visit with Candace and our talk with Buford right before his murder. "But today I came to explain about the delay in setting her up with a security system. I have a friend who can make sure none of Buford Miller's nefarious friends ever bother her, but he's helping the police right now and can't get to the job immediately."

Birdie looked at Theo. "You think I need cameras watching my front porch, Son?"

"This neighborhood has changed, Mama. I wish I did a background check on Buford Miller before you ever allowed him to live here." He looked at me. "Since you have a reliable person who can install a security system, I'll be happy to pay for it."

"Indeed, Miss Jillian knows the most reliable man in town, Mr. Tom Stewart. As for Buford, remember the poor soul is dead. I have prayed for forgiveness because I was impatient with him, even unkind at times. No matter how he came to his unfortunate end, I am truly sorry for how I treated him."

"He brought trouble and worry into your home, Mama. You know what I'll be praying for? Your safety once I leave." He nodded to emphasize his point.

I stood and set my empty mug on the tray. "I would have called if I'd had your phone number, Birdie. But I am so glad I stopped by and got to meet your son." I couldn't say the same for the encounter with Wayne, although I may have interrupted what could have been a difficult conversation between Theo and Wayne. Secrets never stay secret and the one about Birdie and Mr. Jeffrey would be spilling out onto the streets of Mercy very soon.

That was why, when Birdie slowly walked me to the door, I hugged her and whispered, "Don't you think it's time you told your son the truth?"

When she pulled away, I saw tears in her eyes. She nodded.

I walked out and down the porch steps to my minivan. I hoped Candace was at the station. I had a few things to talk about with her.

Twenty-six

I tried Candace's cell once I pulled into the courthouse parking lot. My call went straight to voice mail. Perhaps she was talking to Dirk right now about the will.

I hoped at the very least B.J. would tell me what was happening. I ran into Audrey in the lobby and as usual, she inspected me and the floor around me for cat hair. She pulled an orange hair off my shirt. "This don't belong to one of yours. It's from that cat you were with on TV, huh?"

"You're very observant," I said with a smile. "Did you see Candace or Tom this morning?"

"Saw them come and saw them go. Came separately, left together. You worried about Candace stealing Tom away from you?"

I smiled. "Not at all. When did they leave?"

"Maybe thirty minutes ago. Morris just passed through if you got police business. Grumpy as a bear, though. That relative of Mr. Jeffrey's was with him, hanging on like they was best friends. The way he looked at her, you'd have thought she had a disease."

I stifled a laugh. I was familiar with Morris's demeanor and his expressions left nothing to the imagination. "Maybe he needs rescuing." But which relative came in with him? It sounded like Millicent. I couldn't picture LouAnn or Ida Lynn hanging on to anyone.

My guess was confirmed when I found Millicent sitting in the waiting area. She'd pulled a chair right up to B.J.'s desk and from the look on his face, he wanted her gone. A lot of strange people came in and out of this place, but I wondered how many of them sat so close for a chat.

"Hey there, Millicent." I added plenty of warmth to my greeting. "How are you?"

To my surprise, she stood and gave me a kiss on each cheek, the scent of her perfume strong. Her dress, a leopard print, had a diagonal hemline. My degree may be in fiber arts, but I'd learned plenty about fabric during my college years. Creating a diagonal hem with the stretch fabric in that dress required skill—and skill cost money.

With no Morris in sight, I decided he'd made his escape without my help. I glanced at B.J. over Millicent's shoulder and his eyes begged me to rescue *him*. I could handle that.

"Are you waiting for another interview with Deputy Carson, Mrs. Boatman?" I asked. Candace had said she would be speaking with her again today, so I surmised that was why she was here.

"Yes, but this sweet young man, who has been telling me how he will be joining your little police force next year, has informed me that other business called Deputy Carson away. He wants me to reschedule. I told him my appointment with the undertaker we've hired isn't until this afternoon, so I can wait for her to return."

"But it's so uncomfortable in these old chairs," I said. "Why don't you join me for coffee down the street and come back later?"

She raised a well-manicured hand to one cheek. "Why, do you suppose that would be all right?" She looked at B.J. who nodded solemnly.

This Southern belle act can't be for real, I thought. Her cousins sure didn't talk or act like this. "Have you ever been to Belle's Beans?"

She hooked her arm in mine. "Why, have you forgotten I grew up in Mercy? I most certainly know Belle Lowry, but it has been several years since I have visited her little coffee shop. She's proven herself quite the entrepreneur." She glanced at B.J. "I do believe I will take Jillian up on her kind offer of companionship. You already have my number if Deputy Carson returns and wishes to speak with me."

We turned to leave and I glanced over my shoulder as we walked out the door arm in arm. I saw B.J., who was mouthing "Thank you," hands steepled, eyes to the ceiling.

We walked to Belle's, the threat of rain still a few hours away. I enjoyed the summer breeze, as well as the whiskey barrels of colorful geraniums and gerbera daisies that lined Main Street, despite sharing the walk with the rather odd Millicent Boatman. The only one who hadn't seemed strange in the family was Dirk—but now I'd learned he hadn't exactly been forthcoming. Maybe Candace and Tom were discovering more about him this minute—and learning exactly why he'd lied about the will.

As we made our way down the block, Millicent talked nonstop. She spoke about how much Mercy had changed over the years, from mill town to tourist spot, and described in detail her home on Hilton Head Island with its beautiful ocean view. By the time we made the five-minute walk to Belle's, she'd also informed me about three restaurants I simply had to try when I came to visit her.

Visit her? I didn't think so. But of course I couldn't be impolite and tell her that would *never* happen.

When we reached Belle's, the late-morning-coffee crowd was gone and only a few people sat at the tables.

It was an odd mix of older retirees and young people with their laptops taking advantage of Belle's free WiFi.

I had my usual vanilla latte—a decaf after the industrial strength brew I enjoyed at Birdie's house. Millicent ordered a black iced tea shaken with pomegranate juice. *Huh?* I didn't even realize Belle served anything that fancy.

Millicent didn't protest when I offered to pay, just tottered off to a table near the back of the café while I waited for the order. I'd heard the rich often get richer because they thought their status entitled them to "free stuff." I was beginning to believe it.

When I sat down, I saw Millicent typing a text on her blinged-out phone. The glittery protective cover practically lit the room. Once I set the drinks on the table, she placed the phone facedown on the table and enjoyed a long sip of her tea through the straw.

"Dirk messaged me that Deputy Carson and Mr. Stewart arrived to question him at the Pink House. Now, why couldn't that young man who answers the phones or dear Morris Ebeling tell me as much? Poor Morris doesn't seem any happier than when I knew him way back when. Some folks stay unhappy. Isn't that right?"

I wasn't sure which question to answer—or if she indeed wanted any answers.

Sure enough, she kept on talking. "Dirk is so bothered by this unpleasant business here in Mercy. I will be glad when I can take both Clyde and my boy back home."

Her *boy* had to be forty years old. "Does Dirk live with you?"

"Oh no. He's quite successful in real estate and keeps his own home as of several months ago. I suspect he has a woman friend and moved out of my residence for more privacy. When the time is right, he'll talk with me about whether I believe she's suitable for him. He does visit me often, though, since we both live on the island. I am proud to say he managed to make a good living when most everyone else in his business suffered through those economic troubles. Such a smart man, my son. I always said he took after Norm more than his father."

"From what you said before and the talk about town—you know how people love to chat in Mercy—you, Mr. Jeffrey and your cousins were once close. I realize LouAnn came between you and a man you loved, but what about your estrangement from your brother? Is that just a rumor, Mrs. Boatman?"

Millicent offered one of her nervous giggles. "People are saying we were estranged? That's ridiculous. Norm and I were fine. He did have this misguided notion that I aggressively pursued Oliver the minute LouAnn went off to college, but he realized later on he was wrong. Oliver pursued *me*."

"So it was simply a misunderstanding that lasted a long time?"

She smiled and pointed at me briefly before resting her hand on her phone. "Bless your heart, you've obviously been listening to gossip mongers and probably heard tales from poor LouAnn. I do believe Oliver's death has affected her mental health. She did resent that I had a child, a joy she never experienced. But then, perhaps that's what one might call karma. And you know what people say about that." She leaned forward and put her straw to her lips, her eyes appraising me.

I met her stare. "Hmm. Sounds as if you might still have lingering resentment toward LouAnn."

"No, my dear. Unlike LouAnn and Ida Lynn, I moved on with grace and civility. You'll have to speak with those two about old resentments."

"So you and Mr. Jeffrey were okay before he passed on?"

"You're beginning to talk like a policewoman, dear. I've lost my only brother and I will refrain from disparaging him in any way."

If she felt the need to *refrain*, I believed that answered my question. But I had to smooth the feathers I'd just ruffled. "I'm so sorry if I seem to be prying. Somehow I feel as if we've been friends for longer than a few days and I got carried away with my questions. Friends share everything, right?"

She reached over and patted my hand. "All you need to know is that I loved my brother even if I did not often come to Mercy and visit with him face-to-face. We shared a blood bond that could never be broken by any of the choices he made. I forgave him."

"You're talking about how he took LouAnn's side way back when?" But I wondered if she might be referring to Mr. Jeffrey's relationship with Birdie.

"That is correct, dear. I did feel judged at the time. However, it is all ancient history." Her facade dropped for just a moment. I saw anger in her eyes.

Could a decades-old feud with her brother be reason enough to kill him? Not likely, I decided. It *was* ancient history. "Obviously you loved your brother. I mean, you agreed to take his cat. Taking on a pet is a big responsibility and that was so kind of you."

She seemed to relax and her smile returned. "Why, thank you, Jillian. I'm only sorry the cat slipped out and ran off. I could not bring myself to tell Norm what happened and thank goodness he left this world believing Clyde was safe and sound. And now, thanks to you, he *is* being well cared for again."

"Clyde is doing fine. But are you sure about your decision to take him home? LouAnn would surely love to have him. Clyde has proven during his stay with me that he gets along fine with other kitties."

"He cannot live with anyone but me. We must abide by my brother's wishes, after all. Don't you agree that's how we honor the dead?" Her tone was sanguine sweet, but I hadn't once heard her say she loved cats—and that concerned me. Perhaps I needed to change the subject. Clyde's future was not set in stone, but arguing with Millicent wouldn't be productive and would only put her off. "I suppose you would be honoring Mr. Jeffrey's wishes. When is the funeral, by the way?"

"The day after tomorrow. It is time to put poor Norm to rest." She shook her head sadly. "I simply will never understand why anyone would want to take a sick man's life."

"That is puzzling," I said. "Did you ever meet the other victim, Buford Miller?"

"No. Dirk took on the responsibility of making sure Norm was cared for after he became ill. Now he is berating himself over choosing a caregiver with problems serious enough to get him killed right in my brother's home." She lowered her voice and leaned closer to me. "We both believe that Miller man murdered Norm."

Whoa. Where did this come from? "Really? Why would he do that? And if he did, who killed Buford?"

"I have no answers. We are confounded by the developments here in Mercy. Ida Lynn informed me this Miller person was involved with drugs. As I mentioned to Deputy Carson, he may have been stealing from my brother and—"

"But why kill your brother, then? I mean, he was the goose with the golden egg. Once Mr. Jeffrey died, Buford might have lost future access to any remaining valuables he could pilfer for drug money."

"Obviously he still had a key. Who knows what he would have stolen, given the chance? Dirk is convinced there was nothing to steal in the house, but I knew Norm better than anyone. He had secrets. And the Miller person may have found something worth stealing that we knew nothing about."

"Really?" I finished my coffee and held the empty cup between both hands.

"Yes. But you do have a point about those golden eggs. I never thought about Mr. Miller losing access to money my brother may have been providing to him either willingly or by theft." Her brow creased. She seemed perplexed. "Perhaps he wasn't the killer, after all. Perhaps whoever murdered him, murdered my brother, too."

After last evening's conversation with Liam, that didn't seem likely, but I wasn't about to bring that up. "It's all so sad and again, I offer my condolences. I will definitely attend the funeral. Will the services be at a church or a local funeral home?"

"The Amos Brothers Funeral Parlor in Woodcrest is coordinating with Ida Lynn's church. She is familiar with those particular undertakers. They seemed quite reasonable, and since we have no idea what expenses Norm's estate will be able to cover, we must be frugal."

"LouAnn believed your brother was well-off. You don't think that's true?"

The nervous laugh returned. "You do understand LouAnn is not in her right mind? Besides, Norm would not share information about his money with her—in fact he, like LouAnn, tended to be reclusive and secretive. We accepted their peculiarities."

"*We* meaning you and your son?" I asked.

"Yes. Dirk cared so much about Norm—perhaps because his father abandoned the two of us after carrying on with another woman. Dirk may have been past his teenage years at the time, but he still needed a father. He and Norm would always find things to talk about. As I said, they are very much alike."

"But your son is the executor of his uncle's will. Has he shared any concerns with you about the state of your brother's finances?"

I saw a hint of surprise test her features briefly. Did she even know her son was the executor? Or was that a fact *I* wasn't supposed to know? Surely Candace had asked all the family members about the particulars of the will.

"Medical bills for a person with cancer can drain a bank account," she answered. "Why, he may have debts we do not yet know about." She finished off her tea and dabbed at her lips with a napkin.

"But if there are funds left, how do you think he would divide his estate?"

"I have no earthly idea. You'd have to ask Dirk." She pushed away from the table and stood. She placed her phone in her handbag and said, "I believe I'll return to the police station now. Since I do have an appointment in Woodcrest later today, maybe Morris can take my statement. He was in such a frightful mood earlier, but perhaps he's had time to reflect on the benefit of good manners when dealing with the bereaved."

Yes, no one could accuse Morris of having any Southern charm. "I'll walk back with you," I offered.

"That won't be necessary. I haven't forgotten my way around town despite all the changes since I moved away."

She seemed more standoffish now and I'd probably overstepped by questioning her about family money. She had been so open and talkative at first, but I'd obviously moved the conversation past her comfort zone.

She did give me the double kiss again before she left, so maybe I was wrong. It wouldn't be the first time this bizarre woman had left me feeling like I'd been more confused by talking to her than I was before we spoke.

Twenty-seven

I waited several minutes after Millicent left Belle's Beans before I got up. If she didn't want me walking back to the courthouse with her, so be it. I took out my phone and immediately realized I was about to look at a cat cam feed that didn't exist. This reminded me that whoever destroyed my security system did so for a reason—and it wasn't just vandalism. They were after Clyde. *But why?* The only person interested in cats was LouAnn and she certainly hadn't chased a kitty through my house. But someone had.

Nothing seemed to make sense right now, and I felt the need to go back to Kara's place and visit with my fur friends. Perhaps their presence would ease the anxiety I felt at not knowing what the heck was happening with this family. Maybe then I could think through what I'd learned today.

But when I walked out of Belle's Beans, I spotted Tom's Prius parked in front of the Main Street Diner down the street—and Candace's squad car was right next to it.

A few minutes later, I joined them in one of the wooden booths. To my surprise, Dirk was having lunch with them. I smiled at him and gave Tom a peck on the cheek, all the while wondering why they'd take a suspect to lunch.

Candace hadn't touched her cheeseburger yet and a look at what the guys had ordered showed me that their food must have just arrived. I told them to dig in and I ordered a sweet tea when the waitress appeared. Despite the wonderful smells of grilled onions and fries, I wasn't hungry. Millicent's overdose of chatter and my jangled nerves after meeting Wayne had killed my appetite.

"I just talked to your mother, Dirk," I said.

He stared down at his chili dogs. "She wasn't looking for me, was she? I promised her we'd have lunch, but if I'm forced to eat one more chicken salad sandwich at that doily-infested Victorian B and B, I'll lose my mind."

I smiled. "She was expecting to talk to Deputy Carson at the police station." I looked at Candace. "Or was she mistaken?"

"I figured I'd see her at the Pink House when we went there to talk to Mr. Boatman, but—"

"Please. Call me Dirk, Deputy Carson." He looked at me. "My mother left before I woke up. I had a few too many scotches last night and overslept. Scotch is required whenever I spend more than a day with my mother."

Perhaps he wasn't as devoted to her as she had led me to believe. "She just went back to the police station, determined to finish giving her statement." I rested a hand on Tom's knee. "But the Main Street Diner seems like an unusual place for *this* interview. What's going on?"

Candace said, "We're headed for the bank after we eat. Mr. Boatman—I'm sorry—*Dirk* surprised us by revealing a safe-deposit box key he found."

"Surprised you?" I was a little confused.

Tom, who wasn't about to let his hot roast beef sandwich get cold, had been shoveling in food, but now he said, "Dirk and his uncle Wayne went to the funeral home yesterday to take clothes they'd brought for Mr. Jeffrey to wear for the viewing. The funeral director gave him this little envelope with the key. It had been stuck in the lining of Mr. Jeffrey's pants pocket."

"It was missed at the autopsy?" I asked.

"Remember," Candace said, "Mr. Jeffrey's death wasn't deemed suspicious at first. His clothes were bagged and no one thought to go back and check them. Miss Monk and I will speak about that issue at another time since one of her responsibilities when a body comes in is to examine the clothing and remove belongings from pockets."

I could only imagine how that talk would go down and I surely didn't want to be present. "I'm not sure how it works after someone dies. Will you be given access to the box, Dirk?"

Candace had her cheeseburger poised for her first bite, but paused. "According to the bank, Mr. Jeffrey attached a codicil to the leasing document for the box. Seems only Dirk may access its contents—which saves me from having to wait to get that subpoena."

"Do you know the terms of the will, Dirk?" I asked.

"Here's the only thing I understand." Dirk glanced at Candace. "Can I tell her what I told you?"

"No problem," Candace mumbled around a bite of her burger.

Dirk looked at me. "The last time I came up here to visit him, Uncle Norm said Wayne had been hounding him for money—apparently for an investment. He told me he'd made me executor and said Wayne wasn't getting anything from the estate since the man had never listened to his advice about how to manage finances."

"So," Candace said, "if Wayne knew he gets nothing, that tends to send him to the bottom of the suspect list. Did he know this for certain, Dirk?"

"I got the impression from Uncle Norm that he'd told

Wayne as much. It was a difficult conversation because my uncle rarely shared anything personal."

I reached for the glass of tea the waitress had just placed in front of me. "Sounds like your uncle trusted you. Is that why he made you executor?"

"Maybe, but I deal with contracts all the time. Uncle Norm said I was the smart choice because I would understand what needed to be done."

I nodded. "Ah, makes sense. Sounds like your uncle knew exactly what he was doing."

"He was a great guy." Dirk stared at his food again—the two chili dogs he hadn't touched.

I realized then that for the first time, I was talking to a person who truly seemed to care about the victim and was feeling the loss. I swallowed hard. "You came here often to see him?"

"Yes—and I should have seen that he was in danger. I'll never forgive myself for hiring Buford Miller to care for him. I know he killed my uncle. I'm sure of it." Dirk's voice had risen and he was drawing stares from other folks in the diner. He noticed this and mumbled, "Sorry."

"Nothing to be sorry for, man," Tom said. "We'll figure this out. Your uncle's will and maybe other things in that box will help us solve his murder."

"I sure hope so. But can we change the subject? I don't want to completely lose my appetite now that I can enjoy something other than chicken salad."

They ate in silence for a few minutes and after Dirk finished one dog, he sat back. "I want to apologize again for making that call to the prosecutor's office." Dirk flushed and looked at me. "Like I told them earlier, my mother asked me to call and ask questions. She wanted to know what steps we had to take once we arrived here. She thought it would seem as if all she cared about was Uncle Norm's money when she only wanted to know what procedure to follow. Neither of us have ever dealt with the logistics of a funeral before. It *is* more complicated than I thought."

"It is," Candace said. "But like I told you back at the Pink House, do not lie about anything to the police again. It just creates trouble for everyone."

"I know that now. And I am sorry," he replied.

I stayed around for a few more minutes, hoping I'd be invited to go with them to the bank. I couldn't help but be curious about what was in that box. But that didn't happen. We said our good-byes outside the diner.

As I slid behind the wheel of my van, I decided it was probably a good thing, since I'd been away from Kara's house and my fur friends for too long. Before I drove off, I checked my buddy Emily's GPS location and saw she was at the newspaper office. Maybe she actually was taking Kara's advice to heart and wanted to learn how to prepare herself for a career in the news industry.

Since I'd made the mistake of trusting Emily before, I decided it might be wise to call Kara and make sure Emily wasn't annoying her. After all, I was the one who had brought them together.

When Kara answered, I said, "Emily's there, right?"

"Yes, we can do that." Kara's random reply told me Emily was probably in the room with her.

"Is she bothering you?"

"I'm on a deadline, so I'll have to call you back." Kara didn't sound happy.

"I am so sorry, Kara. Should I come and take her to lunch or something? Get her out of your hair?"

"No, that's not necessary. I'll talk to you later."

"Okay, but if you need rescuing, let me know. I'm headed back to your place."

"Thanks for calling." She disconnected.

From Kara's tone, I guessed Emily was making a pest of herself. Perhaps she wasn't simply an overeager young woman, but rather a narcissist. Despite what Kara had told her, Emily probably truly believed she could get a news-anchor job by presenting her station with an exclusive story about Clyde and the murders. I drove to Kara's house, feeling guilty for pulling my stepdaughter into this situation.

I disengaged the security system and came in through the back door. My spirits definitely got a reboot when six cats swarmed me in the mudroom, which also was home to the washer and dryer. I sat cross-legged on the tile floor and let them nudge me and vie for attention in their own ways. Chablis immediately crawled into the gap between my thighs. Syrah stared at me, blinking slowly in his regal style. Merlot lay down next to me and rolled onto his back for a belly rub. Pulitzer and Prize meowed in unison, begging for scratches under the chin—something they both enjoyed. Clyde watched all this and finally planted his huge paws on my shoulders and rubbed his face along my chin. Now this was cat heaven.

Time to feed this crew. My kitties were given regular meals, but Kara's cats always had food left out for them so they could eat whenever they desired. I knew if all the dishes were empty, one of *my* happy campers had probably eaten more than his fair share. She kept the food and water in here, so I stood with Chablis in my arms and checked the dishes in the far corner.

Sure enough, the kibble had been cleaned out. Merlot and Clyde, the big boys, topped the list of suspects. I went to the kitchen, found a larger bowl and filled it, thinking about the human suspects a little more. I recalled what Dirk had revealed about Wayne: He'd asked Mr. Jeffrey for money and had been turned away. Could this have been a murder about anger and revenge? Had Wayne enlisted Buford's help to get rid of Mr. Jeffrey and then murdered Buford before he could spill the beans?

I rinsed the water dish and refilled it, deciding that my

theory made little sense. Mr. Jeffrey was already dying. If Wayne got Buford to overdose the poor man, he'd probably have to pay Buford to do the deed. If Wayne needed money and was getting nothing from the estate, he'd only be hurting himself. But, maybe Wayne then killed Buford so he wouldn't *have* to pay him. I'd come full circle to revenge as a motive.

Still, someone wanted Mr. Jeffrey dead before the disease took him. Someone desperate. That person could well have been Wayne, especially if Dirk was lying to Candace about Wayne's being cut out of the will after asking Mr. Jeffrey for money. Dirk had lied once that we knew about. But why lie about any will provisions when he seemed so cooperative about going to the bank with Candace and Tom? They'd find out immediately when they read the document. Nope. Didn't make sense.

But what if there wasn't a will in the safe-deposit box? Or what if Wayne and Mr. Jeffrey had mended fences and the will had been changed to include him?

I shook my head, confused by all the possibilities. I went back to the mudroom, set the water and food bowls down, and decided to forget about all of this, at least for now. I smiled as the clowder went straight for the fresh kibble. This was what I wanted—to relax in Kara's wonderful country house with no one around except a lot of cats. I'd brought several quilt squares to appliqué and I could sit in front of the television and stitch. Cats, quilts and a little HGTV would clear my mind.

Twenty-eight

By eight o'clock that evening, I was too anxious to sit still another minute. I'd finished three appliqué squares, binge-watched *Rehab Addict* until I was sure I could refinish one-hundred-year-old crown molding, given the chance, and played with the cats until they finally tired of chasing feathers and stuffed mice on strings. All of them except for Chablis slinked away to find spots to snooze. She stayed close to me as usual, especially since I'd been hearing thunder rumble in the distance for the last hour. Chablis did not like thunderstorms.

Kara had called around five to say she was headed for dinner with Liam and then would be going back to the office. I'd heard nothing from Tom and Candace and was anxious to learn what they'd discovered in that safe-deposit box. Did they finally have a motive for the murders? I'd texted Tom thirty minutes ago, hoping he'd tell me, but he hadn't replied. I was about ready to grab my keys and head for the police station when the doorbell rang.

How strange. Who would be calling on Kara tonight? She never mentioned she was expecting anyone. I went through the foyer, the marble tiles cold on my bare feet. When I looked through the peephole, I couldn't withhold a groan of displeasure. A drenched Emily stood waiting for me to open the door.

How had she found me? And what did she want? I didn't move or make a sound, considering whether or not to open the door. Did I want to deal with her tonight? *No!* shouted a voice in my head.

"Jillian, I see your van," Emily called. "I know you're in there."

I sighed heavily. I couldn't leave her out there in the rain. Besides, I knew she wouldn't leave until I spoke with her. I let her in.

She smiled after greeting me with a wet hug and then took in the curving staircase off the foyer. Her gaze, accompanied by slack-jawed wonder, drifted to the vaulted ceiling, took in the open space of Kara's living room that flowed into the dining and kitchen combination. "This place is gorgeous," she finally said.

Her shoes were soaked and she'd tracked mud onto the previously immaculate floor.

"Before we get into why you're here, would you mind taking your shoes off?"

She stared down at her feet, apparently realizing for the first time that she was soaked. Even her dark hair was plastered to her head.

"Oh. Sorry." She bent over and removed her open-backed slip-ons.

No doubt about it, she needed dry clothes. I asked her to remain in the foyer until I could help her dry off. I'd noticed a basket of clean laundry in Kara's room earlier and hurried to find something she could wear. Although Emily was shorter, they both had a slim build.

I returned with a towel, yoga pants and a gray T-shirt. Once she'd dried off a little, I pointed out the powder room in the hallway off the living room. Fifteen minutes later, Emily sat on the opposite end of the sofa from me, clean and dry and sipping hot tea.

"How did you find me here, Emily?" I'd chosen sweet tea for myself—a much-needed dose of sugar to counteract my exasperation at her having shown up.

"You didn't tell me about the break-in at your place, Jillian. That's awful. Good thing you weren't home at the time."

Cats began appearing from every nook and cranny. Chablis crouched between us on the couch, probably more spooked by the thunder and flashes of lightning than by this visitor. Visitors she could handle.

"Please answer my question." I was beginning to wonder if she'd stuck another GPS on my minivan.

"Oh, how did I find you? You do realize people talk in this town. I mean, a *lot*. Rumors were flying all over that coffee shop about what happened at your home—about the break-in and how Tom's system wasn't as foolproof as he thought. And although Kara is a great teacher—I did learn a lot from her today—her face gives away too much. I knew she was talking to you on the phone earlier and when I went to your place and discovered your house all dark, I asked myself where you'd go if you didn't feel safe. But I knew. All I had to do was head back to the coffee place, ask someone where Kara lived and here I am." She smiled so proudly, you'd have thought she'd found a Picasso at a garage sale.

"Excellent sleuthing skills, Emily. Maybe you're cut out to be an investigative journalist after all. But why not just call me? You have my number." She probably had it memorized.

Emily held her steaming mug close to her nose with both hands, taking in the fragrance of Kara's peach green tea. "This is so good. I'll have to hunt for this brand back in Asheville." She sipped carefully and sighed with pleasure after she swallowed.

"Again, why didn't you call me rather than come here,

Emily?" I tried to keep the frustration out of my voice—
with difficulty.

Syrah must have sensed I was out of sorts because he
sat in front of Emily and stared at her. Pulitzer and Prize
were too timid to make it all the way to the sofa and
greet this new-to-them person. They crouched by a leather
wing chair near the fireplace. But the other four had met
her before and understood she was harmless. Well, harmless to cats, anyway.

Merlot, still looking a bit sleepy, sat on the Oriental
area rug next to Syrah. Clyde, who despite his size apparently considered himself a lap cat, jumped onto Emily to
say hello. She raised her mug just in time to keep hot tea
from spilling all over him.

"I guess he likes me." She put her mug down on the
lamp table near her left arm, making sure to use one of
the stone coasters Kara kept there.

So Emily did have a few manners. But again, she was
dodging the question about why she'd come here.

"If I tell you a few other things I learned hanging
around Belle's Beans, will you please ask Kara if I can
write the story? Because this is amazing stuff and I'd let
her help me get it right."

Let her? Emily still had so much to learn. But I was
intrigued, so I said, "Why don't you ask her yourself?
You did spend the day with her."

"Yes, and she told me that maybe it hadn't been a
good idea that I shadowed her while she created a morning edition layout. I think I asked too many questions."

"In other words, you kept interrupting her."

"That's about right. Would you ask her to give me
another chance now that I have this awesome scoop?"

"I'll try, but I have no idea if she'll agree to whatever
you intend to write. Maybe you need to let her decide
how important it is."

"Oh, it's important." She lifted Clyde off her lap and set him next to her on the sofa. "Gosh, you're heavy. But you are one special cat." She drew her legs up beneath her, facing my direction.

Clyde, apparently unhappy with her decision not to offer him a lap, decided Merlot was a good substitute for some needed attention. He jumped off the couch and wrapped his big paws around Merlot's neck. The two started wrestling playfully.

Emily went on. "My concern is the timing. When I should send off what I write, what markets I should use, stuff like that. And I need to know if it's okay to give away provisions in a will before the family's been informed. Could I get in trouble for doing that?"

She had my full attention now. "Yes, you could—with the police in this town, anyway. What do you know and how did you find out?"

"Shoot," Emily said. "I forgot how much Deputy Carson dislikes me. She might just arrest me, huh? But we do have freedom of the press in this country and I doubt she can keep me from telling this story."

"Back up, Emily. What exactly are you talking about?"

"Okay, here's the deal. I met Dirk Boatman—actually I saw him coming out of the police station and followed him to Belle's Beans. He seemed worried, looked like he could use a friend. We'd talked before, so I became a *better* friend." She smiled, obviously pleased with herself.

"You talked about the will?"

"Not at first. You have to slide into something as touchy as inheritance. When Clyde was discovered hanging around the Jeffrey house and we first learned about how far the cat traveled, Dirk and his mother both gave interviews to the TV stations. So we talked about how a vagabond cat gets a lot of interest. I mean, Clyde brought *me* here, didn't he?"

He had indeed. "What do you know that you want Kara to help you write and sell?"

She leaned forward and whispered to me as if we were in a crowded room and she didn't want anyone to overhear. "Dirk Boatman has a cousin he never knew about."

So Emily knew about Birdie's son. Did Candace give Dirk this information and he in turn told Emily? It was bound to come out, but the only way Dirk could have learned about this between when I saw him and meeting up with Emily was if there was something about Theo in that will. I had to take this slow. "So Dirk told you this?"

She nodded. "Mr. Jeffrey never mentioned this secret son, but he's named in the will. And get this. Mr. Jeffrey wanted his son—his name is Thurman or Thurston or something like that—anyway, he wants this son to have Clyde—*and* all the money that comes along with Clyde. This is a *big* story, Jillian. The family is going to be so upset."

Huh? Money that comes along *with Clyde? Clyde living with Theo?* I was dumbfounded. But I kept my cool. "This son is the only one who benefits in the will?" I wasn't about to share what I knew about Theo Roberts and I certainly wouldn't be telling Emily he was in town.

"I don't know about the rest of the will. Dirk said there were pages and pages of legal stuff, all sorts of provisions. He was just blown away that Mr. Jeffrey never told him a thing about this guy—and he's apparently about the same age as Dirk. Yup, he's pretty bummed that his uncle never shared the information."

The cats were on the move all of a sudden and I wondered if a moth or a fly had come in out of the rain with Emily. All except Pulitzer and Prize, who ran into the hall leading to the powder room and Kara's home office. All three boy cats headed through the kitchen toward the mudroom, but to my surprise, Chablis went to the sidelight window by the front door and peered out. It was still storming, so I was surprised she was brave enough to leave the safety of the couch.

"Where are they all going?" Emily asked.

I stood, wary of all the cats responding at once. If not for this heavy rainstorm, I might have been able to hear what they were hearing. I muttered, "I don't like this. Something's up."

Before I even made it to the mudroom and back door, my heart was racing. The hair on the back of my neck rose. Was someone else in this house?

Like a fool, I'd been so mobbed by all the cats who greeted me when I'd arrived earlier, I'd completely forgotten to lock the back door. The minute Emily arrived, I should have remembered. Too late now.

Twenty-nine

In the darkened mudroom I saw the silhouette of three cats sitting and staring at the back door. I flipped on the light. No Clyde. Where was he? What had just happened?

Then I smelled rain and realized the door was ajar. "No," I cried, running through the small room. I threw open the door and stared out into the blackness. I heard the sound of a car engine and, despite the rain, I ran outside and saw a car, headlights off, backing out of Kara's driveway. I pulled out my phone and dialed Tom's number, knowing whoever had tried to nab Clyde before had just succeeded.

He didn't answer and I wanted to throw the phone as far as I could. I was that upset.

Emily had come outside and was right behind me. "Who was that?"

"Someone's taken Clyde." I pointed to the end of the long driveway where headlights now came on as the car made a turn onto the road.

"I'll get him back," Emily said. "This will be an amazing story."

She ran back into the house. I started after her, but the

rainwater brought in by the intruder who had snatched Clyde got the better of me. I slipped and slammed onto the hard tile. My tailbone hit the floor, and pain shot up my spine. My legs felt like rubber as I used the built-in benches lining one wall for purchase and reached up for one of the coat hooks. Finally I was upright.

By the time I reached the kitchen, walking seemed almost impossible. I had to forget about doing anything in a hurry. I noted Emily's car keys were gone—and a glance toward the front door told me so were her wet shoes.

I still clutched my phone and this time I speed-dialed the police station. Lois, not B.J., answered.

"Is Tom there? Or Candace? This is an emergency." The pain in my backside was subsiding—maybe just because of adrenaline doing its job.

"Jillian, is that you?"

"Yes. I need to talk to one of them right now."

"Something I can do?" she asked.

"Please. Are they there?" Did she not hear the urgency in my voice?

She must have finally understood I wasn't making a social call. "They're both here. Let me get Tom on the phone."

It seemed like forever, but probably only a few seconds passed until he came on the line.

He only got out half of a hello before I started talking. "It's Clyde and Emily and they came for Clyde and she's following them and—"

"Jillian, slow down. Are you all right?"

"I'm fine. But it's dangerous for Emily. You already know Clyde gets the money and that's what this is all about and—oh my gosh." I stopped as it hit me. "We can track them. We have Clyde's GPS and the one on Emily's car." I almost felt euphoric at this realization.

"Start at the beginning and tell me what's going on—I'm confused."

"There's no time to tell you everything. Someone came here and stole Clyde. Emily was with me. She got in her car before I could stop her and is following whoever it is. And, Tom, it could be the murderer. She ran into Dirk and he spilled the details of Mr. Jeffrey's will. That girl is just foolish enough to confront whoever it is if she catches up with them."

"Okay. I'll handle this. I put all the tracking info for both Clyde and Emily on my iPad. I'll find them both."

Relief washed over me. "Okay. Thank God. And please keep in touch. I can't stand not knowing what's happening."

"We'll take care of this. Sit tight." He disconnected.

Sitting was the last thing I wanted to do right now. I probably wasn't capable of doing so, anyway. As the adrenaline rush began to fade, the pain ramped up. I slowly made my way to Kara's powder room, hoping she had some aspirin in the cabinet.

I found a bottle of Motrin. "Even better," I mumbled, cupping water in my hands from the bathroom faucet and downing the painkiller.

I turned to see five feline faces staring at me from the bathroom entrance. Relief came then as I realized the rest of the cats were inside and safe, even though I wasn't sure if I'd closed the back door. I only wished Clyde were with them.

As I slowly walked through the house to secure that back door—how stupid to have left it open in the first place—I had a thought. Just because Tom and Candace were on this didn't mean I couldn't track Clyde, too. So I pulled up the GPS program for Clyde on my phone and sure enough, I saw his little red dot making its way toward town.

The door was closed, thank goodness, and I locked it this time. I should have done that to begin with and none of this would have happened.

I grabbed a few paper towels from the kitchen to wipe up the water. Every muscle in my back protested when I tried to bend over. I dropped the towels and used my foot instead. All the cats seemed quite amused by this and Syrah even attacked my toes a few times. I was glad I could make someone happy tonight, because I'd sure let Clyde down.

Slowly the medicine began to ease the pain and I was able to think through what Emily had told me as I paced in front of the dark flat-screen TV. If Clyde disappeared—which seemed to be someone's plan—what happened to all the money that Theo would have inherited when he took the cat?

A sickening feeling in the pit of my stomach suddenly rivaled the pain in my backside. Aside from the apparently clueless Dirk, the rest of the family knew about Theo's existence, knew that he was Mr. Jeffrey's son. Wayne was aware Theo was in town. But did the rest of them know? Would one of them harm him to make certain he never saw any of that inheritance?

I needed to know the exact terms of that will. If both Clyde *and* Theo were gone, who got the money? This killer hadn't stopped with one murder, and it was probably the same person who'd broken into my home and came here tonight. Yes. Whoever it was might well go after Theo.

Since Clyde was helping us track this monster, I checked the screen and enlarged it to see if they were anywhere near Birdie's address. I released the breath I'd been holding when I saw the little red dot actually moving *away* from her house.

If Birdie hadn't told Theo who his father was, she needed to do so immediately, just so that her son understood he was in danger, if nothing else. But had I gotten her phone number when I'd visited earlier? *Of course not.*

Someone had to talk to Birdie. I could do it, but I knew I should check with Candace first.

I got Lois again when I called the station a second time. "She's busy, Mrs. Hart. There's a situation."

"I just need to ask her one question."

Lois sighed. "Oh, all right."

Candace sounded worried when she picked up and said, "Has something else happened?"

"No. I'm concerned about Birdie and Theo. I'm not sure she's gotten up the courage to tell her son the truth, but you know it will be all over town by morning."

It was Candace's turn to sigh. "You're right, but we're headed out to find Clyde and protect Emily. I'll call her once we have a moment. I really have to go, Jillian."

"I'd be happy to talk to Birdie and—"

"Would you? That's great." She disconnected.

I stared at my cell. I'd been hoping to get a number from Candace, but no way could I call the station a third time.

Finding Clyde and Emily was more important than anything else right now.

So I donned a raincoat that I found in Kara's hall closet, petted all the kitties and said good-bye. This time I made certain to secure the house by turning dead bolts and setting the alarm. When would I learn that nowhere was as safe as it might seem when there was trouble?

The rain had let up some but was still coming down pretty hard. I wanted to rush to the van, but it was a slow go. The next challenge I faced was unexpected—climbing in and finding a sitting position that didn't bring tears to my eyes. But after readjusting the seat, I headed to Birdie's house, praying all the way that she had already told Theo the truth.

On the drive into town, I called Kara to tell her that Emily could be in trouble.

"For real?" Kara sounded unconvinced.

"Yes. She's chasing someone who might be a murderer. That girl is impulsive, if you haven't noticed. But Candace and Tom are on it and will probably rescue her from herself—and maybe catch a killer." I explained about Birdie's son, the cat's abduction, the will and Clyde's GPS tracking that even I could follow on my phone. I didn't mention the fall I'd taken. I was too embarrassed to admit my butt was throbbing. "I'm on my way to warn Birdie and Theo that if whoever it is gets away from Candace, Theo might be in danger."

"Why don't you just call her house?"

I explained how Birdie's name sure wasn't listed on any of the white pages I'd searched on my phone.

"Did you do a reverse lookup? You have her address, right?"

"I tried that the other day when I was hoping to call her, but nothing came up. Besides, I don't mind getting out. Hanging around your house waiting to hear what's happening with poor Clyde and Emily was only making me anxious."

"I'm not surprised. But do you really need to do this tonight? Can't you wait until Tom and Candace have done their job? I worry about you."

"I can see on the GPS that whoever took Clyde is far from Birdie's place. I'll be fine. If you hear anything on your police scanner, call me. I'm worried about that cat and even more worried Emily will get herself into big trouble. Thank goodness for that tracking collar."

"Tom can track Emily's car, too, right?"

"Yes. He said he'd do both."

"Sounds like Candace and Tom might have someone in lock-up by tonight. Maybe Emily will be locked up, too, if we're lucky."

I could picture Kara's smile and knew she was kidding. I apologized again for hooking her up with Emily in the first place and disconnected.

A few minutes later, I parked in front of Birdie's house and carefully made my way along the rain-slicked cement walkway to her front steps. The last thing I needed was another fall, so I hung on to the railing tightly as I made my way up.

I rang the doorbell and, while waiting, I closed my small umbrella and slid it into the pocket of Kara's raincoat.

No answer.

I tried peeking through the crack in the lace curtains covering the door's window. Lights were on. I rang again and this time I called, "Birdie? Theo? I just need a minute of your time."

Finally, I saw Theo's silhouette through the lace as he approached the door. But he didn't open it. He just pulled the curtain aside and spoke to me through the glass. "My mother is asleep. Can you come back another time?"

Something about his voice—the lack of the assured professorial tenor I'd noticed before—told me something wasn't right.

"Are you okay, Theo?" Perhaps after my last visit his mother had finally told him the truth and he was shaken by the news.

But no. I saw fear in his eyes.

"We're fine," he said loudly. But then he pressed his face closer to the glass and mouthed, "Call 9-1-1."

I reached for my phone and held it up. I also didn't speak, just pointed at the phone and mouthed the word, "Trouble?"

He nodded, but before I could get a finger on the keypad, Theo turned and shouted, "No!"

The door's glass shattered around me when Theo

crashed into it. I dropped my phone. I heard it thud onto the porch floor somewhere behind me.

But what I now saw through the hole in the glass made me forget about my phone.

A jagged circle of blood on the left shoulder of Theo's white shirt was spreading fast.

Too fast.

Thirty

My hammering heart thrummed against my ribs as I crouched on the porch. This position sent a shock wave of pain up my spine. I didn't care.

I have to find my phone. Have to. Where did it go?

"Stop what you're doing this instant, Mrs. Hart," commanded a voice from beyond the broken glass.

That sweet drawl had an edge to it, and I turned to see Millicent Boatman grasping Birdie by the shoulder of her dress and holding a gun to the terrified woman's temple.

I rose to my knees and raised my hands. "Whatever you say. Please don't hurt her."

Millicent shoved Birdie and said, "Roll your son's body away from the door. We surely would enjoy it if Mrs. Hart came in out of the rain and joined us."

I heard Theo say, "I can move, Mama. It's all right."

"But you're bleeding, Son." Poor Birdie sounded as terrified as I felt.

"Don't you two believe for one minute that your fussing after each other will buy Mrs. Hart time to phone the police. I'll shoot her next if she tries anything."

A second later, the door opened just enough for me

to enter. Theo, his shoulder bleeding profusely, sat leaning against the wall.

"All of you march your precious selves into the living room and allow me to reconsider how to deal with the three of you." Millicent waved the gun at me. "You have created quite a dilemma by showing up here."

Theo put his right hand out to me and I pulled him up, the strain of doing so making me catch my breath. We walked down the hall as instructed, and I wished for once that I still had a tracking device on *me*. Kara knew where I was. Candace might, too, but we all believed the danger was with Clyde and Emily.

Not at this house. Not now.

Millicent told us all to sit—but not together. Birdie eased onto the Victorian sofa, but her eyes never left Theo. He took the armchair near the window, his right hand pressed to his bloody shoulder. His face didn't reveal any of the agony he must have surely been experiencing. He wanted to protect his mother by maintaining his composure despite the shooting. His self-control bolstered me. I sat on a padded straight-back chair, refusing to let the pain I felt by the mere act of sitting show on my face, either.

"I suppose," Millicent said more to herself than to us, "that once the police show up here, they will conclude that Jillian Hart was in the wrong place at the wrong time." She smiled. "Oh, this will work well. The Mercy police officers will assume that the drug-dealing ne'er-do-wells came here looking for what Buford owed them. And out of pure spite, they decided to take their revenge on the innocents visiting Miss Birdie tonight." She looked at me. "That sounds like a plan—don't you think?"

"Why are you doing this, Millicent?" I wished I hadn't said anything as soon as the words left my lips.

"What business is it of yours, dear? You believe that because LouAnn thinks you hung the moon or you took in that infernal cat, you have the right to put your nose in our family business?" She glanced at Theo and sneered. "And that includes you, doesn't it?"

"You are *not* my family," he answered.

"Funny you should mention that," Millicent said. "I had the exact same thought. Unfortunately, my brother didn't see things the same way. He decided to hand over far too much of his wealth to you along with his beloved and *stupid* cat. Why? Because he felt *guilty*, that's why."

"You knew what was in his will before Dirk found out today?" I had to keep her talking—perhaps give us all a chance to stop this insane woman from killing us. In an attempt to ease the agony in my lower back, I shifted in the chair and felt the compact umbrella against my thigh. I leaned to my right so it wouldn't press so hard against me.

"Keep still while I think, Jillian." She slipped her hand into the pocket of her dress. I feared it might be another weapon, but she pulled out a phone and tapped the screen with her thumb. She muttered, "I do need help to pull this off. Why hasn't he called me yet?"

Who was she talking about? I didn't know, but she was concerned about taking three lives and staging the scene by herself to make it look like drug dealers had broken in. That meant we might have time to escape or talk her out of all this. But looking at her cold eyes and set jaw, I had serious doubts I could talk her out of anything. I couldn't lose hope, couldn't let the fear that chilled me to the marrow take over.

She stared back at me. "You're such a well-known cat lover. How long would it take to drown Clyde?" Her sugary tone as she made this threat made me want to vomit.

I closed my eyes briefly, determined not to let her bait me. She had help from whoever had taken Clyde— from the person Candace could be arresting this very minute. The endgame was to get hold of Mr. Jeffrey's money. But why use such desperate measures? Why all the killing?

I briefly looked at Theo when she checked her phone again. His face had paled and his golden eyes looked as if they were glazing over. He'd lost too much blood. I had to do something. But how could I stop this woman?

Two could play the baiting game, I decided. "You knew the money would go to Theo because your brother couldn't stand you, could he? My only question is why would he ever let a person like you take his cat?"

I saw color rise on her throat and reach her cheeks. I'd gotten to her. "*A person like me?* What is that supposed to mean? I was nothing but good to my brother and he then tells me he's leaving his money to a damn cat? I *need* that money."

She came closer as she said this, the gun leading the way. I gripped the sides of the chair and realized the umbrella handle was right by my hand.

Without another thought, I whipped it out and swung hard, striking her wrist with a thwack. She screamed in pain and the gun toppled to the floor. But before I could get up, she was already scrambling after it.

That was when Birdie, every generous, beautiful pound of her, landed on top of Millicent, pressing her facedown on the wood floor.

I rose quickly, not caring how much it hurt—and oh, did it hurt. I grabbed the gun.

We all ignored Millicent's muffled cries.

Birdie adjusted her knee into the middle of Millicent's back and pinned both her wrists to the floor with her two chubby but strong hands. "Take care of my son, Miss Jillian. I got this witch."

I took several steps in Theo's direction, but he was pointing at the telephone on the stand in the hallway to my right. In a rasp that frightened me more than the gun I now held, he said, "Call for help."

As Birdie, the same woman I'd once helped upstairs and believed to be a frail arthritic, continued to keep Millicent contained, I made the call. Then I hurried to the kitchen for towels and ice, which I hoped would help stop the bleeding. I held on to the gun and used my free hand to wrap a frozen bag of peas in a dishcloth. When I pressed it to Theo's wound, he only nodded his thanks. He was fading.

The sound of sirens approaching couldn't have taken more than two minutes. The first person through the door was fireman and good friend Billy Cranor. Billy said, "You want to hand me that, Jillian?" He nodded at the weapon. "Real easy. Point the barrel down."

I'd never let go of the gun and was pointing it at Millicent. I vaguely recalled telling her not to move or I'd shoot her. Thank goodness she believed me and stayed still, because I could never have pulled the trigger.

Marcy and Jake, two paramedics I also knew well, came rushing in right after Billy took the gun from me and unloaded it. Only then did he take over for Birdie to restrain Millicent.

As Marcy and Jake assessed Theo, I helped Birdie get up. My fireman hero was now holding down a ranting Millicent with plenty of force.

Birdie went straight for Theo, but Jake held up a hand. "Please, ma'am. Help him by letting us do our job."

"Yes, sir. Most certainly." She slumped into the chair I'd vacated, tears streaming down her face.

Lois arrived seconds later. I do believe I have never been so happy to see a pair of handcuffs in my life. After securing Millicent's hands behind her back with Billy's help, she lifted the woman off the floor like a rag doll and read her the Miranda rights. "Now march your ass into the dining room and sit yourself down." Lois pushed the woman in the back to encourage her.

As she passed us, Millicent turned her venom on Birdie. "This is your fault. It's all on *you*."

"If I were you, ma'am, I'd be thinking real hard about my right to remain silent. Keep moving."

Once Millicent and her personal police escort left the room, I felt like I could breathe again. Billy stood guarding the gun that now sat on an end table. It would have to be bagged as evidence. He was well versed in police procedure and understood the less it was handled, the better. No one would be getting near that thing and if I never saw it again, it would be too soon.

We watched as the paramedics set up an IV and placed oxygen cannulas in Theo's nose. The oxygen seemed to bother Birdie more than the blood that had soaked through the pressure dressing Marcy had taped onto Theo's shoulder.

She bowed her head. "Dear Lord in heaven, I don't ask you for much. I'm asking now. Please save my son."

I rubbed circles on Birdie's back and she reached back and gripped my hand tightly. They had just put Theo on the stretcher when Kara burst into the room, looking frantic.

"Jillian, what's going on here? Are you okay? When I heard the police scanner go off with this address, I freaked. Especially when B.J. said GSW."

Thanks to Tom, I understood that GSW stood for gunshot wound, but I hoped the reference went over Birdie's head. She was upset enough already.

But clearly not too upset to tell Kara, "Your stepmama done right fine by us, Miss Kara. You got lots to be proud of."

"You didn't do so bad yourself," I said. "Are you a secret ninja?"

Birdie smiled a bit, but I could tell her thoughts were with her son.

Marcy said, "Mrs. Roberts, do you drive? You can follow us to the hospital."

She stood, her gaze intent on Theo. His eyes were closed and I assumed they'd given him pain medicine. "I can't ride with him? Make sure he's okay?"

"Sorry, ma'am. But you can stay close behind us. We'll be working on him all the way to the hospital, but we need to move fast." They began wheeling the stretcher into the narrow hall and it was a miracle the thing fit around the corners of the old house.

"Wait," Birdie said. "I have to find my keys. And the car is in the back in the garage and—"

Kara took Birdie's hand. "I'll drive you." Kara looked at me. "You want to come, too?"

"I believe I'll need to give a statement to the officer waiting in the dining room to transport her *suspect*. Although there is no doubt this suspect will be convicted of what she did tonight."

Kara's eyes widened and she whispered, "Who is it?"

"The high-and-mighty Millicent Boatman." Birdie, her eyes misting, didn't bother keeping her voice down. "I will gladly take you up on your offer, Miss Kara. I doubt if I could get my car out of the garage, my hands are shaking so. But can we hurry? My son needs me."

They followed the stretcher out of the house and I wondered what officer would come to help Lois transport a prisoner she certainly didn't want to haul off alone. Candace probably still had her hands full rounding up Millicent's accomplice. My question was answered when Morris arrived, looking like he'd been asleep when the call for help came in.

He nodded at me and Billy, and I pointed toward the dining room. "They're in there."

Tucking the tail of his uniform shirt in at the back, he went in the direction I indicated. Over his shoulder he said, "Tom picked me up so me and Lois can take her squad car to haul this idiot off to jail. Seems Tom and Candace have had a night of it, too. He'll be right in."

When Morris disappeared, Billy said, "What in the heck is this all about, Jillian?"

"In a word, greed. But I don't have all the answers and I'm not sure anyone will until—"

Tom walked in, carrying Clyde. If my backside could have taken one more round of torture, I might have collapsed on the chair in relief.

He wrapped his arms around me with Clyde between us. "I am not letting you out of my sight for the rest of our lives." He rested his forehead against mine.

Clyde apparently wasn't thrilled being squished between us. He struggled to free himself, jumped down and headed straight for the chair where Theo had been sitting. Blood dripped from a spot on the left arm of the chair. Clyde sniffed at it before leaping onto its seat. He put one huge paw on the blood and sat staring at me like a sentry. The blood belonged to someone he'd traveled two hundred miles to find.

See, Clyde had finally found a small part of Mr. Jeffrey here.

I blinked back tears and Tom pulled me to him again.

Thirty-one

Once Morris bagged the gun, took pictures of the broken front door and collected the spent shell casing in the hall, they took Millicent out to the squad car. He gave Billy a roll of crime scene tape and asked him to do the honors before they left. Billy said he'd take a few minutes and find a temporary fix for the broken window and we left him to that task, Clyde held tightly in Tom's arms.

Morris told me I could give my statement at the station, but I had a million questions swarming around in my head. I wanted answers right now. But getting Millicent out of this house was more important.

If we hadn't had two vehicles, Tom could have filled me in on his part of tonight's adventures in crime. As we walked out to the porch, the pink protective case on my phone almost glowed in the dark. Why couldn't I have found that thing when I needed it?

I tried to stoop to pick it up and cried out when my rear end seized up in protest.

Tom stood on the top step and swiftly turned when I yelped in pain. "What's wrong, Jilly? Did that woman hurt you?"

"Long story. It happened earlier. Would you mind picking up my phone? Gosh, I needed it when Theo was shot. And oh, how I wish I could pull up my cat cam and see my fur friends right now."

"I'll have that fixed as soon as possible. You want Clyde to ride with you? That might help."

"I could sure use his company for the next few minutes." Soon, Clyde sat on the van's passenger seat. He studied me in the glow of the streetlight with what seemed like concern, an interesting addition to his usual smile. Such a great cat. I sure hoped Theo would recover quickly—and he *had* to be okay. He would. I just felt it. I remembered then that Birdie told me Theo already had a cat. Clyde belonged to Theo now and I was glad he would not be an only "child." From how quickly he'd bonded with my three, that was perfect.

I drove almost at a snail's pace, hoping to avoid a bumpy ride. Tom had to slow down several times, I guess keeping his promise to not let me out of his sight. The unhurried ride also ensured that we wouldn't run into Millicent during her walk into the interrogation room.

Thank goodness we went around back to the jail entrance where there was an elevator. I had only two steps to climb rather than the dozen that led up to the courthouse entrance. I clutched Clyde close as we headed down the musty hall leading to the elevator. Tom pushed open a door that said AUTHORIZED PERSONNEL ONLY.

An officer I didn't know sat behind a desk and beyond him were the holding cells. The man waved at Tom. "Need this guy upstairs again?" He nodded back toward the cells.

"Nope. Just making sure he's where he's supposed to be. Check it out, Jilly. There's your vandal, your killer, your liar, your catnapper, your all-around jerk."

Wayne Jeffrey sat in a cell, his back against the wall,

fingers laced behind his neck. He didn't acknowledge us in any way and I was grateful.

Appropriately, Clyde hissed and Tom quickly shut the door.

The big boy had dug his claws into my arm but released them as we moved on. I'd been scratched and clawed plenty of times and he'd actually not dug in all the way. It was no big deal compared to the pain from my fall.

I said, "Thank goodness Dirk wasn't the killer. After Emily's visit tonight to Kara's house and all she told me, I was worried he might have been lying to us all along."

"He did lie about one other thing. Apparently Mr. Jeffrey gave Clyde to *Dirk*. He told Dirk it was a temporary arrangement and that Dirk would understand in good time. But Millicent Boatman insisted on taking the cat, telling Dirk that Clyde would be better off with her because he was too busy with work to care for a pet. A few days later, Clyde disappeared. I'll bet Millicent and Wayne never counted on that cat traveling all the way back to his home."

"So she let Clyde out on purpose—because he was an obstacle to money she wanted?"

We stopped at the elevator and Tom stabbed the button. "I'm guessing as much. She probably thought he was long gone. See, Wayne told us plenty. He's decided it's in his best interest to cooperate in hopes of a plea deal now that he's been caught red-handed—caught partly thanks to GPS technology he thought he was using for *his* benefit."

As the elevator arrived, I asked, "What does that mean?"

"We made an assumption—and I should have known better. I've been away from the job too long and broke a cardinal cop rule: Never assume. Emily didn't put that GPS slap-and-go on your car. *Wayne did*. He's a pretty tech-savvy guy, does electrical contract work. When we switched the device to Emily's car, he didn't even realize he was tracking *her* rather than you. She was on your tail so much, it made no difference—until she made it to Kara's house. When she arrived there, he was quite pleased he'd found you and Clyde."

The elevator car lurched to a halt and I squeezed my eyes shut. Every little unexpected movement seemed to hurt. Clyde nuzzled my neck and I decided he could get a job as a therapy cat, given that he was that intuitive.

Tom didn't need to hear any words. He was pretty intuitive himself. "Jilly, please tell me what happened. I'm worried."

"I'll be okay."

"Come on. We're about to share our lives and you know you can trust me with anything." He took my elbow and helped me off the elevator.

As we walked to the police offices, I relented and explained about my fall. "But don't say anything. I feel so foolish."

"I won't say a word—until I take you to the doctor so you can get this checked out."

"Tomorrow, please? I might feel better after a good night's sleep."

"Okay, tomorrow." He opened the door to the Mercy PD waiting area. Emily, looking like the proverbial drowned rat, sat huddled in the corner with a concerned-looking Dirk.

She jumped up when she saw us and ran to hug me. Thank goodness I held Clyde and this stopped her. So she gripped my upper arms and squeezed. "Thank goodness you're okay."

I wondered what part she'd played in Wayne's takedown. Or how they'd taken him down *in spite of her* might be a better question. But these were only two of my many questions. The most pressing issue right now was whether I could sit long enough to give my statement about the events at Birdie's house.

"I am so sorry I took off like I did, Jillian." Emily sounded contrite.

"You should be." Tom didn't hide his irritation.

He turned to talk to B.J., who sat at the dispatcher desk. From his obviously unintentional bedhead hairstyle and red-rimmed eyes, I guessed he'd been called in to work tonight just as Morris had.

Emily lowered her voice. "Tom's pretty mad at me for leading that despicable man to Kara's house. But you guys are the ones who put that tracker on my car."

"Sorry about the GPS thing, but we thought you put it on *my* car."

She grinned. "Oh, wow. That's too funny. Makes sense you'd stick it under my bumper. I'd probably do the same thing if our roles were reversed."

"It's all behind us now," I said. "I'm just relieved you're all right. What happened when you left Kara's house?"

"I followed the guy to a boat launch dock at Mercy Lake. He spotted me, even though I killed my lights and thought he couldn't see me. Guess I have a lot to learn when it comes to criminals. If Candace and Tom hadn't shown up right then, I might have ended up at the bottom of the lake—which is where he intended to put poor Clyde."

Dirk, who'd been sitting quietly gnawing on a cuticle, said, "Would you mind if I petted Clyde?"

"Do you want to hold him?" I shuffled toward him. "Be careful, though. You know how he likes to roam." I smiled and Dirk managed to return a half grin.

Clyde's purr came almost instantly when Dirk took the cat in his arms. He buried his face in orange fur and mumbled, "I am so sorry, Clyde."

Everyone was full of apologies tonight. But I had the

feeling Wayne and Millicent didn't have any regrets aside from getting caught.

Candace appeared in the hallway. I was so glad to see her, my smile almost hurt, too.

She blinked hard and I could have sworn she was about to cry. But she quickly regained her composure. "I should have never told you to talk to Birdie, but if I hadn't, this wouldn't have turned into a victory. Thank you, lady. And now, I want to hear what happened tonight right from the horse's mouth." She waved me through the swinging gate.

I asked Dirk if he'd hang on to Clyde and he happily agreed.

As we walked down the hall, I said, "Is she here?" I nodded to the closed door of one of the interrogation rooms.

"Yup. Waiting on a public defender, but since we have only two for the whole county, that'll take a good long while. Morris will be taking her down to the holding cells in a minute."

I took my time as Candace led me to the chief's office and of course she noticed.

She opened the office door. "You hurt, Jillian?"

"Took a spill earlier. No big deal—but if I could sit in the boss's chair, I'd sure appreciate it."

That's how I ended up behind Chief Baca's desk with Candace and her legal pad across from me. It was the most comfortable I'd felt since all the trouble started.

She said, "You should know that Wayne Jeffrey has spilled his guts, so we know the whole convoluted story. What a sorry two Millicent and Wayne are. I mean, seniors are supposed to be sweet and gentle and wise. Not them. No way."

"Can you fill me in? Because Millicent said a few things to me back at Birdie's house—like how she needed money. But not much else. And here I thought she was well-off."

"She is flat broke. About to lose her fancy house. And she and Mr. Jeffrey were far from a loving brother and sister. Mr. Jeffrey despised her lavish lifestyle and was angry that she refused to follow his advice about her finances. They were estranged and that's why she never came here to Mercy to visit. But she was friendly with Wayne. When he told her that he'd had a blowup with Mr. Jeffrey about a loan and confided that both he *and* Millicent were about to be cut out of the will, the two of them concocted a plan."

"So," I said, "they murdered Mr. Jeffrey before he could change the will?"

Candace fiddled with the pencil in front of her, spinning it one way and then the other. "Nope, though they planned to. Thing is, Buford heard the whole argument between Wayne and Mr. Jeffrey. When the old guy immediately called up his attorney, Buford considered this an opportunity to maybe make a few bucks. He called Wayne up and asked for money and in exchange he'd give Wayne inside information concerning Mr. Jeffrey's actions. When Buford was recruited to witness the new will, Wayne probably felt like everything was lining up just right."

I said, "Wait a minute. Buford figured Wayne could pay him for information after he'd just ask Mr. Jeffrey for a loan? That doesn't make sense."

"I told you it was complicated. Let's take this step by step. Wayne was furious once he learned about the change. Tonight he told me his idea was to kill the old man just for spite. But Millicent talked him out of it. She convinced him there might still be time to get Mr. Jeffrey to change the will back to the way it was."

I closed my eyes. "Figures. She is such a manipulator."

"Their original plan was to eliminate poor Clyde first and then get rid of a completely unsuspecting Theo. See, Millicent was certain she could talk Dirk into sharing how much money was involved—because Dirk was next in line once the cat and Theo were out of the way. Like you said, she's a manipulator and knew how to get Dirk to talk. Her first task was to convince him to give her Clyde. For some dumb reason, he agreed. Wayne said Millicent planned to take a boat out and throw the cat in the ocean, but Clyde knew what was about to happen and scratched her up pretty good the minute they walked out the door. He escaped. She and Wayne figured it was fine, that Clyde was out of the picture and that's all that mattered. Then the waiting began—for Mr. Jeffrey to go downhill. Once he was near the end, Theo would have a subway accident or become a tragic victim of a mugging gone wrong way up north in New York City. But a couple months passed and Buford got antsy. See, Wayne convinced him he'd be paid for everything he told them about Mr. Jeffrey, his will, his activities, and how soon he might succumb to the cancer. The cat was taken care of, but Theo would have to have his little accident before Mr. Jeffrey died or his 'accident' might draw unwanted scrutiny. So Buford was told he would have to wait for his payday until the poor man died."

I said, "I get it now. Buford became their inside man."

"Right. An impatient and untrustworthy inside man. In other words, their criminal conspirator."

"Pretty foolish of Wayne and Millicent to trust a druggie." I shifted my weight, wishing I had a cloud to sit on. "Do you have an aspirin by chance?"

"The drawer to your left. Chief Baca has a little first aid kit in there." She stood. "Let me get you some water." She left the room briefly and returned with a bottle. Two aspirins and several healthy swigs of water later

I said, "Okay, did Buford get antsy because he was being pressured?"

"Oh yes. Remember those drugs and the gun we found?"

"Uh-huh."

"Seems the folks he was doing business with wanted their money from the cocaine he'd been selling for them. Trouble was, he had spent everything he'd earned and though he offered to give them back what was left of their product, they told him he'd better sell what was left for twice as much. Otherwise, he was a dead man."

"Turned out he was a dead man anyway," I said. "Did the drug dealers kill Buford, then?"

"Nope. Here's where everything turned upside down for Millicent and Wayne. Buford overdosed Mr. Jeffrey, thinking it would be considered a natural death—or even a suicide. He thought Millicent and Wayne would be thrilled and pay him handsomely for getting rid of Mr. Jeffrey—and of course Buford would get the cash they owed him right away. He was wrong. They were furious, worried Mr. Jeffrey's death would look suspicious since he still had months to live. Buford messed everything up."

"So *they* killed him," I said softly.

She nodded. "Wayne copped to that murder. Buford demanded money and said he'd implicate Wayne and Millicent for conspiracy if they didn't come up with cash right away. Seems Buford had been smart enough to tape his conversations with Wayne about taking out Theo—but not smart enough to know he was dealing with people far more evil than he was."

I sighed. "It all makes sense now. Or at least I understand—because killing people for money will never make sense. What's scary is that if Buford hadn't messed things up, they could have gotten away with murdering Theo. And it's no wonder they were after Clyde. Bet they never planned on a cat traveling all that way to return to his true home."

Candace smiled. "I guess Clyde helped solve this just by being so determined to get home."

"He's a smart boy," I said.

Candace straightened the legal pad in front of her and poised her pencil over the paper. "Now, I've heard secondhand what happened at Birdie's house, thanks to Morris and Lois, but I need to hear it from you."

So I told her everything, including how we'd made a mistake ourselves by thinking the GPS tracker had been Emily's doing. And what a fortuitous mistake it had been.

Thirty-two

I awoke the next morning in Kara's guest bedroom to see strips of sunshine coming through the blinds. The rain had swept through overnight. Four cats surrounded me, but Pulitzer and Prize were nowhere in sight. They were probably happy to be hanging out with Kara. Chablis was curled up next to me. Her usual spot in the morning was on my chest, but since I couldn't lie on my back, she was happy to accommodate me. Clyde, Tom and I had returned to Kara's house after I gave my statement, while Kara went to the newspaper office to write her story for the *Messenger*. Tom checked all the doors and windows and then set the alarm system before he tucked me into bed. I could tell he was still beating himself up over the break-in at my house. Even though the bad guys were locked up, he apparently didn't want to take any chances. He said I could find him on the couch if I needed anything.

A glass of water sat on the bedside table along with the Motrin bottle—courtesy of either Kara or Tom. I sat up carefully and took another pill. I plumped my pillow and lay back down to give the medicine time to work.

I still had questions that hadn't been completely answered last night. I understood that Millicent probably manipulated Dirk into letting her keep Clyde. But why didn't he know just how awful his mother was? I mean, he'd grown up with her, lived with her for years. When I'd taken Clyde from his arms last night, he'd seemed so devastated by what had happened, I understood it was not the time to question his decisions concerning her.

Maybe I could talk to him soon, but I wanted to get out of this bed and check on Theo. I was concerned about Birdie, too, worried about how she'd fared after getting so physical taking Millicent down. Was she as achy as I felt?

I moved Chablis out of the way and eased out of bed. The information we got last night about Theo was that he had been in shock by the time he'd arrived at the county hospital. The good news was they'd stabilized him quickly and he then went to surgery to have the bullet removed.

After a long shower that did wonders for my back, I made my way to the kitchen.

Kara sat at the breakfast bar with her coffee and smiled at me. "Tom went home to shower and change. Cats are fed and now they're frisky."

As if on cue, Syrah raced out of the mudroom and tore by me, with Clyde on his heels. Merlot followed at a much more leisurely pace. Meanwhile, Pulitzer and Prize wrestled on the living room floor. Chablis was the only one who was by no means frisky. She was sunning herself in the bay window overlooking Kara's huge backyard.

"Where will you be most comfortable sitting?" Kara had slid off the stool and was headed for the coffeepot.

"That's a good question. How about nowhere? I'll stand around for the next week or so."

"Coffee?" But she was already pouring me a cup.

I leaned on the counter and watched her fix it just how I liked it. She put the mug in front of me and lifted

a copy of today's *Mercy Messenger*. The headline read
TWO WOMEN DISARM ASSAILANT.

"You went with that?" I laughed. "Good thing it's all
written down for me to read later because this morning,
how it all happened is pretty fuzzy. I only know I never
want to cross Birdie. That lady is fierce."

"I checked on her and Theo—I know a friend who
works at the hospital. No details because of confidenti-
ality issues, but apparently Theo is doing fine. He's not
even in ICU."

"That's great news. What a bad day for that poor man
yesterday. First he finds out who his father is and that he
will never get to meet him. Then the aunt he never knew
about nearly kills him. Did you hear anything about
Birdie? Did she stay with Theo last night?"

"They have recliners for relatives to spend the night
and my friend tells me she never considered leaving his
side. Maybe we can convince her she needs to get better
rest than what a hospital recliner provides. Theo will be
home soon and he'll need his mom. Bet she'll be a wonderful nurse to him."

"Can we head over to the hospital today? You've got
your big story written and—oh, that reminds me. Will
Emily get *her* big story?"

Kara smiled. "Read the byline."

Emily Nguyen had her name in print, sharing the byline with Kara.

She went on. "She came over to the newspaper office
after she left the police station. She apologized, felt she
was responsible for causing all sorts of trouble for you
and me and I guess the entire world. I offered her a
chance to prove she could be more responsible. We
wrote the piece together and it's already been picked
up by the AP. She now has her toe in the door. But, I
have to say, I sure will be happy to see her pursue her
dream elsewhere."

I laughed. "Me, too."

"Breakfast? You know I'm still learning how to really use this kitchen, but I can scramble eggs and toast bread."

I rubbed my tummy. "The Motrin seems to have upset my stomach. Maybe toast—and though I'd love this coffee, I'd better wait until my tummy settles down."

We spent the rest of the morning playing with the cats and talking about what had been put on the back burner for the last week—my engagement. I told Kara that Tom would be selling his house and moving into mine with Finn. But though she pressed me, I couldn't give her a timeline. Tom and I still hadn't told his family we were getting married.

Around noon, Tom showed up with Dirk in tow.

What was this about? I wondered.

They refused the coffee Kara offered and took her up on her offer to sit in the living room. Before I had an answer to why Dirk was with Tom, my fiancé had a question for me—probably because I was still standing.

"When's your doctor's appointment, Jilly?"

"I didn't make one. I feel a lot better today. I probably bruised my tailbone and it will just take time to heal." I may not have felt *a lot* better, but I did believe what I said about the tailbone.

"But if it's not better in a couple days, promise me you'll make that appointment?"

"Deal." I eased down into the wing chair by the fireplace.

"Did you get injured in the fight with my mother last night?" Dirk asked.

"No, I took a spill. Don't worry about it."

"But she held you at gunpoint. She shot Theo Roberts. She helped murder my uncle Norm." He looked so upset—just as he had last night—but it was Clyde to the rescue again. He sauntered into the living room from wherever he'd been napping and immediately rubbed up against Dirk's black khakis, leaving a generous amount of orange tabby hair behind.

Dirk almost smiled and scratched Clyde between his ears. "I want to visit Theo. He needs an explanation. You have a bond with his mother, and I was hoping you'd go with me and convince her to let me talk to him."

"Today?" I said. "Can it wait?"

"The funeral for his father is tomorrow. I want to speak with him about my uncle Norm before he's laid to rest. The terms of the will tell everyone just how much Theo meant to him—and how much he trusted him since that's where he wants Clyde to live. He should hear that as soon as possible—and from a member of his family. I just wish my uncle had told me about Theo before he died. I never saw the will until I read it along with Deputy Carson and Tom."

"I have a question that's been bothering me, Dirk," I said. "Your uncle didn't care for your mother—something you probably knew all along. Why did you let her take Clyde when Mr. Jeffrey wanted you to care for the cat?"

"Just stupid, I guess. I know my mother's faults. But did I know she'd do something criminal? Did I believe she'd harm Clyde? Maybe I was deluded, but I figured she was being kind when she said Clyde shouldn't spend his days alone while I was at work. She said she could take care of him and I believed her. Obviously, I was wrong—wrong about everything." He hung his head momentarily and then looked up at me again. "I'll be candid. I owe you that much. My mother has lied and connived from as far back as I can remember. I never gave up the hope that she'd change—until now."

He stared down again, but not before I saw his eyes glisten with tears. No matter how terrible a person a mother is, the children always want to believe in her. I totally understood where he was coming from.

"Your mother was in deep financial trouble," Tom said. "Her bank and credit card statements came through yesterday. Deputy Carson and I were ready to bring her back in and question her further—but that's when all hell broke loose in Mercy."

"I didn't know, but I'm not surprised," Dirk said. "Her spending was out of control. But back to Theo and his mother. It might make their situation a little easier if they knew my uncle wanted them to be taken care of for the rest of their lives."

Tom pulled a business-size white envelope from his shirt pocket. "We found this in the safe-deposit box. It's addressed to Birdie. We'd like to give it to her."

Kara said, "You sure you're up for a hospital visit, Jillian?"

"Absolutely, especially now that I understand why we need to go today. But only if I can talk to Birdie in private first and make certain she wants to talk to Dirk."

He nodded. "I'm fine with that."

"I don't want Birdie to think I'll be listening in, ready to report on her private affairs," Kara said. "I'll stay here and play with the cats."

A trip to the hospital felt like the right thing to do. Now, to find a pillow that would make the thirty-minute drive bearable.

As it turned out, Kara had a wonderful memory foam pillow that became my new best friend on the trip. I was sure it would be my constant companion in the days ahead.

Theo's room was on the fourth floor. As I requested, Tom and Dirk stayed in a waiting area by the elevators while I went down the hallway and found Birdie sitting by her son's bed. I guess I'd expected to see Theo with tubes everywhere, maybe a unit of blood hanging from a pole by his bed, but it was nothing like that.

His eyes, clouded by pain and shock last night, had

returned to their sparkling green-gold color. An IV still gave him fluids and his shoulder was bandaged with his arm secured against his chest, but that was it.

"My hero has arrived." He reached out with his free hand and patted his mother's arm. "My other hero, I should say."

Birdie rose and though she was obviously tired, she had less fatigue in her step than I'd anticipated. She gave me a monstrous hug and kissed my cheek. "Nope, Theo. It's all this lady right here. She's the one who saved your life."

He gave me a warm smile.

"Come on and sit with us a spell," Birdie said. "They got a little kitchen across the hall with juice and soft drinks. Can I get you anything?"

"Nothing for me. I do have a request, though."

"Anything, Miss Jillian."

"Dirk Boatman wants to meet Theo, and my friend Tom has something to give you, Birdie."

I couldn't read her face, but she didn't respond.

Theo said, "I'd like to meet Dirk. From what Deputy Carson told me when she came by this morning, he had no knowledge of what his mother and his uncle were up to aside from allowing his mother to take Clyde without Mr. Jeffrey—I mean, *my father*, knowing."

"That's true." I glanced at Birdie and could tell she wasn't as forgiving. "Birdie, Dirk's devastated by what happened. He couldn't fathom that his mother would end up behaving so heinously."

"You're saying the man is feeling what his mother isn't capable of? She's one reason I never did marry Norman. She and Ida Lynn talked so mean all the time. I never wanted my child raised anywhere near such poison."

"My mother needs this meeting as much as I do," Theo said. "I welcome his visit."

Birdie nodded at me. "Okay. Go on and fetch them. My son needs to know he has kin who have good intentions."

A few minutes later, Tom and Dirk walked into the room after me. After Dirk introduced himself, he pulled a chair up next to Theo's bed.

But when he began apologizing for his mother, Theo stopped him by raising his free hand. "I don't care about her. I want to know you—because I always wanted a brother and at my age, you're about as close as I'll ever get."

Birdie laughed. "You got that right. My oven shut down a century ago."

We all joined her in that laughter.

Then the conversation began—two gentle, intelligent men in their forties catching up on the decades they'd missed together. When football became the most passionate topic among the three guys in the room and I was tired of standing, I motioned for Birdie to follow me.

"Can you show me where those drinks are?" I asked when we were out of the room.

"Sure I can, but did you hurt yourself in that scuffle last night. I see pain in your eyes."

As she led me to the kitchenette, I explained how I'd fallen earlier last evening and assured her I'd be fine.

I chose water and Birdie took an apple juice. We walked down the hall and I was glad to get my muscles moving. I wished I'd brought Kara's magic pillow into the hospital with me.

"Men don't get to the point as quickly as women, so I need to ask you a couple questions. First, did Candace explain about Mr. Jeffrey's will?"

"She did. I always knew Norman did well—he was such a smart man. But I was surprised to learn about that million dollars. Honestly, I don't know why anyone needs so much money, but Theo will put it to good use. I'm thinking future college students will benefit."

"I'll bet he left you money, too." I unscrewed the cap on my water and took a long swig.

"Honey, that man has provided for Theo and me all these years. Why he had to go and add on more is beyond me."

"Was it you or Mr. Jeffrey who decided to keep Theo's paternity a secret?"

"That was my doing. Like I said, I didn't want my boy around Norman's family—and didn't want gossip about Norman and me, neither. He would have married me—he begged me in fact—but a black woman and a white man back then was cause for trouble. Still is for some folks, though we've come a long way."

"Thanks for explaining. My other question is about Clyde. You do know that Mr. Jeffrey wanted him to have a home with Theo?"

"Oh, Theo is pleased as punch. I think I mentioned he has a cat back there in New York City. My son is a bigger animal lover than I ever was. Every time I see Theo loving on his cat, I think, 'There's the Norman in him.' They shared a passion for numbers and for cats."

I breathed a sigh of relief, remembering Clyde's paw on that spot of Theo's blood.

"That eases my mind. Clyde is a special boy, and I am so glad he'll have a loving home and have a part of his beloved Mr. Jeffrey with him from now on."

"Things work out as they should quite often—don't you think?"

I had to agree.

Thirty-three

The next day, with my rump feeling far better, Tom, Kara, Candace and the remaining members of Mr. Jeffrey's family attended his funeral. But I was surprised that a reclusive man drew such a big turnout of Mercy citizens—until one after another, people spoke about the man's philanthropy. The Mercy Animal Sanctuary, the YMCA, the Red Cross, the local hospice, and scout troops had all received generous donations from Norman Jeffrey over the years—but they had been sworn to secrecy. He'd told them, they all recounted, that he couldn't control what they said after he was gone. If they wanted to speak, he couldn't stop them. Shawn and Allison Cuddahee showed up, too, and Allison talked about how much Mr. Jeffrey loved each and every cat that he'd been privileged to own—and everyone had a laugh when she said that every one of them had been named Clyde.

As we were leaving the cemetery, I caught a glimpse of Birdie by Mr. Jeffrey's grave, her head bowed in prayer. She held a piece of paper in her hands and fiddled with it nervously. This was probably the letter from Mr. Jeffrey that Tom had given to her yesterday. I was certain she would never share what he wrote to her, and that was as it should be. Two people who were meant to be together had instead spent their lives apart. I wasn't sure I would ever understand, despite Birdie's explanation.

The church organized a potluck lunch after the funeral. There was enough fried chicken, ribs, pulled pork, potato salad, coleslaw, macaroni and cheese, baked beans and fresh rolls to feed an army. Dirk, LouAnn and Ida Lynn had been huddled together for most of the day, but once we were in that basement community room, it was time to offer my condolences to them as a family. They'd not only lost a cousin and uncle; they'd lost Wayne and Millicent, too.

I filled a plate and made my way to their table. Dirk stood and LouAnn smiled up at me. She'd had her hair professionally cut and colored an attractive silver, and I couldn't help but notice she looked very much like Millicent—though a much kinder, gentler version.

Ida Lynn spoke up when I approached the family. "Will you break bread with us, Jillian?" She was dressed in a black vintage suit, which should have been appropriate. But the hat she wore had long, thin feathers that flashed around, and she had on elbow length black gloves and a mesh veil that covered half her face. It was flamboyant for a funeral, but I guess Ida Lynn had to be true to herself.

I put my plate down on the table and pulled out the folding chair. Sitting was easier than two days ago, but I still took it slow. "I wanted to again offer my condolences to all of you over losing Mr. Jeffrey. Today revealed a side to him that we didn't realize existed. He will be missed by the community."

"We used to play cards when I'd visit," Dirk said. "I'll miss those talks we had over gin rummy." He stared down at his uneaten food.

LouAnn patted his arm. "I hope you'll keep visiting us in Mercy. I can play gin rummy, you know."

He smiled at her and picked up his fork. "I'd like that."

"We all played cards together when we were children," Ida Lynn said. "I could join you."

LouAnn and Dirk stared at Ida Lynn as if she'd spoken to them in a foreign language. But after a beat, they smiled and nodded.

Maybe she was speaking a foreign language, I thought, *but I liked it.* I dug in to my mound of mustard potato salad. Why was funeral food always so delicious? Maybe because loving hands took part in its creation.

We all ate in silence for a moment, and then I was surprised to look up and see Birdie standing at the table, her eyes fixed on Ida Lynn. Dirk stood immediately and offered her a chair.

"Thank you, Mr. Dirk, but I have to be getting back to the hospital. I did want to pay my respects to your family—to Norman's family."

"How is your son?" LouAnn asked.

"He's fine. He'll be coming to stay with me to recover starting tomorrow. His name is Theo, by the way. And no matter how much it bothers you, he does have your family blood. All I ask is that you respect him."

Ida Lynn did the most unexpected thing. She stood, walked around the table and embraced Birdie. When she pulled away, she said, "I apologize for my past behavior and I apologize for the people not here, who harmed Norm and who harmed your son."

LouAnn nodded. "Theo isn't the only one who is family. You are, too."

Tears welled in Birdie's eyes. "There is a forgotten soul in all this. Before you hear it on the street, I have made arrangements for Buford Miller's burial. He was an instrument of the devil, as my pastor would say, but I forgive him. I hope all of you can, too." She looked at me and smiled. "This here is our guardian angel. Don't you ever forget what she's gone and done for all of you."

Before anyone could speak, Birdie turned and left the church hall. She was a proud woman and perhaps one of the strongest people I'd ever met.

She hadn't seen the last of me.

Thirty-four

Clyde hadn't exactly enjoyed the bath I'd given him, but today he was traveling to New York to begin his new life. My new security system had been up and running since right after the funeral and I'd been glad to return home with the cats. Theo had come by and visited with Clyde several times in the last few weeks as he recovered his strength.

It was a big day for me, too. Tom's mother, Karen, her partner, Ed, as well as Kara, Liam, Tom's stepson, Finn, and Candace were all sitting on my deck enjoying one another's company. Since there was wine and beer involved, I heard plenty of laughter coming from outside.

Tom had helped me bathe Clyde while Syrah, Merlot and Chablis watched. If cats can gloat, my three gloated, glad Clyde was the one suffering through this torture rather than any of them. After we dried the big boy with a towel, I put his GPS collar back on and let him run off. The three amigos chased him, wanting a sniff of Clyde's shampoo.

Theo and Birdie arrived five minutes later, just as I was putting a vegan cake in the oven. I had to be careful about Kara's diet these days—it seemed to change with the weather—and a vegan cake was the safest option. Tom had finished filling a tote with the treats and toys and food I'd learned Clyde enjoyed the most.

Tom took the carrier Theo brought and set it in the middle of the living room. I lined it with the kitty quilt Clyde had used during his stay and Birdie eyed it with admiration.

"You make pretty quilts, Miss Jillian. Got to give you that."

"Thanks, Birdie," I said.

Tom looked at Clyde, who was already examining the carrier. "We thought we'd let Clyde get used to the thing before—"

But he walked into it, circled and sat down. He wasn't wasting any time. That was Clyde—affable and adaptable. What good traits to have. I knelt and rubbed his cheek with the back of my hand and heard his rumbling purr one more time. I blinked back the tears that threatened. "Good-bye, friend," I whispered.

After I stood and backed away, Theo reached in and scratched Clyde's head before latching the door. "My plane leaves from Charlotte—had to get a nonstop so Clyde wouldn't have to change planes. We have to be going."

Tom handed Birdie the tote bag. "Make sure your son takes all this Clyde stuff with him."

Birdie took the bag, hung it over her elbow and hugged Tom. Then she gave me a bear hug and told me not to be a stranger.

"I won't. I promise."

Theo bent to embrace me and said, "Thank you again for saving my life."

Before they left, Tom offered to carry the cat since Theo's shoulder was still healing, but he said he still had one good arm and he wanted to use it.

I felt tears sting my eyes once again after their departure. Clyde, with his perpetual smile, was one fine cat. I was glad he would have a fur friend and loving human friend in New York. But gosh, I would miss him.

Tom put his arm around me. "You ready for our announcement?"

I smiled up at him. "I am."

We walked out on the deck hand in hand. Mercy Lake was still, the sun's orange glow spreading its warmth and beauty across both land and water.

The happy conversation among our friends and family stopped when Tom cleared his throat. Everyone looked at us.

Tom said, "We have something to tell the people we love the most. You ready, Jilly?"

I nodded and in unison we said, "We're getting married."

Tom took me in his arms and kissed me to the sound of their cheers and applause.

There was no blinking back my tears of joy anymore. This felt, well . . . perfect.

Read on for a look at the next book in Leann
Sweeney's Cats in Trouble Mystery Series,

The Cat, the Sneak
and the Secret

Available from Obsidian in August 2015.

The cramped office that served the Mercy Animal Sanctuary smelled like . . . *love*. There was nothing I enjoyed more than cuddling with a cat or dog starved for affection.

But on this particular sunny October morning, I had not come to comfort the shelter's inhabitants. Instead, I sat beside my future stepson, Finn, as we waited for the shelter owners, Shawn and Allison Cuddahee, to bring out a very special cat. Whenever Finn was in town on a college break, he volunteered at the shelter. He was in town this time because his stepdad, Tom Stewart, and I were getting married in a few days. But we were here today because he wanted me to meet a little tortoiseshell kitty—or "tortie," as they were usually called.

Since his last time volunteering, Finn couldn't get this particular cat out of his head. Since she was still available, he wanted to adopt her. But the cat would have to live with Tom and me until Finn moved from the dorm into his own apartment next semester.

As we sat on folding chairs in the cluttered office, Snug, the African grey parrot who believed he was in charge of the place, entertained us. He promenaded back and forth on the horizontal pole Shawn had installed near the ceiling, saying, "Hello, Jillian Hart. Hello there," and "Finn, clean the dog crates. Clean the dog crates."

When Shawn finally came rushing through the door that led to the kennels and cattery, his face was flushed with agitation. And he wasn't holding the tortie. "Sorry, Finn, but she's gone again. She is the sneakiest little girl we've ever had."

Finn stood. "That's okay. I planned on working today anyway, and she always comes back. She'll probably be here by the time Jillian picks me up." He looked my way. "Anything I need to do to help you guys with the wedding setup when I'm done here?"

I laughed. "Though I'm certain you're dying to wrap vines and rosebuds onto Kara's banister, we'll take care of it." Kara was my stepdaughter—my late husband's only child. She was hosting the reception at her gorgeous new house.

"Yeah, I'm probably more useful here." Finn looked at Shawn. "Where should I start?"

Snug piped in with, "Clean the dog crates, Finn. Clean the dog crates."

Shawn still seemed a little annoyed and preoccupied, but not with Snug. He bent and retrieved a shoe box from under the desk and set it down on the battered metal surface. He glanced back and forth between us. "You sure you want a cat who brings this kind of stuff home all the time?"

I leaned forward and examined the contents of the box while Finn merely seemed amused.

Shawn picked out a shoelace and held it up. "This couldn't hold anything together, it's so old."

I spied what looked like a ragged sock, several coins, buttons, more shoelaces, a filthy little sachet pillow and a baby's knitted hat. I looked up at Finn and smiled. "Are you adopting a cat or a magpie?"

Snug said "Magpie" three times and did a wolf whistle to top it off. None of us could keep a straight face after that one.

"That's it." Finn grinned. "I'll call her Magpie. It's perfect, Jillian."

Shawn shook his head. "All I can say is, you'll have your hands full turning her into an indoor cat. She's semiferal and those types can usually be transitioned to house cats. But this one? She's always out hunting for anything she can drag back here." He waved his hand at the box. "And this is just from the last few days. Jillian, I want you to see what you're getting yourself into if you plan on keeping her through the holidays."

"She said it would be no problem." Finn glanced my way. "Right?"

"Absolutely. We'll manage just fine." I smiled.

Finn went on as if Shawn and I needed more convincing. "Plus I'll be living with her and Tom starting the first week in December and through most of January. I'll have plenty of time to help her become an indoor cat."

I could tell this kitty was indeed special. Finn really wanted to bring her home.

Shawn's phone rang, and he answered with, "Mercy Animal Sanctuary." After listening for several seconds, he said, "This cat is wearing one of my collars? You're sure?" He nodded and glanced at Finn. "What does the kitty look like?" More listening and more pointed looks at Finn. "I'll be right there."

Finn cocked his head and stared at Shawn. "Was that about Magpie?"

"Oh yeah. Did you bring a crate for that girl?" Shawn asked.

I nodded. "Someone found her, I take it?"

"Yup. And you'll never guess who. Let me tell Allison we're headed out. You can follow me and then *please* take this little troublemaker off my hands." But Shawn smiled. He had a soft spot for troublemakers.

We left the office with Snug bobbing his head and chanting "Magpie" over and over.

The route Shawn took confused me at first. I'd only lived in Mercy for seven years. There were more back roads than people in this town. But then I recognized where we were headed and turned to Finn sitting beside me in my minivan. "How did Magpie end up at Ed's Swap Shop?"

"You got me. This should be a fun mystery to unravel, Jillian. I love it."

We considered Ed Duffy a relative. He was the lovable, gentle, live-in companion of Tom's mother. He'd been collecting junk for years and actually did a steady business either swapping his treasures for different items that caught his fancy or just taking cash. Finn spent almost as much time with Karen and Ed as he did with Tom. In fact, when we pulled onto the neglected patch of asphalt Ed called a parking lot, he opened the door and Finn's rat terrier, Yoshi, came racing straight for him. Ed often kept Yoshi at the shop when Finn or Tom didn't plan on being home. Tom must have dropped the dog off before he went to pick up the new suit he'd bought for our wedding.

Finn opened his arms and the dog leaped into them. After licking his beloved Finn's face and wiggling with joy, Yoshi jumped down and greeted me as he'd been taught—by sitting in front of me and waiting for me to pet him. Then it was time to say hello to Shawn, who was already crouched and waiting to scratch Yoshi behind the ears.

Ed called, "Y'all come on and help me with this little feline problem I'm presented with."

Soon we all crowded into the store. Decades ago it had been a family home, and the stacks of toys, tools, small appliances, magazines, books, lamps, fishing gear and so much more made what had once been the small living area seem even tinier. And there before us was this battered old love seat—obviously a new addition. It filled what little space had been in the center of the room, and since we couldn't get past it, we all stood staring down at its dingy brown upholstery.

Ed stroked his gray beard. "This here is the problem." He looked down at a whining Yoshi. "Help me out, fella. Make some noise."

Yoshi complied by jumping on the love seat and yelping at the space between the back and bottom cushions.

We all heard a cat meow in reply. I would have expected a hiss if one of my three cats found themselves trapped in this sofa, but Magpie had been at the shelter so long, she was probably used to dogs barking.

I put my hand to my mouth and muttered, "Oh my. Is she stuck?"

"Darn right," Ed replied. "Only good thing is she can almost get her head through that crack. I reached down and felt the tag on the collar, got a flashlight for a better look. Like I said on the phone, she's one of yours, Shawn. But I've been working for an hour to coax or help her out of there and it ain't happenin'."

"Actually, Gramps, she's now my cat." Finn smiled at Ed. He'd taken to calling him Gramps not long after he came to live with Tom.

Ed's bushy eyebrows rose in surprise. "Well, there's a new development. Guess she needs savin' right quick, then."

Shawn addressed Finn. "Yoshi's done his job. Maybe he needs to go in the back while we work on this problem. The cat's probably scared."

As soon as the dog was in the back room, I fit my fingers between the back of the love seat and the attached cushions. I used a soft, coaxing voice. "Hey, baby.

You okay?" I wiggled my fingers. The sofa was old and dirty, and I was thankful the dark brown of the cushions hid a lot more than the stickiness I could feel.

It only took a minute for Magpie to wriggle her head out. Finn laughed and immediately took out his phone and snapped a picture. "Got to think of a caption for this when I put it up on Instagram."

"Such a pretty girl," I whispered, stroking the side of her face.

Meanwhile, Shawn was looking underneath the love seat in the back to check if she'd gotten in there through a rip or tear. He stood after checking. "She either got in there the way she's trying to come out, or came in through the bottom."

"There's no hole in the bottom, Shawn," Ed said. "I woulda seen it."

"So she can get out, but she's choosing not to." Shawn wore a wry smile. "Typical cat."

Sure enough, Magpie began to worm through the space and finally Finn couldn't stand it anymore. He grabbed hold and pulled her out.

It was then that we saw she had a thin gold chain wrapped around one front leg.

"Ah. So you were Dumpster-diving again." Finn held her up and looked into her eyes while Shawn unwound the chain. It seemed to have a locket attached.

Magpie, with her mottled black-and-gold fur and pale green eyes, was indeed a beauty. But as I held her back legs so Shawn could untangle the chain, I felt a stickiness. When Shawn was finished, Finn held his new friend close and I glanced at my hands.

My palms were rusty red. I held my fingers to my nose and immediately recognized the smell.

Blood.